UNTETHERED

Praise for Shelley Thrasher

Autumn Spring

"Thrasher's unique and exquisite take on romance in a small town offers a new and welcome perspective on mature relationships…The focus on the empowerment of older women serves to underscore both the charm of life at a slower pace and the sweetness of new relationships. Readers will find it deeply refreshing to see female characters who are defined as much by their kindness and grace as by their chosen roles in life."—*Publishers Weekly*

First Tango in Paris

"So initially I read this book to indulge in my love for Paris; that was the defining factor in my choice of novel. I didn't know what the subgenres of the book were (incidentally they are LGBT, family drama, history, romance, etc.) but what I got was a captivating story of love, not only of another person but also love of oneself. The historical elements of the story are fascinating…this subject makes for interesting reading and made me want to read further into some of the key figures in French history. I really enjoyed *First Tango in Paris*. The storyline flowed with effortless ease and the characters had me rooting for them. I can't ask for much more in a novel."
—*Lisa Talks About…Blog*

"Great debut novel. Easy read, likeable characters, and good thoughtful plot."—*Rainbow Book Awards, Honorable Mention*

The Storm

"*The Storm* is very well researched and Shelley Thrasher does an excellent job weaving together fact and fiction. The references to historical events such as the Galveston hurricane, the Spanish Flu epidemic and the suffrage movement add depth and interest to the overall storyline. Overall an entertaining and enlightening read that fans of historical romances will enjoy."—*Library Thing*

"The Orient Express" Short Story in ***Women of the Dark Streets***

"Fantasy and dreamlike story aboard the Orient Express, is imaginative and super sexy. Bon voyage!"—*Rainbow Book Reviews*

By the Author

The Storm

First Tango in Paris

Autumn Spring

Hidden Dreams

Untethered

Visit us at www.boldstrokesbooks.com

UNTETHERED

by
Shelley Thrasher

2024

UNTETHERED
© 2024 By Shelley Thrasher. All Rights Reserved.

ISBN 13: 978-1-63679-636-9

This Trade Paperback Original Is Published By
Bold Strokes Books, Inc.
P.O. Box 249
Valley Falls, NY 12185

First Edition: August 2024

THIS IS A WORK OF FICTION. NAMES, CHARACTERS, PLACES, AND INCIDENTS ARE THE PRODUCT OF THE AUTHOR'S IMAGINATION OR ARE USED FICTITIOUSLY. ANY RESEMBLANCE TO ACTUAL PERSONS, LIVING OR DEAD, BUSINESS ESTABLISHMENTS, EVENTS, OR LOCALES IS ENTIRELY COINCIDENTAL.

THIS BOOK, OR PARTS THEREOF, MAY NOT BE REPRODUCED IN ANY FORM WITHOUT PERMISSION.

Credits
Editor: Jenny Harmon
Production Design: Stacia Seaman
Cover Design by Tammy Seidick

Acknowledgments

I prefer not to travel alone, so my good friends Lou Anne and Brenda graciously went to Indonesia with me on a luxury cruise last year. Little did we know what we were getting into.

Finally back home and crafting a new novel, I have thoroughly enjoyed working with Rad, Sandy, Cindy, Ruth, Stacia, and the rest of BSB's outstanding publishing team.

And my editor? Wow! Jenny went above and beyond.

As for my extended support system, I couldn't have made it without my family and my weekly writing group, as well as Justine, my longtime beta reader, and Ann, my new one. They've all been invaluable.

My fellow BSB authors and the best group of readers imaginable round out my outstanding gang of literary companions. It's exhilarating to be in such good company.

For Ann,
who has held my hand through every inch of this writing journey
and helped me begin to become the writer and the person
I've always wanted to be.

January 2023

PROLOGUE

Sitting in my sister Kitty's den, in her recliner, I notice a small magazine lying on the arm of her large, comfortable chair. As I do with almost anything in print, I pick up the magazine and leaf through it. Kitty majored in health and recreation, which she taught in the local public school system for decades, so I'm not surprised she subscribes to this periodical.

A brief article questioning why the author always felt different from everyone else catches my attention. Having no idea what subject she's writing about, I start reading the brief story of an attractive young woman in her late twenties, as told to another woman.

Olivia, the author, talks about not liking to go to parties and sleepovers when she was young and the fact that crowded, noisy situations such as these always overwhelmed her. She says that though she can be sociable, after she spends a lot of time interacting with people, she's exhausted for days.

I'm mesmerized. The writer's already tapping into my feelings on a level I've never experienced before. This is me, I keep thinking as I read.

She describes her emotional instability in high school and being diagnosed with anxiety, depression, and PTSD, saying how relieved she felt with each assessment. But after a time, she would realize that none of them seemed right for her.

In her early twenties, Olivia happened to talk frankly to her best friend's aunt one night, who asked her if she'd been tested for autism. The woman's teenage daughter had just been diagnosed with autism spectrum disorder (ASD), and that information sent Olivia on a research mission. As she read, she realized she was finally on the right track.

However, her therapist dismissed her revelation, saying that she was able to carry on a conversation, which autistic people can't do. That analysis discouraged Olivia so much she dropped the subject for two years, but one day she asked her own mom if she thought she was autistic.

"One hundred percent," her mother said immediately, surprising Olivia.

At that point, I'm so excited, I jump up and go grab a glass of ice water. Trying to calm my pounding heart and racing brain, I sit down again and finish reading the article.

Olivia saw another doctor, who *did* assess her as being on the spectrum. This news thrilled her. "I finally had the answers to my questions about why I reacted to certain things the way I did," she states in the article. Because she's found a diagnosis that fits, she can stop pretending to be who she thinks she should be and simply be who she is. And for the past few years, that's exactly what she's been doing.

Reading this young woman's brief story sets me on fire!

February 3, 2023

Family Ties

My cousin Lou and I—who live near one another in the houses where each of us grew up—often sit in her small, knotty-pine-paneled den. She prefers her dad's old brown leather recliner in front of her always-on television set. But I choose her mother's slightly smaller, crimson lounge chair, with its worn velvet cushions and armrests. We usually discuss current events but sometimes share confidences in this cozy, dimly lit room.

On this raw, cold night, though, we sprawl on her shag carpet, pull old pictures out of an ancient-looking woven straw basket, and sort them. Lou's large male Siamese cat stretches out between us.

"Look at this one, Helen," Lou says. "Mama's wearing that old flapper hat pulled down so far you can't see anything but her eyes, nose, and lips." She laughs.

"Check out her long cigarette holder. I bet she drove the boys wild." I take the photo from Lou. "Can you believe she and the family moved here from West Texas almost a hundred years ago? Time sure flies."

She nods. "Well, I can't believe they stayed in this Podunk town after the big East Texas oil boom played out. I've heard that back then this area was like the California gold rush."

"They probably stayed for the same reason you moved back here after living in Houston. It's a nice little place, safe and—"

"Boring." Lou wrinkles her small nose. "If my folks hadn't been here, I'd have never set foot in it again."

I reach out to pet Lou's Siamese but jerk my hand back when he glares. He's fast and has sharp claws and teeth. Took me just once to learn my lesson.

"Do you have any other shots of my dad and the rest of the family during those early years?" I rummage through the stack I've been sorting.

"Here's one of my favorites." She hands me a creased black-and-white picture, one corner torn off. "They were driving to California on a vacation in the early 1930s."

"Oh, yeah. I've seen that one." I study the photo, twirling a piece of my long, curly, white hair between two fingers. "I still can't believe they drove. That's halfway across the country."

"I guess it was either that or ride the train. Mom said they stopped at what motels and cafés they could find along the way. I suppose they decided to enjoy some of their dad's fortune from the oil boom before he drank it all up or gave it away to his 'women.'" She shakes her head. "I bet it took forever to get there."

"How long were they gone?"

"Several weeks, maybe more. Can you imagine five kids and two grownups cooped up that long in that old-timey car?"

I lay the photo between us and brush back a strand of hair that's fallen in my face. "What an adventure, though. It would have taken two or three days just to get up to Amarillo and hit Route 66. Then even longer to make it straight across New Mexico and Arizona. Wow! Route 66 would have been practically new then. That trip was probably as exciting for them as my cruise through Indonesia's gonna be for me."

"Mama said they even stopped by the Grand Canyon." Lou glances at her huge, muted TV set. "With no air conditioning, not many nice motels, and greasy-spoon food? Yuck."

She places several shots of my dad in one pile. "And don't forget what a moody bunch they all were. Our granddad and his two youngest kids probably never shut up, and our grandmother and the older three probably never said much of anything, especially your dad."

I nod. "Isn't that the truth?"

"I wonder why he was so quiet most of the time?" she asks. She glances over at the framed portrait of her parents that hangs above her large, unused, stone fireplace, then lays the picture of the family trip to California on the carpet between us.

"Guess we'll never know." I shrug. "Mama would warn us when he withdrew and refused to talk to any of us, especially her. Though we could certainly see it for ourselves."

"How long would he stay that way?"

"It varied." I shrug again. "Sometimes a month or so. We didn't try to say anything and avoided him. Not that we ever talked to him much. Poor Mama. It really bothered her."

Lou frowns, and I swallow the lump in my throat. "Mama left us about thirty years' worth of her daily journals, and I want to cry when I read some of her entries. She always thought *she* caused him not to talk."

Lou shakes her head, her long, bottle-black hair gleaming in the light of a nearby brass floor lamp. "My mom acted like your dad did, though not for that long. We never knew what set her off."

She smooths her small hand down her cat's back. "Mama seemed to think nobody liked her, at least that's what I figure. And she sure made it clear she'd rather be by herself."

Lou's Siamese claws at her, and she jerks her hand away. "She never let anybody try to help her deal with whatever she was feeling. She just brooded. I get that way sometimes too, though I've tried to work through it."

Lou's quiet for a minute but then hops up and carries her empty glass into the nearby kitchen. "Sure you don't want some wine?"

"No, thanks. This water's fine. Healthy."

She disappears, then comes back and sets a bowl of chips on the leather hassock between us, crunches on a Frito. "I've talked to some of our younger cousins about their parents." She shakes her head again. "They all say the same thing. Total withdrawal, silence. Obviously not normal behavior." She flips a strand of hair out of her right eye.

I blow out a long breath. "You know, I thought only Daddy acted that way."

I'm tempted to ask for some wine, but my oncologist recommended that I avoid alcohol. Lou sips from her already half-empty glass. "If you hadn't left town so long ago and just dropped by to visit during a few holidays every year, you might have found out about this earlier." Her smile's crooked. "I guess we thought you'd escaped."

"Humph. Escaped? When I was growing up here, everybody in

the family used to say I acted and looked just like my dad, but I didn't want to believe them." I run my fingers through my bangs, trying to keep my hair out of my eyes.

"For a very long time now, I've tried not to act like him." I sigh. "But I've never had much to say to most people. I have a hard time expressing what's on my mind and don't feel like people understand what I have to say when I do try. Maybe that was how he felt too. It's easier to play games like dominoes and Scrabble, like we usually did when we got together as a family, than to try to carry on a conversation." I frown, finish my glass of water, and stand up. "Gotta go. It's late."

Lou's cat opens his eyes and stretches, then curls into a ball again.

I touch his back briefly. "Interesting subject, Lou. I enjoyed our little talk. It's nice to know I'm not the only one with such an antisocial parent."

She smiles as she strokes her cat lightly. "I suppose that's one good thing about families."

I sigh, pull on my lined leather jacket, wrap a wool scarf around my neck. "Maybe I'll have some new insights during the next few weeks while I'm enjoying my cruise on the other side of the world."

Lou gets up too and hands me the old picture we've been discussing. "Here. Take this, since you love to travel so much." She gives me a one-arm hug around my waist.

"Thanks." I glance down at her and slip the photo into my pocket. "Hey. I just remembered. Today's Daddy's birthday. He would have been a hundred and two."

She grabs her wineglass and holds it up. "I always liked the old bastard, especially after he finally became a bit more sociable. He even talked to me a few times. May he rest in peace."

I put my hand on her shoulder and squeeze it. "May we all rest—and live—in peace. You stay warm."

She looks up at me, her gaze as intense as her mom's used to be. "If I don't see you before you leave, have a great time. Maybe you'll meet somebody special." She winks.

I shrug. "Maybe so, Lou. I'd like that."

Eight Days Later: February 11–13, 2023

WAITING IN AUSTRALIA

"Did you ever think you'd be sitting in the Brisbane airport?" I ask Martha Jo, one of my travel buddies.
"Not in my weirdest dreams." Yells from the TV in the bar behind us almost drown her out. She shifts from one slender hip to the other as she slumps in a hard, plastic chair in the waiting area. I've rarely seen Martha Jo slump. She slicks back her short gray hair. "So far, so good."
I nod. "Yep. I'm tired, but that's no big surprise." I'm eighty-one, three years younger than Martha Jo, but I'm not ready to admit how exhausted I already am. *Hmm. Five more hours to go after this six-hour layover. I can make it.*
She stands, stretches her thin arms over her head. "I'm looking forward to a nice, luxurious cruise," she says. "I do want to spend my mornings exploring some of the remote islands where we stop. But *then*, every afternoon and night, I intend to take it easy on board the ship."
I nod. "You deserve some rest after that long drive to the Dallas airport. The traffic's ferocious."
She gazes at me with calm, blue eyes. "And you deserve to unwind as much as possible after the past few years you've been through."
I take a deep breath. "You're right. It has been rough."
"Rough? I'd say backbreaking and catastrophic. I don't know how you've managed."
My face heats. "Oh, Martha Jo."
"Don't 'oh, Martha Jo' me. I've seen what you've been through, at least most of it, so I should know. How do the words divorce, surgery, relocation, car wreck, and cancer sound? Have I missed anything?"

I push my hair back from my face. "No, except the death of my mom. That's when everything began to unravel."

She puts her smooth, unblemished hand on the back of my rough, liver-spotted one. "I know what you mean. That's probably the hardest one of all."

"Hey, girls." Amy, Martha Jo's wife, bounces up behind us, the thick lenses of her wire-rim glasses reflecting the overhead fluorescent lights. "Aren't you gonna watch part of the game? It's Super Bowl fifty-seven. Only happens once a year." Amy squeezes Martha Jo's shoulder.

"Mmm. That feels good." Martha Jo rolls her creaking, popping neck. "You can give me a massage right here in the airport, and I won't complain a bit."

"Later, babe. Later." Amy's voice is soft and sweet. "Right now, I want to see the rest of the game." She glances back at the few fans at the bar yelling. "It's almost over. Let's do something then. I'm tired of just sitting."

Martha Jo straightens her back. Though she's not as tall as I am, she does have a few inches on Amy. "What about playing Rummikub?" she asks. "I packed the tiles and trays in my carry-on."

Amy laughs. "Why am I not surprised?" She squeezes Martha Jo's shoulder again, adjusts her glasses. "Why not?" she asks. "Though we'll probably have gobs of time to play while we're on this cruise."

"I sure hope so," Martha Jo says. "I'm really looking forward to relaxing. And I'm sure you are too, Helen." She glances at me like she's checking to see if I've been paying attention.

I nod. "Yes. It's just what my oncologist ordered."

"I wouldn't mind a little downtime either." Amy glances over at the bar area again, her cropped, graying red hair shining under the bright, overhead lights. "But first I have a Super Bowl to finish watching. See you two in a bit."

Martha Jo and I settle back into our rigid seats. My eyes close, yet too soon, loud cheers shake me awake. "Sounds like the game's over," I say, pushing my shoulders back.

Amy strides over like we're sitting in their living room. "The Chiefs won," she says.

Martha Jo raises her arms over her head and lowers her dainty feet from her roller bag to the floor. Then she slides her makeup pouch from its front compartment. "Let's play Rummikub after I go freshen up." She's apparently had a nap too. "See you in a minute."

Amy plops down in the vacant seat beside me.

"Did you enjoy the game?" I ask.

"Sure. At least watching that bunch of big guys tough it out kept me awake." She jumps up and paces back and forth in the empty area behind our row of chairs.

"Getting in some of your steps for your big hike?" I turn around and ask.

"You better believe it. If I'm gonna walk half the Appalachian Trail this summer, I've gotta be in top shape. Sitting cramped up on that plane was the worst thing I could've done. I need to exercise while I can." She bends over and touches her toes, then stands on her tiptoes.

Martha Jo rushes up. "I found a vacant table just the right size in the bar! Grab your things and come on before somebody else claims it." She's snatched up her belongings and hurried to the bar area before Amy and I have a chance to gather ours.

"Come on." Martha Jo waves us to a small, round table, and Amy and I roll our bags over and cluster them nearby, then sit down. "Anyone hungry or thirsty?" Martha Jo hovers like she's entertaining guests back home.

I shake my head no, but Amy pipes up. "All that yelling made me thirsty. How about a beer?"

"If that's what you want, sweetie, I'll get you one. And I'll have a soft drink. Do you want anything, Helen?"

"No, but thanks." I just want to sleep but try to be as sociable as possible.

Martha Jo hurries back. "Here you go, sweetheart." She sets a can of Great Northern and an empty glass gently in front of Amy. "The bartender recommended this brand." She cups one of Amy's plump cheeks briefly.

"Why, thank you, babe." Amy looks up at her. "You're too good to me."

Martha Jo simply smiles. Then she hands me a tall glass of water. "You need to stay hydrated, Helen, especially after all that time in the air. Doctor's orders, and mine too."

I thank her. Hopefully I can take her advice. On this trip of a lifetime, I don't want to miss anything huge, though I have promised myself to try to relax and rest. After all, this time last year, I hadn't even started my five weeks of radiation. And the chemo's another story.

Martha Jo puts her Coca-Cola in her own place. "Cokes are the favorite soft drink here down under too, just like at home."

"You don't say?" Amy takes a swig of her lager. "Hmm. Good. Getting chummy with the barkeep, Martha Jo?"

"It never hurts to know the people in charge of the food and drink." She returns the tray to the bar. Then she comes back and, from her carry-on, pulls out three small, black, plastic trays, each about nine inches long, and, finally, a purple felt bag, *Chivas Regal* stitched in gold thread on one side.

Amy sips her brew again. "Well, when it comes to food and drink, you're the queen and the king." She gazes at Martha Jo as if they've been together only a few months instead of twenty years.

Seeing their obvious love for each other comforts me, makes me feel safe after my recent cancer scare. I'm also relieved to be sharing a suite with them on this adventure. It's like traveling with my mother and my sister, I muse as each of us picks fourteen small tiles from the *Chivas* bag.

We play Martha Jo's favorite game for a while, each trying to place all our tiles on the table first. The familiar activity soothes me, as if we're back in Texas camping in our RVs instead of in a far-away country, poised on the edge of a new experience.

As we compete, though, we glance up at the arrival and departure boards. Flights to and from Sydney and Canberra come and go, but none from or to Darwin, our final destination here in Australia. A worm of anticipation crawls through my stomach.

"Looks like Darwin's a small town," Martha Jo says. "Not many people going there."

We have no idea what to expect. I'd never heard of the city before we booked this trip. I know only that it's on the north-central coast of Australia, and we'll board our small cruise ship there, bound for Bali.

Eventually, Amy stretches her fleshy arms above her head. "I've let you two win enough. I need some exercise. Think I'll see what's down that hall over there. Be back in a bit."

After she leaves, Martha Jo and I take turns going to the restroom, then move our belongings back to the waiting area. Like Alice staring at that famous rabbit hole, I wonder what lies on the other side. Do I really want to go down it, or should I have stayed home so I wouldn't be tempted to exhaust myself?

Amy finally shows up again, and after Martha Jo also takes a long walk, I stroll through the busy adjoining mall. It's like the ones in every airport facility I've ever seen—glitzy, overpriced, and crowded—though many people are wearing shorts instead of heavy corduroys, T-shirts instead of sweaters. Something clicks in my head. I'm on the other side of the world, suddenly immersed in summer instead of winter.

On my way back, I notice several huge black-and-white photos on the walls, depicting some of the long-ago effects of WWII. Hmm. I was a baby when those nurses and doctors I'm now looking at were risking their lives in a major war. Gazing up at those brave strangers, I try to imagine what they were going through. Times have certainly changed.

After I return, we sit silently in the waiting area's uncomfortable chairs again, stare through the huge windows at the arriving and departing planes and passengers. I doze off, dream I'm reaching out to pet Lou's cat, as Lou says three words: "Meet somebody special—"

"May I have your attention, please." A loud voice forces me to listen. "Flight 38 from Brisbane to Darwin will be leaving from Gate 9 at eight p.m."

We come alive, gather our belongings, move halfway around the terminal from where we've been. Then we sit down again, near our gate, and I promptly fall asleep.

Eventually, I rouse. A woman with long brown hair stands in front of us. "Hi, there. Are you meeting a cruise in Darwin?"

Amy jumps up. "We sure are."

"So are we," the stranger says. "From Darwin to Bali. My husband's over there, and I'm Heather." She gestures. "We're from California. So, I guess we'll be on the same ship. Aren't you excited?"

She and Amy chitchat for a while. Then, after Heather rejoins her husband, Amy, Martha Jo, and I settle down again and stare, hypnotized, at the steady stream of airplanes rolling across the tarmac. Finally, we board.

Martha Jo and Amy sit in the front of the small plane, and I'm in the very back row, which seats only two passengers. A youngish woman next to me is already reading a thick paperback, so I relax. At least I won't have to make idle conversation with a stranger. That's one of my worst nightmares—and it takes so much energy. I recall the magazine article I read last month, about that young woman who discovered she was autistic. She said she felt exhausted for days if she spent too much time interacting with people. Am I like that too? Or am I just old and tired?

I'm about to fall asleep when the woman beside me says, with an obvious Aussie accent, "Excuse me, but I need to get my jacket from the overhead bin. It's chillier than I expected." She's wearing a colorful, flowing dress as thin as Kleenex. After all, I remind myself again, it's summer in Australia.

I flinch yet nod. Will this person want to talk, or do I simply have to move out of the way? That, I can handle, but trying to converse with a stranger almost always seems like a death sentence. I can never respond appropriately, even if I can come up with anything to try to say. It's like having to climb the pinnacle of the Empire State Building on a windy day. I keep worrying I'll fall.

"No problem," I say.

She quickly grabs a lightweight jacket and settles down with her book again.

Aah. Perfect.

But then she says, almost as if talking to herself, "I've just been to see my mum in Brisbane. She has Alzheimer's, and I wish I could visit her more often."

After that, she simply picks up her book again as if she hasn't spoken.

What prompted that statement? My white hair?

Since she's given me a choice, I risk a conversation. She seems honest and real and obviously has a serious concern.

"I can relate to your situation," I say, then wait.

She merely nods, and I gather the courage to continue. "My good friend back home, whom I've known forever, was recently diagnosed with Alzheimer's. I visit her often, but she's only in stage one. What a horrible disease."

She nods again, and soon we're intimately discussing our mothers and our interests in a way that sometimes only strangers can. We'll never see each other again, so I enjoy our brief exchange for what it is, revealing personal things I rarely share with anyone back home. And she appears to do the same. Evidently, conversations like this feed something in me instead of drain me, which most personal interactions do. What's going on? Why am I gaining energy instead of losing it? Is she a special type of person? Is it the subject matter? Strange.

Our exchange, which lasts all the way to Darwin, leaves me with a rare glow of confidence. Technically, I'll be alone on our cruise, and maybe I'll be able to converse with at least a few new people. Perhaps I'll get to know Heather from California, who's sitting with her husband about ten rows in front of me. She seems honest and down to earth.

The hours speed by. It's almost midnight when we arrive in Darwin. Still, oddly rested after connecting with my congenial seat mate, I'm ready to tackle this new venture and try to forget my catastrophes of the past few years.

A prearranged minibus meets us and Heather and her husband, then whisks us through hushed, well-lit streets, past large buildings, downtown to the city's Hilton.

At last, we sleep in actual beds. Finally here at our jumping-off place, we can begin this trip we've anticipated for months.

February 14, 2023

WAITING FOR OUR FIRST EXCURSION

"Wow. This breakfast buffet's great." Amy plunks her plate down where Martha Jo and I already sit. "I'm going back for more coffee. Anyone need anything?"

"Uh-uh," I say—Texan for "No, thanks."

I've just noticed a woman sitting alone a few tables away. Perhaps Australian? Somehow, she reminds me of the one on the plane last night that I clicked with.

I take a bite of omelet made to order. "This sure beats my breakfast yesterday in economy," I say.

Finally, Amy shows up again. "Long line for the coffee bar, but I didn't have any trouble finding these delicious-looking pastries."

The woman's still sitting by herself, studying a small pamphlet with the word Advantage in large print near the top. *She's obviously with our group.*

People bustle around, but, jet-lagged, we take our time. Amy says, "Most of these folks probably got here yesterday afternoon, when we were originally supposed to." She finishes her second cup of coffee and her baked goods.

The woman puts her pamphlet into her backpack and heads toward a nearby restroom. Short, her medium-length brown hair streaked with gray, she appears younger than I am and in good shape. What's her story? Married? I vaguely nod at Amy's praise of the food. But why even ask such a question about the stranger? I'm not really in the market. Three strikes and you're out. At least that's what I keep reminding myself.

Amy sighs loudly, obviously content, then gets up. "Let's go see what's happening. I don't want to miss our bus trip to Kakadu National Park." She takes off her glasses and polishes the lens with her shirt tail.

Martha Jo and I gather our sun hats and daypacks, crammed with water bottles, sunscreen, Band-Aids, sunglasses, soft toilet paper, etc. "Okay, sweetheart," she tells Amy. "Let's go."

The huge lobby is crowded. Strangers fill the sofas and large chairs, mill around the vast space and cluster in small groups. Normally, I'd retreat to a secluded corner, but Martha Jo and Amy meet people with ease, so I follow in their wake.

A man a little younger than Martha Jo and I walks up. "Are you latecomers? I don't remember you from last night."

We nod, and he says, his eyes bright, "We were some of the lucky few who got here on time." His New York accent obvious, he looks at his wife as if checking in, then back at us. "Several of us walked along the coast after dinner and took some nice pictures, didn't we, dear?" A top-of-the-line Canon hangs around each one's neck. "We're professional photographers." He chats like he's known us forever, and Amy reciprocates, while his wife, who doesn't make eye contact, stares at the crowd. She seems to enjoy conversing with strangers about as much as I do.

Most of our group, assembled in the huge lobby, look older—sixties through eighties, a few men in their nineties sprinkled in. Some use canes or walk with a limp or have a humped back. Harder to determine the women's ages. Gray hair does dominate though.

A few women have long, curly hair, like I do. Mine reminds me of the sixties, though it's no longer dark brown. Back then, I let it grow out and frizz, which always embarrassed my much-younger sister, Kitty. She ironed hers to straighten it. Lately, I've let mine go wild again. I also lost forty pounds during my bout with cancer last spring. Changing my appearance so drastically at my age makes me feel free and a little unbalanced.

Late arrivals like us share horror stories as we wait. "My first flight was delayed in Cleveland, so I missed my connection," a woman about my age says. "It made me so nervous."

"I tried to call the number Advantage gave us, but no one ever answered," someone else says. "I ended up in Canberra, totally frustrated because I didn't get any response at all. I could certainly have used some help."

The woman I noticed at breakfast, who's drifted into our small group, quietly speaks up. "When I reached Melbourne, I discovered my flight to Darwin had been canceled. Worse, none flew out for two days. By the way, I'm Grace, from near P-town."

We all introduce ourselves.

Grace has an East Coast accent and a calmness I envy, and her name reflects her demeanor. How can she be so at ease around all these strangers? Without Martha Jo and Amy, I'd be hiding in a corner.

"What did you do?" someone asks.

"Like you, I tried to call Advantage. But when no one answered, I simply bought a ticket from another airline. Otherwise, I could have missed the cruise. I expect our tour company to reimburse me for that extra charge."

Just then the photographer from New York joins us again. "Would you four ladies pose for me? I'm doing a series of shots of our group on our first full day here."

We glance at each other, and when no one seems to object, Amy says, "Sure. Where do you want us to stand?"

"Over there, away from the crowd."

He arranges us at the base of one of the colossal white columns that dot the lobby, lining us up by height. I stand on the left, then Martha Jo, Amy, and Grace.

"Thanks for your cooperation," he says as he finishes, then heads over to another group. We rejoin the crowd, and Grace disappears.

Resuming our earlier conversation, Amy says, "I'm certainly glad our flights have gone smoothly except for our long layover in Brisbane."

Martha Jo nods, frowning. "But we could have gotten here a lot quicker and more comfortably if Advantage hadn't mysteriously changed our original schedule at the last minute."

Maybe Amy feels more optimistic because she's quite a few years younger than Martha Jo and I are. At our age, do those extra years make such a big difference? Maybe they do.

An hour later, still in the overflowing lobby, Martha Jo says, "This is ridiculous. You'd think they'd at least tell us something."

Amy and I nod, try to relax into one of the comfy couches we've managed to find. Less talkative now, most everyone's lounging around in a stupor since we had to get up so early for this excursion.

Suddenly a man rushes in, bellows, "We'll be leaving soon." Everyone jumps up and crowds toward the front doors.

Then we all burst outside and flock geese-like toward several large, air-conditioned buses pulling up in front. "Which way should we go?" Martha Jo asks.

No one seems to know. Amy raises one shoulder.

A middle-aged man with a toupee abruptly breaks through the crowd, shouting with an Aussie accent, "Plenty of room on my bus, people. Follow me." He leads us to bus number three, muttering, "How disorganized can you get? I'd replace whoever's in charge right now."

We climb steep stairs into bus three. "Want to sit near the front?" Amy asks us.

"Sure," I say. "Why not?"

Amy slides into a plush seat, Martha Jo sits next to the aisle, and I take the aisle seat across from them.

"Plenty of room here," our new leader says. "Just make yourselves comfortable while I go save more people."

He scurries away, returns with a gaggle of followers. Then, loaded with now-eager, elderly adventurers, our bus roars through downtown Darwin.

Our vacation trip with Advantage certainly has not begun in a restful manner. We hurtle down the smooth highway. *Surely things will calm down soon.* Then I glance around our bus, check to see if Grace boarded with us. No such luck. Would talking to her energize or exhaust me?

Kakadu National Park

Our leader, Bill, a retired forest ranger, adjusts his toupee, then picks up a microphone. "We're driving through the city's outskirts now," he says. "Then we'll turn east and south toward Kakadu, but we'll see only a small part of this huge UNESCO World Heritage site." He fills us in on Darwin's business community, detailing the history of a local hamburger joint we've just passed. "They retained some of world-famous McDonald's icons," he says as we head out of town.

The man behind me yells, "Good for them."

Soon, in the middle of nowhere, though still on a smooth highway, Bill points. "See that huge mound, taller than a man's head?" We crane our necks. "Termites built it. And I've seen some a lot taller than that." He shows us wallabies, cockatoos, and other native animals as we motor over the flat terrain. No kangaroos though.

Finally, we stop at a complex of white buildings that looks like an old-fashioned motel in New Mexico or Arizona. *Daddy and his family might have stayed in a place like this on their trip to California way back when.* I wonder how Lou and everyone at home are doing. They seem so far away.

"You'll find the toilets right over there," Bill says, and almost everyone on the bus heads toward them. He definitely understands the needs of our age group.

After we relieve ourselves, he says, "You can see some water buffalo in that first pen, imported from Asia, though they're smaller than your American bison."

To give Martha Jo and Amy some time to themselves, I walk over to the animals by myself. Behind a metal fence, a big black creature and a pinkish-beige one graze on hay covering the muddy ground, their sharp, pointed horns branching out and then stretching upward. They're about the size of the Black Angus bull that services the cows that my across-the-road neighbor in Texas raises. Not an animal I'd like to get close to, but impressive at a distance.

Suddenly, I'm so homesick I grab one of the metal fence rods. *What am I doing here all alone in this unfamiliar country about as far away from home as I can get?* But I'm not missing my family. Instead, I think of my former spouses, all three of them, who, during the past sixty years, traveled with me all over Europe and the Far East, who sheltered me so I never felt this solitary. I don't like being alone like this. I feel so vulnerable, almost naked, almost scared, and certainly unsure of myself.

I'm terrified to converse with strangers in a social situation. Martha Jo and Amy safeguard me, but they're with each other. I'm here by myself. Maybe I can find a companion, someone like Grace, the woman we just met. I wonder if she feels the same way I do about being alone in this crowd of strangers?

Bill strolls up, and I snap out of my sudden panic. He waves toward a small, swampy area. "You can see some crocodiles over there"—he points—"but keep your distance. I don't want anyone's feet or hands to go missing."

Everyone rushes toward the sturdy enclosure like it's the Second Coming. I wander over and spot a few of the creatures in the water. But I once lived near the bayous of southern Louisiana, where alligators are as common as mosquitoes. These crocs don't look much different from those gators, though someone from New York or LA might find them unusual. I'm being a jerk, but I'm not feeling great right now. Jet lag, maybe? *More likely fear.*

We head back toward our bus, and I bump into Amy, who's snapping pictures with her phone. "Look at these beautiful bushes," I say. "Those white blooms remind me of gardenias." *And of home.* I'm still a bit raw from my attack of self-doubt.

"Yes," she says. "And those glossy leaves look familiar too."

Amy's a master naturalist, so she and I mill around the grounds while some of our crowd visit the facilities again, "just in case." Several large, white cockatoos in a huge, gnarled tree appear as curious about us as we are about them and call out in a raucous tone, emphasizing how far away from home we are.

People struggle onto the bus, and we finally pull onto the ruler-straight road. Sitting in a double seat with no one beside me threatens to pull me into the doldrums again, but I try to focus on the strange countryside we flash by. *This is an adventure. This is an adventure.*

After riding in silence for a long while, someone calls out, "Hey, Bill. How far have we been?"

"About two hundred and forty Ks," he says.

"Two hundred and forty," the guy behind me says. "That's impossible. We'll never make it there and back."

"Yes, dear," his wife says quietly. "But remember. The Australians use kilometers, not miles. That's about a hundred and fifty miles, so not as bad as it seems."

He grunts, and others mutter, stretch their backs.

Sitting nearby, one of our most senior members, probably in his mid-nineties, groans. "For God's sake, man. We just flew halfway around the world to get here. Isn't this a bit much?"

"Hey. I'm not in charge," Bill says. "But we'll be there soon."

I shift from one hip to the other.

"Wish you could see the large hotel in Jabiru shaped like a crocodile," he says. "We're on a tight schedule, though. Everything's bigger in Australia."

"Watch it, Bill," Amy says. "We're from Texas."

He grins. "Guess you understand long drives, then."

She and Martha Jo and I nod.

"But the people who planned this trip don't seem to," Bill says, though he doesn't speak into the microphone.

He's certainly not a peacemaker.

We keep driving. At least the road's smooth, and the weather's clear and cool. "Here's Jim Jim Road," he suddenly announces. "We're almost there."

A huge, craggy, red rock rises from the lime-green horizon and dwarfs our bus. We finally park near Nourlangie—a gigantic, ancient Aboriginal rock-art site—then walk to a cleared area. The prospect of seeing this famous rock art dulls my anxiety about being here without a partner.

"You have a choice here," Bill says. "Either take that path, on flat ground, or climb up that one." He gestures to a narrow, steep trail dotted with large stones. "You'll end up at the same place, but you'll have to work harder on one of them, though the view's better in a lot of spots."

"I'm taking the easy trail," Martha Jo says immediately.

Amy and I look at each other, then nod. We've chosen the more rugged one, Bill leading us. After heading almost straight up for a while, we stop to rest and look back at the flat, wooded area we drove through earlier. We sip water, then trudge on, in some places almost having to squeeze between the rocky walls. The excitement of the uneven trail that leads us through lush woods studded with cliffs and overhangs helps me forget that I don't have a permanent partner to share this experience with. Besides, though out of the sun now, I'm panting and have to focus on keeping up with the group. Finally, we stop at the world-famous rock paintings.

Another guide stands there, supposedly an expert. "Some of these paintings are 30,000 years old," he says.

"Look how faded and dim those designs over there are," I whisper to Amy.

She points at another section. "But those are still really vibrant. Check out those orange, black, white, and purple swirls and figures."

Our guide says, "These ancient people obviously used natural pigments, which have lasted very well."

We stop at the central painting of the group, where he gives a mini lecture, stating, "The male figure clearly dominates this painting and this civilization. The women nearby obviously exist only to serve him."

I bristle and stop listening, instead noticing Grace. She must have been in the group in front of us and is lagging behind them. She frowns as well. At least somebody seems to agree with me.

After he finishes and walks away, I whisper to Amy, "You know, those figures of the ancient Aboriginal ancestors make me realize that the relationship between men and women hasn't changed much in all these thousands of years. Men were dominant then and still are."

"I agree," Amy says.

I glance behind us and notice Grace is still there. In fact, she's standing close enough to overhear Amy and me and grinning. Hmm.

Our group slowly climbs out of the rocky cliffs and slabs protected by overhangs, and a few of us follow Bill on the long trail around more of the site, but I don't see Grace again. The warm February sun, the pleasant shade of the scrubby trees, and the opportunity to stretch my legs provide welcome relief, as does wondering about her and her situation.

When we're back on the bus, Bill says, "Glad we didn't run into any crocs in the wild. They filmed a lot of the first two *Crocodile Dundee* movies here."

"Why didn't he mention that earlier?" I whisper, leaning across the aisle toward Martha Jo.

She nods. "A lot of us would have enjoyed knowing more about that, since those movies were so popular back in the '80s. And we probably wouldn't have had to go rock-climbing to see where some key scenes were filmed. After all, none of us are spring chickens."

I nod. Though Amy and I did enjoy the trek, most of our fellow travelers obviously couldn't or didn't want to try to navigate such a site.

"I hope things suit our group better after we get on the ship tomorrow." Martha Jo nods vigorously. *And I hope we keep bumping into Grace. I want to know more about her.*

Yellow Water Billabong

We pull onto a bumpy road and soon arrive at a small congestion of buildings.

"The toilets are over there," Bill says immediately.

Martha Jo jumps up, and Amy and I follow her.

"Whoa. I'm tired," Amy says as we wash our hands and pat some water on our cheeks.

"Yeah. I'm hungry too. Where do you think we'll eat out here in the middle of nowhere?" I push my fuzzy white hair back over my ears several times. *What am I doing in a run-down restroom in Northern Australia?* I take several deep breaths. *It's an adventure.*

Yeah. Right, my sensible self says. *Is this adventure worth such crushing exhaustion?*

As we exit the building, Bill shouts, "Over here."

We follow him down a well-worn path, surrounded by weird trees and foreign bird calls to a large body of green, murky water.

"Welcome to the Yellow Water Billabong," a large Aboriginal man calls, and we cluster around him. "In case you don't know, a billabong used to be part of a river but was cut off somehow."

We file into a covered aluminum barge, the man walking to the rear of the boat and standing behind a big steering wheel. "We will be out in the sun for ninety minutes, so drink plenty of water. But don't worry. We have a toilet aboard."

Some people chuckle, though everyone seems tired and hot and hungry, like I am.

"I am the owner of this tour company, here today as a guide because of the large crowd." He starts the quiet motor. "I want to show you my home." He points out a group of small houses and trailers in the distance.

Appearing as serene as the billabong, he says, "We Aboriginals take care of this huge area of Australia as its custodians and prefer to live as we always have—in our clans. We regard this sacred billabong as part of our Dreamtime, our story."

I think of my small hometown, where I returned several years ago after spending my adult life in larger cities. Rejoining my family has been gratifying.

Steering slowly through calm, swamp-like water, our guide shows us pink and white waterlilies and various grasses. "Look at those little birds over there," he says. "They're so light they can walk on the vegetation in the water to find bugs and other things to eat." He later alerts us to a sea eagle perched in an ancient, gnarled tree, reminding us to take turns moving to one side of the boat to photograph it. "The crocs don't treat drop-in visitors well," he says, and we chuckle nervously. But his gentle tone and the peaceful setting seem to wash away much of our former hostility and frustration.

Time sails by. We land, walk back toward our bus, and enjoy a buffet lunch on a cool patio. As we're finishing, Grace stops by our table. "May I join you?" she asks.

I nod eagerly, but Martha Jo, always gracious, says, "That would be nice, but we're about to leave."

Grace glances at our empty plates, nods, and then sits with the couple from New York.

I feel like joining them just to satisfy my curiosity about her. But she must be on a bus that's due to leave slightly later than ours, and I don't want to miss my ride. When we board our ship, surely I can discover more about her.

On the bus, we speed back to our hotel, most of us dozing on the way.

Mutiny at the Tables

"I can't believe we haven't eaten yet and that no one from Advantage has made a general announcement," Martha Jo says. "Isn't someone in charge?"

Amy looks at her watch. "It's almost nine o'clock, and we got up at six this morning. I'm tired and hungry."

"We want dinner! We want dinner!"

"What in the world?" Martha Jo asks, then points. "Look over there at that group in the middle of the room."

Amy laughs. "Some of our tour members have had a little too much of the free wine the waiters have been handing out."

"Well, I can sympathize," I say. "They're just doing what we'd all like to. Look. Heather and her husband—you know, the ones we flew in with—are part of that gang. You know how Californians are."

"No. How?" Martha Jo asks.

"They aren't afraid to say what's on their mind."

"Well, I think they're being a little rude," she says, but then she grins. "Though if it works, I'm all for it."

Amy nods. "I agree."

Martha Jo frowns. "But they don't have to beat on the table in time with their chant. I just hope I taught my four children better table manners than that."

"I feel sorry for the waiters," Amy says. "It's not their fault they don't have any meals to serve us yet."

I'm not sure whether to be embarrassed or join the protesters. The frustration that the flight problems caused has resurfaced, but magically our servers soon arrive with our meals.

Finally, after we've eaten and are preparing to leave, a young woman associated with Advantage drops by our table and shares a bit of information about tomorrow's activities. But by that time, it's old news.

As we head back to our room, Martha Jo says, "I've been on a lot of cruises, and I've never seen anything like this."

Amy chimes in. "Yeah. It's like no one's in charge. Or if they are, they don't have a clue what to do next."

I say only, "I traveled with this company seventeen years ago, and nothing like this happened."

"Things change, I suppose," Amy says.

I inwardly sigh. I'm the one who suggested we take this trip, but I'm beginning to be sorry I did, except for the possibility of meeting Grace.

February 15, 2023

SIGHTSEEING IN DARWIN—GETTING ACQUAINTED WITH GRACE

"Where's Bill?" Amy asks as we climb onto bus three the next morning.

"That young woman who finally visited with us after dinner last night probably heard some of the nasty things he said about her and fired him," Martha Jo says.

"Well, I'm not surprised," I say. "He was a little unprofessional. But he was right."

The rock-art expert from yesterday narrates the history of Darwin as we drive through its skyscrapered downtown. "We're mostly a modern city," he says, "because of the Japanese and a cyclone."

We perk up. *What did the Japanese have to do with a cyclone?*

"Everyone knows about Pearl Harbor, right?" our guide asks.

We all nod. Some of our group probably lost a relative there.

"The same fleet that bombed you hit us also—two months later."

Several of us make eye contact and nod. I would have been a month old when that happened.

"But they used more bombs here in Darwin and attacked the downtown area as well," he says. "And on top of that, they came back here fifty-eight more times."

I look at the relatively modern buildings we pass with new eyes.

Someone asks, "What about the cyclone you mentioned?"

"That hit us about thirty years later," he says, "in 1974."

I think back to 2005—the year of Katrina, then Rita. Rita made the subdivision where I lived near the Gulf Coast in Southeast Texas look like a war zone, so he has my attention.

"The winds here were estimated at more than 200 kilometers per hour," he says, "about 125 miles per hour. They destroyed most of our population as well as the older historic buildings that had survived what we call our Australian Pearl Harbor. The people who weren't killed were airlifted away."

Some of our group nearby are shaking their heads.

Our guide continues. "But we built Darwin back, using special construction techniques, so hopefully we can survive anything now, except maybe the crocodiles who've invaded since then."

We drive along the bay and the coast, passing huge water parks.

"Why are water parks so popular here?" someone near the back asks.

Our guide rolls his eyes slightly. "Like I said earlier. Crocodiles."

"What about them?" someone else asks.

We've heard rumors, references to them, but that's all.

He stands up, shakes his head slightly. "They were declared an endangered species here in the '70s. Because of all the hunting, only about 3,000 were left."

"So how many are around today?" a man asks.

"Approximately 400,000 in Australia as a whole," he says. "And about a fourth of them live here in the Northern Territory. That's why you see all these *No Swimming* signs along the highways. The crocs are in our ocean."

He definitely has our attention.

"During the wet season, from November to March, many of them head inland and hang out in the swamps and rivers. It's a wonder we didn't see more yesterday in Kakadu. It's also their mating season now, so maybe they were busy."

We snicker, recall the few we did spot. At least this young man isn't as uptight as he seemed to be during his lecture yesterday.

"But in the dry season, from April through October, the crocs prefer the estuaries and the open sea," he says. "And they're the world's largest reptile. Even though their jaw muscles aren't as powerful as you'd expect, they have sixty-odd teeth, which grow back quickly after they lose any."

Someone in the rear of the bus whistles, then asks, "So when you head to the coast for vacation, you think water park, not beach and surf?"

"Righto," our guide says. "Crocs are cold-blooded in more ways than one."

We take a deep, collective breath. I'm almost glad we missed that scheduled stroll along the beach last night.

"And now we're headed to lunch," he says. "Then to the Museum and Art Gallery of the Northern Territory, where you can meet Sweetheart, the most famous croc in this part of the country."

❖

I do see Sweetheart at the museum/gallery—a stuffed male sixteen feet long and fifty to eighty years old. Presumably he attacked the outboard motors on small boats for years because their noise resembled the sound other males made. Then, after terrorizing the people in the area, he repeatedly accosted aluminum dinghies at a popular fishing spot and finally drowned while being captured.

I also walk through a room full of paintings of and by talented Aboriginal artists. One features an older man wearing a gold-colored shirt—arms crossed, stern, straight lips, large nostrils, steady gaze. His gray mustache and long, unruly hair contrast to his black cowboy hat.

After wandering around the facility, I stumble upon four large screens, in a small, dimly lit room, playing clips from classic Hollywood films, each segment focused on a common theme.

Here, I'm drawn to "Love," from 2003, an early video collage in this series of eight. Carefully selected brief film clips depict romance and intimacy, revealing dark themes such as codependency and the abuse of women.

Looking at this variety of clips, I can almost feel the blows, both physical and verbal, that famous movie stars such as Marlon Brando and Vivian Leigh give each other on-screen. If the film artist had spaced these segments farther apart, they might be bearable to watch. But, locked in a tight sequence like this, they overwhelm me and, apparently, other viewers, most of whom don't linger here.

Glancing away from the screen, I spot Grace several times. She's sitting nearby, and when she and I make eye contact, we shake our heads, sigh, and continue to watch the collage of violent movie clips.

"I've had enough," I finally say, then leave to breeze through the rest of the museum. But later, when I return for one last look at the intense, disturbing exhibit, she's still sitting there—eyes wide, shoulders drooping.

"I've watched all four of the episodes being shown here in Darwin," she says, shaking her head as if waking up. "I wish this entire amazing collection, which is touring Australia right now, would make it to the States."

"You must be tough," I say, and motion to the video screens. "To watch all that."

"I am." She glances around the practically empty room and then at her wrist. "Oh. We should get back to our buses. And we better step on it."

"I'm in the first bus today," she says as we hurry out the front door, "and it looks like they've almost finished loading."

"I'm in the third one. See you on the ship," I say, and she strides away. She seems sure of herself and willing to look at life in depth, judging by her absorption in those graphic film segments. Maybe we can spend some time together. By now I'm almost positive she's traveling alone.

Grace. I like her name. It makes me think about my flapper great-aunt, as well as positive qualities such as forgiveness and beauty of movement.

The buses deliver everyone to the docks, where we board our small ship, chattering about setting sail and enjoying a relaxing day at sea tomorrow.

Martha Jo, Amy, and I meet our steward and inspect our cabin, with its three separate beds. It'll be a little cramped, though we probably won't spend much time here.

Then we attend a mandatory safety drill and explore the ship.

Finally, we walk down to our first nightly briefing, which goes smoothly—at first.

Shocking First Briefing

"Mmm. It's so good to settle down after our hectic past few days," Martha Jo says. "Maybe now we can have a little peace and quiet, at least for a while."

We've gathered in the large meeting room/lounge next to the bar—a comfortable, downward-sloping area, dotted with small booths, benches, chairs, and cocktail tables. It features a stage/dance floor, musical equipment to one side, and AV screens in the rear.

"Yeah." Amy takes a swallow of her complimentary drink. "The entire crowd seems a little more mellow tonight, probably thanks to these." She holds up her glass, and I nod.

Our young, handsome cruise director from Italy introduces the entire crew and, finally, the captain, who welcomes us.

"The ship's international crew seems friendly," Martha Jo says. "Our cabin boy acts like he'll do everything he can to make us happy." She laughs. "Now this is what I envisioned."

Each of the handful of the twenty- and thirty-year-olds in charge of our daily activities takes a turn at the microphone and explains his or her various roles and expectations for the trip.

"Wow. They're all so young," Martha Jo says. "Much younger than any of my children."

Amy chimes in. "And they seem truly excited about being part of this cruise, don't they?"

Up front, the young man says, "We've just completed Advantage's first Bali-to-Darwin voyage. And on our way back to Bali, we'll stop at some places we hadn't planned on. So they'll be as new to us as they are to you." He gives us a beautiful smile. "Now we want to share some details about our activities during our next ten days of exploring small, relatively isolated, Indonesian islands."

A young geographer from Scotland takes the microphone and introduces herself as our sea-kayak master.

"I thought we were supposed to go snorkeling, not kayaking," Amy whispers.

Martha Jo sighs. "Here we go again."

The young woman announces, "We have only five seaworthy, two-person kayaks, with just one opportunity to use them." Immediately people nearby start whispering.

A fit-looking, gray-haired man asks, "Where do we sign up, and how do you plan to choose the ten lucky people?"

"You'll need to fill out a questionnaire," the speaker responds. "Then we will evaluate them and choose the ten best-qualified kayakers."

"Uh-oh," Amy whispers. "I bet the competition's gonna be fierce."

"Yeah. And she still hasn't said anything about the snorkeling equipment they promised us," Martha Jo says. "I'm looking forward to that activity."

A different young man takes the stage. "Just to make sure you know, the Indonesian government has suddenly demanded we change our itinerary and go ashore at some islands we haven't anticipated."

"So that's why we'll encounter some places different from the ones this ship stopped at on the way here from Bali," a woman sitting nearby says.

Politics. We shrug. No one seems to mind, though, because none of us know enough about any of our remote destinations to care. Most everyone just seems to want to take it easy and see the highlights of an unusual part of the world at a very good price.

After other discussions about what to expect during this voyage, an abrupt, no-nonsense Brit stands before us. "You're on an *expedition*, not a cruise," he states brusquely, clearly unapologetic. He stares around the meeting room, probably appalled at how many old people he sees.

Almost everyone nearby appears puzzled and begins murmuring to their neighbor.

He stares at us until we settle down. "I have been in charge of Advantage's expeditions to Antarctica for the past few years," he says, "and I consider this voyage as complex and as difficult as those have been."

A few people nearby gasp quietly and stare at each other.

His tone grows even more serious. "First, because of our new schedule, we will be stopping at some islands no tourists have visited since COVID began." Dead silence. "There, we will have to drive long distances over rough roads in un-air-conditioned vehicles to see most of the sights we have hastily planned to visit. So forget the leisurely afternoons the old schedule promised you."

Feet shuffle. A few snorts sound.

"And at every island except three, you will have to ride a Zodiac to go ashore."

"A Zodiac," someone calls out. "What's that?"

Our tall, thin expedition director snorts this time. "Didn't you read about them?"

Most of us shake our head. One bald man says loudly, "I knew we'd have to take a tender at a few ports, like I've done on many other cruises. But our schedule states in black and white that we'll be able to walk right off the ship to see most of the islands we stop at." He waves the document in the air.

The Brit frowns. "Well, the recent mandatory changes have invalidated that schedule. You'll have to ride in a rubber raft that seats ten people. That's a Zodiac. The sea will be moving up and down, sometimes a lot, so the crew will have to help you on and off the small boat. It won't be easy. And you'll definitely have to wear a life jacket. We will teach you more about riding in your Zodiac in the morning, so everyone who wants to go ashore *must* come to the mudroom when we call your group."

An older man waves his hand in the air, then says, "I have a bad leg."

"We'll help you as much as we can," says another youthful director of some sort, frowning slightly, apparently concerned at the direction this discussion has taken.

"I'll say it again. You're on an expedition, not a cruise," the Brit states, almost scowling. "And when we reach the shore, we'll have either a wet landing or a dry landing."

A sophisticated blonde sitting near the front of the crowd speaks up. "What's the difference?"

"In wet landings, expect to get your feet wet and sandy. You'll have to walk ashore through the surf."

She winces. "At least I brought some old shoes."

The man behind me mutters, "I wish I'd known all this ahead of time. I wouldn't have come."

The tall expedition director continues. "With a dry landing you won't get your feet wet. But most of the time, the steps up to the dock will be slippery, so rubber soles are best. You'll have to be careful not to fall."

Mini comments and conversation sprout all over the room. Yet our informant has saved the best for last.

"Once ashore, it's hot, so carry and drink plenty of water. However, we won't have access to many Western-style toilets. You need to either be prepared to hold yourself or find a private spot and squat like the people who live here do."

Thinking of our group's median age—about seventy or seventy-five—I almost laugh. The crowd reacts like football fans booing the referee after a bad call.

We finish our first evening briefing and walk to dinner in rather stunned silence. *What have we gotten ourselves into? I came here to relax and recuperate.*

February 16, 2023

DAYBREAK: LOOKING BACK

It's early morning, quiet and peaceful after last night's bombshell announcements, and I'm relaxing in a slatted chair on the ship's rear deck. Gazing back toward Australia, I think about the small section of the large country we've briefly encountered.

The waxing moon high over my head reminds me of a shining boomerang tossed by an Aboriginal. In contrast, a blue-gray cloud stretches along the distant, dark horizon. Some clouds to its right boil, which makes me think of how the Japanese repeatedly bombed Darwin eighty years ago. What a horrible sight that must have been. And to have endured it?

Suddenly I recall a phone call from my gastroenterologist almost a year ago. "I have the results of your colonoscopy," she said.

That February morning, I perched on the edge of one of the olive, tan, and mauve straight-backed chairs in my small living room. *How nice.* No one has ever given me my test results so personally, I thought.

"I'm sorry, but we found a growth, and you need to take care of it immediately," she said. "You have anal cancer. Hopefully it hasn't spread to your lungs."

I felt like she'd dropped a bomb on me. And the chemo and radiation that followed made me afraid I didn't have a chance to survive. Each day I grew weaker, more subdued, drained. Finally, I could barely walk.

The inhabitants of Darwin must have questioned their survival every time they heard those planes buzzing overhead, just as I questioned mine during my six weeks of chemo and radiation.

For me, however, the harsh treatments succeeded. After another battery of scans, my doctors at MD Anderson declared that I was in remission. And during my last checkup, they encouraged me to sign up for this cruise. "Go ahead. It'll be good for you to take it easy and see someplace new and interesting," they said.

Now I'm sitting on the deck watching the clouds grow farther away and thinking about being on the other side of the world. But apparently this cruise isn't what my doctors and I expected. I'm afraid I'm taking part in a rigorous expedition instead of spending a carefree two weeks at sea, and that possibility unnerves me.

These thoughts wash through me like the waves that slap against our ship. The cool sea air bathes me, and I try to clear my mind. *I'm here. Why not simply enjoy the moment? And no one will force me to go ashore at every island we visit.*

Slowly, the sky brightens, and the moon begins to fade.

In the east, the clouds are glowing pink and gold now, and I watch the sun finally come out of its hiding place behind them.

I wish I could be like the sun, as sure of my place in the universe as it obviously is. When this cruise ends, I'd love to feel like a new person.

And I'm more than ready to forget the past few years of my life as one tragedy piled up on top of another.

I'll try to imitate the sun. I realize I'm alone, just like it is, and I'll do my best to be as sure of my place in the world as the sun is. I'll also try to follow its lead and shine on people, help them feel warm toward themselves and others.

Simply sitting here, I already feel better. The ocean breeze cools me as I watch the moon grow dim. Tonight it'll be even larger and brighter.

I smile and promise myself to go slowly, to not push myself. I'll try to keep on recovering from all the traumas of the past few years, and by the end of this trip, I'll be stronger, ready to leave my past behind and enjoy whatever future I have left on this earth. Also, along the way, maybe I'll gain more insight into why I always feel so different from everyone else, like that girl in the *Prevention* magazine article I read last month talked about.

As I sit here at the back of our ship and watch all traces of the down-under continent disappear, an older Asian man pulls himself from his deck chair and murmurs as he nears me, "What a beautiful world. Thank you, God."

I'll be okay.

Exploring the Ship

"Wow. This breakfast buffet looks as good as the Hilton's," Amy says as she fills her tray. "So many choices, plus everything else you could ever want."

Even on my restricted diet, I find plenty to eat, though I forgo most of the tempting, unusual fruit. My digestive system is still delicate after my regular rounds of radiation and chemo, plus a radiation burn that hospitalized me for almost a week. My treatments ended late last May, but their effects have lingered and will probably last for quite a while longer. Most food still doesn't taste very good, and I fluctuate between resorting to the BRAT diet of bread, rice, applesauce, and toast and having to choose bulking-fiber foods such as wheat bread, brown rice, and various types of beans. I'm still on a dietary roller coaster and am more than ready for it to slow down and stop.

Our waiter from last night walks up. "Good morning, ladies. Please to come with me."

We follow him to a table for six.

"I thought we had open seating on this cruise," Amy says after he has pulled out our chairs and taken our hot-drink orders.

I shrug. "After last night's surprises, I don't know what to think."

"The food situation looks really good," Martha Jo says. "Maybe the rest of the trip will go the way we expected." She butters a flaky croissant and takes a bite. "Mmm. Delicious."

"May I join you for a cup of coffee?" someone standing behind me asks, the voice clear, distinctive…familiar.

"Of course," Amy says.

I turn, and there stands Grace. She sits beside me, and my AFib heart beats its irregular rhythm so loud the people two tables away can surely hear it. *What's happening to me?*

"What did you think about last night's meeting?" She looks at Amy and Martha Jo.

Martha Jo addresses Grace's question. "It's a real shame a tour company would mislead us this way." She takes a bite of her scrambled eggs. "Zodiacs, wet landings, no sit-down toilets. If I were in my forties, I wouldn't mind so much." Martha Jo attacks a piece of guava as if it's just frowned at her. "But I'm in my eighties, and I bet none of the passengers will see fifty or maybe even sixty again."

Grace scans the dining room. "You're probably right. And a lot of them aren't happy about their flights to Australia and our disorganized stay in Darwin."

Martha Jo sips some kind of pink juice, then pulls another piece from her croissant and butters it. "But we're probably all just tired. A nice, restful day at sea should help."

Amy grins, her tense shoulders seeming to drop a bit. "Maybe that British guy was exaggerating, and the facilities won't be as primitive as he says."

Grace smiles, then changes the subject. "Do you plan to go ocean kayaking? That should be fun."

Martha Jo and Amy shake their heads *no*, and I say, "I've kayaked several times, but usually on a calm lake. Once, in a river, I got caught in the current and had to stand in the raging water and pry my kayak away from a tree where it was wedged." I shake my head and laugh. "Not one of my finest hours. How about you, Grace?"

She puts down her cup and speaks emphatically. "I've had a lot of experience in the ocean. Have bought and sold several kayaks, including two-seaters like we'll be using here. I've also taught several groups of beginners how to handle different types of kayaks, so I plan to try out for a place."

My slight bit of experience in a one-seater seems puny contrasted to her broad exposure to the sport. "I think I'll forget about kayaking and focus on snorkeling later in the trip. That's a wonderful way to spend an afternoon."

"Well, if they provide us with some decent equipment, I'll join you," Grace says, and Martha Jo nods.

"Not me." Amy frowns. "I prefer to keep my head out of the water. I'll beachcomb while y'all splash around with the fish."

"I don't want to be a wet blanket," Grace says, "but with this cruise company, you never know what may happen." She pushes her heavy chair backward, away from the table. "I plan to just play it by ear." She stands and tugs at her well-fitting, knee-length, blue shorts. "I've enjoyed chatting with you and will see you later. I need to get ready for our Zodiac lesson. I don't plan to miss a single trip ashore."

Soon, Martha Jo, Amy, and I head back to our cabin and sit on our small balcony. We've been there maybe ten minutes, when suddenly we hear an announcement over the ship-wide speakers, "Yellow group, report to the mudroom for a mandatory meeting." We jump up and hurry to the rear of the ship, where we join a long line of passengers in our group.

Finally, we reach the head of the line, and our lessons begin. "You'll find your life jackets in the locker with your cabin number on it." A crewman directs us to ours, where we pull out our jackets.

I stand like a grade-school student, clutching my unwieldy red contraption as if it's a firecracker about to explode. It feels foreign, somehow different from the uncomplicated ones I used to wear as a young person, when forced to.

Our instructor yawns, then says, "Hold up your life vest like you're planning to shake hands with it and slide one arm in, then the other. After that, buckle the straps around your waist."

So much information. It's like trying to operate a new cell phone or computer.

"You'll have to wear a red jacket like this every time you go ashore, so please practice until you get it right," our instructor says. "Without it, you cannot leave the ship."

Oh, the pressure, I think. I wrestle with mine several times but still don't feel sure of the process. "I can't figure out which end's up and where to put which arm," I say, raking my fingers through my hair several times.

Why is this simple task so difficult all of a sudden? I used to be able to do things like this in my sleep.

"Don't worry," the young man replies. "You'll get used to it."

Easy for you to say.

Too quickly, we progress to the next station to learn how to grip each other's arm double-handed. "So, I have to remember to grab your forearm at the same time you take hold of mine?" I ask our instructor, who could be my grandchild.

"That's right," he says. "The Zodiac may be rocking and rolling, both when you're getting in and getting out of it."

"Okay. That's easy enough," I say, still trying to recall how to put on my life jacket. *When did I start having so much trouble learning new basic skills?*

"And, finally," he says, "as soon as you're safely on the watercraft, *sit down. Immediately.* Then the driver will tell you which way to move along the side of the raft."

"So, I'll be sitting somewhere on the edge of it?"

"That's right. You'll find a rope there to hold if you want."

My head's spinning. "Didn't life vests used to be easier to put on?" I whisper to Martha Jo.

She nods sympathetically, then asks me, as we leave the mudroom, "Did you get all that?"

I simply raise my eyebrows.

"I probably won't be going ashore very often," she whispers, her shoulders drooping.

"I *think* I understand the routine," I say, trying to fool myself. "At least I plan to do my best. I just hope the surf's not too rough."

Amy pipes up. "You two don't worry. I'll help you. It'll be fun."

Martha Jo sighs. "Huh. I hope so. It's a good thing I'm married to a younger woman who isn't afraid to try new things."

After that ordeal, we climb several flights of stairs to one of the upper decks, where we inspect the two hot tubs and the small pool at the rear of the ship. No water in any of them.

A worker with a broom walks up and responds nonchalantly to our inquiries. "The pool has a leak, so it won't be available for this trip. But the hot tubs should be ready this afternoon. We're cleaning them."

"Well, that was a bust," Amy says. "Let's check out the gym."

It's on the same level, and it's small.

"Look. Five treadmills," Amy says, "and they're all in front of floor-to-ceiling windows, so we can look outside while we walk."

"I may try the rowing machine," Martha Jo says. "That should be fun."

"I'm used to free weights," I say, "but these pull-downs will work, plus here's a full-length mirror and an open space where I can do tai chi."

"Maybe not many passengers will want to exercise much," Amy says, "so this should suit us fine."

"Okay. At least that's settled." Martha Jo opens the plate-glass door. "Let's go see the rest of the ship, especially the library."

We stroll along the outside walkway, sliding our hands over the smooth, wooden side railing, warm air embracing us.

"Here's the bow," I say, hoping I've used the correct term for this area. "I can't keep that famous scene from *Titanic* out of my mind."

Amy and Martha Jo move to the very front of the ship and do a safe imitation of DiCaprio and Winslet pretending to be flying while I take their picture.

"Hey, don't jinx us," I say, a slight tremor running down my spine when I think about the *Titanic*'s fate.

"What could go wrong?" Amy asks. "We got here without that much trouble. It should be smooth sailing from here on out."

Martha Jo frowns slightly, but then she says, "Oh. Look over there, behind those glass doors." She points. "It's the library."

Amy pushes through them. "And it has coffee machines and snacks."

"Plus, during our free afternoons, we can play Rummikub on that small table," Martha Jo says. "It's perfect."

As she points to the table and some chairs, Amy murmurs, "If we have any free time."

I nod, thinking of last night's meeting. "I'll take it easy," I murmur to myself.

We wander back to our cabin to enjoy what's left of our one full day of leisure at sea.

Alone on Our Balcony

Sitting in the shade of our balcony that afternoon, I prop my bare feet up on the metal rails and let the equatorial sun's rays bake them. Their warmth makes me as pliable as biscuit dough, and I almost doze off.

The MS *Odyssey Adventurer* pushes leisurely through the placid waves, transforming the calm, clear water into swan-white foam. Farther away from the ship, the sea strangely reminds me of the deep blue of the ink I used in my fountain pen as a girl.

How long ago it seems. That innocent child certainly never imagined that, in seventy years, she'd spend ten days on a luxury liner on the other side of the world. She had probably never heard of Indonesia. I smile at that gangly girl and all the changes she'll encounter as she ages.

She'd love to know that all her best friends from school and many of her family members would still be alive today.

But she would probably shudder at her future self's three divorces, her parents' deaths, and her own battle with cancer.

A fugitive gust from the ocean chills me, and I smooth my windblown hair back from my face several times. *Just try to enjoy the comedies and tragedies of this trip and of your life, including your cancer experience*, I counsel myself. *Your scans are clear. Your doctors are amazed at your progress. Let yourself heal completely. Listen to me. Relax.*

The sun warms me again. Piles of gray-white, wispy clouds divide the aquamarine sky from the peacock-blue ocean.

It's as quiet as the desert. Only the constant whoosh of the Timor Sea against our ship breaks the silence.

I stare at the straight line of the distant horizon, inhale the salty air as it bathes my sun-warmed skin.

What will tomorrow and the next nine days traveling on this ship bring?

February 17, 2023

First Zodiac Ride

"Yellow group, please report to the mudroom. Your Zodiacs are waiting to tender you to the beautiful island of Yamdena. Bring your sunglasses and hats, plus plenty of drinking water. But remember, the toilet facilities are limited."

Amy and I jump up, but Martha Jo just sits there on the side of her bed. "Plenty of water and not many toilets," she says, as she removes her beige safari hat from where it hangs by its cord against her back. "I'm afraid to chance it because of the diuretics I'm taking."

"You're not going?" Amy stops on her way to the door. "After we flew all this way?"

Martha Jo nods. "Sorry, sweetie. But that's how it goes when you're married to an older woman."

"Well, I'll stay here too." Amy turns around and sets her water bottle on a nearby desk.

Martha Jo slides her slim arms around her. "We've had this discussion before. I'll be fine. I'm sure a lot of others will feel the same way, so I won't be alone."

Amy cuddles into Martha Jo's embrace. "Are you sure? You know I'll gladly stay with you, don't you?"

Martha Jo smooths one hand down Amy's back. "I do realize that, sweetheart. And I appreciate your offer. But like I said, I'll be fine." She takes off her hat. "You two go have a good time."

"Well, all right." Amy picks up her water bottle and her daypack, and we leave our cabin. Immediately we're part of a crowd hurrying to the mudroom.

"There's our locker," Amy says, leading us right to it.

"How did you remember where it is? They all look the same to me."

"Just a little trick." She grins. "It has the same numbers as the ones in my second son's birthday—719."

She hands me a life jacket and then slides into hers like a pro. I hold mine up as if I've never seen one before. Four pieces of Styrofoam covered with red cloth dangle from white straps, and I can't distinguish up from down, inside from outside. I try to stick one arm through two of the straps but can't figure out where they fasten together.

Amy asks, "Need some help?"

"No. I think I have it." I shove my right arm between two of the red pieces tangled with the straps. Both my mind and my heart race. Why can't I do something so simple? A hailstorm seems to be raging inside my brain. I put my right hand to my head and stroke my coarse hair back from my forehead. Once, twice, three times. But the icy pellets in my brain persist.

Amy stands there as I keep brushing back my hair, other passengers walking around us and joining the line to board the waiting Zodiac.

"Oh, okay. I give up." I hold out the contrary foreign object. "I can't believe I'm so dumb about something that used to be so easy. Sorry."

"Nothing to be sorry about." Amy's tone soothes me like Martha Jo's did earlier in our cabin. "You're an eighty-one-year-old woman in a strange area of a small ship in the middle of a big sea you've never sailed on before, about to visit an island we barely know the name of." She takes the unruly jacket pieces from me, and I let my shoulders drop. She's kept me from totally losing it over a simple task. My mental hail melts and drains away as quickly as it formed. What a relief to be rational again.

"Thank you for being so kind, Amy." I sigh long and hard. "I couldn't have made this trip by myself, not in my condition. You and Martha Jo are a godsend."

"You're welcome. It's our pleasure." She takes my right arm and magically slides it between two of the jacket pieces. "And we wouldn't have known about this interesting cruise if you hadn't told us." She snaps my life vest into place around my chest and nudges me toward the long line of about thirty chattering tourists that inches toward the exit door barely visible in the distance.

"What's this island's name?" I ask her. "I can't remember."

She shakes her head. "They announced it this morning, but I wasn't paying attention."

She taps the shoulder of a tall, thin man standing front of us and asks him.

"I heard someone call it Yamdena," he says. "And the port town's named Saumlaki."

"Oh. Thanks," she says. "After breakfast, we noticed a bunch of Indonesian officials meeting with some of our ship's officers."

"Yes. Yamdena's evidently one of the unscheduled stops the Indonesian government has mandated," he says. He jerks at his brown daypack slipping to one side of his back.

Amy and he strike up a brief conversation, which I feel at ease enough to join, saying, "When our Zodiac reaches that old wooden dock where we're supposed to get off, I hope I don't have as much trouble with it as I've had with this life vest." We all laugh, and I begin to relax. Since I normally feel awkward and tongue-tied around strangers, Amy must be helping me with more than my life jacket.

❖

"We have two Zodiacs running today," one of our young leaders announces as we finally near the exit door. "I'll take the next ten of you, and then another boat will be here in about twelve minutes to pick up the final group." He starts loading passengers.

When the Zodiac's almost full, Amy says, "Looks like I'm number ten, so we'll be separated." She half-turns toward the crewman who's motioning her toward him. "See you when we get there."

The friendly man Amy has just been talking to has left with her, and it already seems like I've been waiting twelve hours instead of twelve minutes. As I listen to strangers chatter, I double-check my belongings, gaze out to sea, and adjust my greenish cloth sun hat. I'm alone for the first time on this trip, except on the plane.

I tense, missing the easy camaraderie I felt earlier with Amy and the friendly man. My arms tingle and grow rigid against my sides as an all-too-familiar panic grabs me. I look around, see nothing but strangers, indifferent to me and to my panic. Am I invisible? They're all laughing and talking, but their words seem foreign. How can they be so at ease in this group of people they've just encountered? My shoulders rise, stiffen, and a tornado seems to howl through my head. I'm sweating, heart racing. No one speaks to me, and I don't utter a sound. I stand there as stiff and mute as a metal piling.

Somehow, I remove my hat and run my fingers through my hair, take a deep breath, then exhale as slowly as possible, try to breathe into the sudden unsteadiness, the panic. So much energy is suddenly blazing inside me, I'll explode like one of the volcanoes so common in this part of the world if I don't release it somehow.

Then I realize I'm pushing my hair back repeatedly, and its soft smoothness is calming me, so I focus on the repetition, think of my mother brushing it when I was a girl. Gradually, my shoulders begin to drop, my heart rate slows, and a cool sea breeze bathes me.

At long last, it's my turn to board the rubber raft that has pulled up alongside the ship. *I don't have to talk to these strangers I'm alone with. I can move, do something that interests me instead of simply standing around feeling like I should make meaningless conversation.*

Attempting to remember the boarding procedure we learned yesterday, I hand my daypack to a crew member, who has to remind me what to do next. "Grab my forearm while I grab yours." I stifle a stab of panic. Lesson learned. But how could I have forgotten something so simple, so basic? Then I put my foot onto the side of the heaving boat, and it gives under my weight. Finally, our driver half-pulls me aboard, a crewman gently pushing me from the ship's opening.

"Sit down right now," our driver orders me.

So, I do.

"And now slide to your right and stay put."

I do that too.

After we've all boarded, we slip around until we're equally spaced and lined up like targets in a shooting gallery, five on each elevated side of the Zodiac. "Ready?" our driver asks.

She revs the outboard motor, and we're off—fresh air blowing in my face. With one hand, I clutch my hat, now jammed onto my head, and, with the other, white-knuckle the rope running along the slick side of the raft I perch on. Recalling summers in East Texas water-skiing, fishing, joyriding in a motorboat, I'm suddenly exhilarated, back in my element from seventy years ago.

All too soon, we arrive at the end of an old, barnacled pier, where

I finally remember to use the required double grip. With a helping hand and a nudge from behind, I scramble up a series of splintered wooden steps. Thank goodness I've been walking several miles a day at home.

After struggling onto a rickety dock that juts out from a large, ramshackle building, I take my daypack from a crewman, jerk off my life jacket and toss it into a pile, then walk, alone, down a long wooden deck dotted with pots of red begonias and dining tables and chairs. I'm heading toward what appears to be a hotel in a rather large town, trying to forget my panic attack and embrace the recent exhilaration of riding in the fresh sea air.

Saumlaki and Sangliat Dol

As I walk through a long, wood-paneled hall, I glance to my right through an open doorway. It looks like a hotel room—a regular-size bed, small side chair, and, voilà—a gleaming-white, Western-style toilet. Martha Jo could have used the restroom here.

But it's too late. I follow the trickle of my Zodiac mates and head for the front door. On a noisy street now, I spot assorted buses lined up on the other side and hurry toward them, dodging dented trucks and old motor scooters crowded with multiple riders.

"Here, over here." A young man waves a small flag, calling me. Up some battered steps and I'm in a well-used bus about four times the size of a minivan, its seat covers torn and faded. Its windows lower only a third of the way, but at least we'll have a bit of a breeze.

Where's Amy? I look around.

Probably already on her way to wherever we're going.

I head toward the back, slide into the only remaining seat. A tattered advertisement partially covers its window, so there goes my view of the countryside. My heart starts to pound, but I take a deep breath, run my fingers through my hair to calm myself again.

Where am I? Near the equator between Southeast Asia and Australia. Check. On one of Indonesia's 17,000 islands. Check. In the central part of this huge west-to-east chain stretching thousands of miles. Check.

Okay. I'm set, my mental geography review complete. The bus

revs, takes off over bumpy roads. Brakes squeal as motorcycles dart around us like minnows in a pond.

No familiar faces. Am I on the wrong bus? *No. Whew.* I spot a younger couple from the lobby of Australia's Hilton the other day. Seems like a week ago. *Calm down.*

"Ladies, gentlemen." Our local guide's obviously cheap microphone crackles. The roar of the engine and the traffic noise overpower him. Everyone in our group either talks or stares out the bus windows. Poor guy. Having to deal with all of us old foreigners.

He's like a rookie teacher in front of a class of rowdy high school students. His staticky microphone has only low volume, so he finally shouts in broken English, "Will take one hour, thirty minutes to reach village." Then he points out some of the larger buildings, especially the public schools, that we pass on the outskirts of the town—Saumlaki—according to a large sign we whiz by. Our guide grows silent as we roar through the sparsely populated, lush, green countryside.

Palm trees, banana trees, abundant, unfamiliar vegetation. Cows graze, staked to the side of the road. Chickens range freely around tin-roofed houses sprinkled along the way. We're climbing. Motorcycles whip past us, buzzing, honking. Oncoming trucks roar.

A woman three seats behind me, on the other side of the bus, complains incessantly about her poor health, her negligent daughter, and on and on. I'll walk back from our destination rather than listen to her when we return.

Finally, we're unloading at a small village in the hills. *Welcome to Sangliat Dol* says a sign nailed to a tree.

As I climb off our bus, Amy walks up. "There you are, Helen. I decided to wait for you here. My guide had to take care of some business, but she's offered to meet those of us who want to stay with her during the day. She speaks English well. Plus, she grew up on this island and works for the local government."

"Ah. Wonderful." I plop down on a rock wall in the shade of a banyan tree and thank the Buddha for the cool breeze and the sudden hush.

A young, tan woman eventually strides up. Her brown eyes bright and alert, she says, in fluent English, "So, welcome to our model Indonesian village, the best of the ones our national government has funded to attract tourists from all over the world."

"So that's why our schedule was changed," I murmur to Amy.

She nods. "Evidently."

"This village overlooks the ocean." Our guide points at a cracked, narrow, asphalt road. "Over there, from the top of a cliff down to the water, you can see a wide, stone walkway, built by these people's ancestors—a beautiful sight and a work of art."

"Oh, thank you, Amy," I whisper. "I thought I'd have to stumble aimlessly through the area."

Amy smiles. "Stick with me. I know the best people."

So do I, evidently.

We walk in the center of one of the village's few streets, lined with young trees and bushes, then down a steep hill past small stucco, tin-roofed homes—green, blue, pink, yellow. Small wooden posts support each home's front porch, and flowers bloom in every clean-swept yard.

"These crotons and geraniums look just like the ones at home," I say, and Amy nods. Women wearing T-shirts and pedal pushers sit on their small porches or peer out their front doors, waving and calling, "Hello." The children stare at us round-eyed, as if we're aliens. "Everyone seems as curious about us as we are about them."

We soon reach an open area, where several dozen men dressed in traditional garb sit on an odd formation of rock walls. "The village center." Our guide gestures. "The walls are part of an ancient stone boat."

"A stone boat?" Amy asks. "Why a boat?"

"Centuries ago, families or tribes joined each other and formed this village, mainly for protection. Many of the people came here by boat, so they made their most sacred landmark resemble one."

We briefly visit the small Catholic church on the highest hill in the village, then return to the boat area, where indigenous women dance for us. Through their movements they show us how they perform everyday tasks such as sweeping and washing clothes. Then several shirtless, barefoot men—wearing colorful sarongs and elaborate textile head wraps adorned with feathers—dance for us. The ceremony then ends with loud speeches from five of the men and an exchange of gifts between them and two of our fellow tourists.

"That was different," I say. "These people really seem to be trying to reach out to us."

"Well, I intend to reach back and go see what's for sale over there," Amy says. "Money's obviously a universal language, and those women behind those tables look eager for some business."

But before she can leave, several young girls wearing bright-colored, mismatched blouses and shorts sidle up to us. We mime taking their picture, and they cluster near Amy. "They want you to get in the shot with them," I say, so she joins them.

Most of the girls have cell phones, but none are wearing sunglasses. They point at ours, seeming fascinated. Fingering her pair, Amy says, "I'd give these to them, but they're prescription. Wish I'd brought a box full of cheap ones from the Dollar Tree back home for them."

Suddenly it's time to leave, and our guide leads us back to our buses. "An interesting day," I say. "I keep thinking about the Native Americans back home, how our European ancestors invaded their homeland and changed it totally. Wonder what these people think about us."

Amy nods, looking rather sad, and heads toward her bus.

Talking with Grace

I sit in the same seat as before. Hopefully, the woman with the irritating voice has changed buses, which I probably should have done. Group members keep trickling on, and suddenly I hear it—that unmistakable nasal sound. "Can you help me up the stairs, please?" the woman asks someone, and I brace for the return trip. Maybe I can manage a long nap.

Suddenly, though, someone says, in a clear, loud tone, "Here. Take my seat. It's near the front. It'll be easier for you up here."

And then, in the blink of an eye, Grace swings into the empty seat next to me.

"Do you mind?" she asks, and I shake my head *no*, relieved. "I felt sorry for that poor woman," she says, and now I nod, glad to have someone to talk to but afraid I won't be able to think of anything interesting to say. *Why didn't I change buses and sit with Amy on the way back?*

Panicked, I try to prepare myself. Grace and I haven't conversed much, and I have no idea what we might have in common besides film clips and kayaking. Maybe I can fake exhaustion and fall asleep? I slump and rest my head on the bare metal near the window.

Out of the blue, she asks, "Do you have anyone to travel with on a regular basis?"

Whoa. She doesn't waste any time. And she wants to discuss one of my favorite subjects. I have plenty to say about that. She couldn't have gotten a stronger reaction from me if she'd offered me a Turtle Pecan Blizzard from the Dairy Queen.

"No. I don't have a steady companion," I say promptly. "But I'd love to." I sit up straighter in my seat, turn halfway toward her.

As she begins to describe what countries she's visited and where she'd like to go, I study her out of the corner of my eyes, actually seeing her as if for the first time. She's short and thin, with medium-length, gray-brown hair and outstanding turquoise eyes. Young, though. Probably not quite seventy.

"I'd like to rent a small camper and tour England in it," she says, "and I'm looking for someone who enjoys driving one."

Her dancing blue eyes attract me much more than her mention of a camper does. "Been there, done that," I say, uncharacteristically blunt. "I've owned five different RVs in the past twenty or so years, from a sixteen-foot pull-along to a thirty-foot, self-contained rig." I try to hide my shudder. "That one did me in, especially when I had to drive it."

She doesn't flinch and tries again. "What about meandering up the West Coast and staying in Airbnbs?" She smiles wistfully. "I've been dreaming about a trip like that for a while, especially since I'm closing in on seventy."

Aha. I was right about her age.

Again, I shrug, my enthusiasm beginning to fade. "I spent a lot of time out there before Airbnbs became a thing. It's a beautiful, interesting part of the country, but not an area I want to experience much more of."

Even though Grace is quite a few years younger than I am, age doesn't make a difference when I'm on the road. And when I'm single, I'm always looking for a suitable companion. I'm here mainly because Martha Jo and Amy agreed to take this trip with me. But Amy prefers to go on hiking treks, and Martha Jo has some age-related health issues.

"Getting older makes you think about what you truly want to do with the rest of your life, doesn't it?" Grace asks, evidently sensing that I have quite a few years on her. I don't mention how many but appreciate her easy acceptance of the honest way I've responded to her suggestions.

"I'm dreaming of touring the ancient sites in Turkey, Eastern Europe, Greece, Italy, France, and the British Isles connected with goddess worship thousands of years ago," I say.

She grimaces, seeming about as interested in my suggestion as I've been in hers. "I hate history," she remarks, which dampens my enthusiasm for this potential companionship. I adore history.

We don't drop the subject, though. She says, "I'm also looking for inexpensive trips for me and my best friend since kindergarten. She can't afford to go much of anywhere since her husband died, so I take her with me as often as I can."

Now I know that she's here alone and why.

"Something like this cruise costs too much, though." She motions to the shabby bus we're bumping along in, but our fellow tourists' wardrobes and our brand-new small ship itself tell a different story.

We ride in comfortable silence. I like Grace, but our age difference could be a problem. Plus, she wants to go places and experience things I'm over and done with. At least it's easy to carry on a conversation with her. What a relief.

But how can anyone hate history? Traveling without learning about the past culture of wherever I visit would be like being blind. Half the fun's discovering as much as possible about a country and its people, past and present, before or after I go.

"So, are you married?" she asks. At least she chooses another easy subject.

"No." I shake my head. "Not right now. Been there, done that. Three times."

She shrugs, obviously not surprised or even concerned.

"Hard to get it right, eh?" Her face tightens, and I notice a few lines I haven't been aware of before.

"Yep. At least it has been for me."

She gazes out the window as we whiz past several children playing in the dirt yard of a tin-roofed house. "I can relate."

"What? You've been married three times too?" I try for a chuckle.

"No." She doesn't fall for my attempt to lighten the mood. "Once has been enough."

"So?" For some reason, a lot seems to be riding on my question and her answer.

"So, that's one big reason I'm on this cruise."

I turn a few inches, look at her more carefully. She's slumped in her seat, her hat in her hand, sunglasses now shading her lovely eyes.

"One reason?" I'm drawn in, holding my breath.

"Yes. I've been married for more than forty years to a man I spend most of my time leaving to take trips like this one."

"He doesn't want to go anywhere?"

The lines in her face harden. "He absolutely refuses. As a career military pilot, he got his fill of being away from home long ago, a lot of the time while I was stuck there taking care of our daughter."

"He doesn't want to go anywhere?"

"Correct. I have trouble even getting him away from the house for anything local."

"And he doesn't mind if you leave for two and a half weeks, like you're doing this time?"

"Nope. Doesn't seem to faze him."

"Is your daughter married?"

"Oh, yes." The lines of her face soften. "I have the cutest, sweetest little granddaughter imaginable."

I smile. "Does she live near you?" That should take some of the strain off her husband's need for solitude.

"No. That's part of the problem. She lives almost 400 miles away. In fact, I may move there so I can watch my grandchild grow up."

"What does your husband think?"

"He likes where we are and refuses to budge. Honestly, he might not even notice if I weren't there." She turns her head and stares out the window for a long minute.

"Have you thought about divorce?"

She looks toward me, her gaze as intense as when we watched the video collages back in Darwin. "Every day for as long as I can remember." Her slow, measured words reek of pain and resignation.

I remain silent.

"In fact, I'm surprised he's never brought up the subject." She shifts in her seat, as hard and unyielding as her tone.

"He wants you to stay together?"

She nods. "I suppose. If I were him, I'd have divorced me many years ago. But we get along okay. We simply don't have anything in common."

Her sigh reverberates through me.

"Well, if you do decide to leave him, you're welcome to stay with me as long as you want."

She stares at me, one eyebrow rising a fraction. "But we barely know one another. That's so kind."

"I mean it. I have an extra bedroom and quite a bit of experience with divorce."

But her telltale eyebrow has inched up a bit more. She probably thinks I've just made a pass at her, but she's too polite to say so.

I think back to my friends and family and their generosity when I've experienced such hard times. Their support means a lot, and I'm more than willing to help someone like Grace. I glance at her, but that eyebrow is still higher than its mate. *Duh.* I chide myself. My friends and family knew me, and of course I knew them as well, so none of us questioned our motives for our acts of kindness. But Grace and I are nearly strangers. How could I be so dense?

Thankfully, we roll into the outskirts of Saumlaki, our Zodiacs waiting offshore. Grace and I climb off the bus and head for the pier, the hurrying crowd separating us. I slow my pace and, on one of the wooden lattices that decorates the pier, notice a spiderweb shining in the sun.

In my mind, and in spite of my rash offer, I visualize a similar web forming between Grace and me. On the bus, I suddenly felt a connection to her that's totally out of proportion to the length of our acquaintance and the content of our few brief conversations. Something about her suggests that we have a lot in common, and I want to see what it is. But am I strong enough to explore our connection without losing myself in her, without giving away my power to her and regretting my own weakness? I've certainly done that often enough in the past and have regretted it.

Standing in line there on the pier at Saumlaki, waiting to board a Zodiac, I notice several square pots on one side of the platform. The tall, thorn-covered cacti in them sport occasional brilliant red blooms. Grace stands five or six people ahead of me, pulling on her life jacket, her shirt the same color as the vibrant blossoms.

I finally have an answer to the question I asked myself in Darwin what seems like many days ago. Grace definitely doesn't exhaust me. Right now, I'm bursting with energy.

February 18, 2023

Dawn at Sea

I slip out of bed very early, hoping I don't wake Martha Jo and Amy, pull on my shorts and an old workout shirt, then head for the small gym on the ninth deck. Alone, I spend several minutes at the weight machine, then stand in front of a huge mirror and practice tai chi.

Being on a rocking ship ups the difficulty factor, but it's easy to compensate, since tai chi has helped improve my balance. My mind wanders as I stretch overhead, bend to touch the floor with my palms, rotate my torso as far as I'm able, stretch my legs, balance on one foot at a time, and kick gently.

Thoughts of Grace drift through my mind, and as I move into my set routine, I dwell on how adept I am at following patterns. With how many women have I felt this strong energy? The process certainly started long ago. My third-grade teacher stands out, along with an occasional older girl in school, though my choral-music teacher in both junior high and high school definitely dwarfs my memories of my obsession with older women. I was infatuated with her until she died. And though she never encouraged my unspoken passion, her apparent fondness for me kept my longing alive all those years.

However, as a child and as a teenager, I didn't really expect the objects of my strong feelings to reciprocate. So when I eventually realized nothing would ever come of them, I wasn't totally devastated. But as I aged, things changed.

In my early thirties, my lust for an older married woman helped cement my first divorce. My husband couldn't compete with my passion for her, and though she promised, at least hinted, that she would get a divorce if I would, she didn't. I did. I was devastated.

Yet I didn't learn my lesson. Another married woman I fell for, encouraged by her seemingly strong interest in me, ended with her dramatically rejecting me totally. Why did I keep setting myself up like this?

Finally, I became friends with a strong older woman, a fellow teacher, who kept me at arm's length and promised me nothing but friendship, in which she became the increasingly dominant force. When she and her husband moved to another city, I grieved my loss but also welcomed my freedom from our unequal bond.

I spent the first fifty years of my life craving a relationship with an unattainable woman, and the next thirty with one to whom I feel like I relinquished more of my power every day. I finish my tai chi routine and gaze out the side window of the ship at the ocean's relentless waves.

Then I stare at myself in the gym's mirror. *Surely, after all these years, you can keep a little distance, not let yourself become totally obsessed with Grace, like with all those other women.*

Cooled down and determined, I drink a large bottle of water, then stroll out onto the deck. The calm sea resembles royal-blue raw silk. I'd like to rub my hands over it, feel its smooth texture, slide into it, bathe in it.

I think about Grace as the sun rises, seems to spew molten gold into the sky, sets it on fire.

Hopefully she isn't having a similar fiery effect on me, like these women in my past have. But I'm afraid she already has. I sigh. Why can't I hold my own with women I'm attracted to? I'm such a weakling.

Breakfast Conversation

"Thank goodness we don't have to leave early this morning to visit Kisar," Amy says as we finish breakfast.

"I slept a bit better last night," Martha Jo says, "so I'm looking forward to seeing a little of this island, even though I'll have to get my feet wet." She drinks the last of her morning coffee, and she and Amy head back to the cabin.

Grace and I linger at the table.

She immediately says, "You know that I'm married, though not very happily. What's your story? You seem to have lived a charmed life."

I sip my herbal tea, stare out the restaurant window at the sea and the clouds for a long minute. "Well, as I mentioned yesterday, I've been married three times. And the third time, which was the longest, was to a woman."

And just like that, I'm out to her.

She doesn't blink or change expression. But maybe she hides her feelings well. Yet, living near P-town, she should be used to queer people.

"Which did you prefer, male or female?" she asks. We could be discussing the difference between vanilla and strawberry ice cream.

"I was with the woman almost thirty years, three times as long as I was with the two men combined, so I'd say female."

She raises an eyebrow. "If you don't consider length, what's your choice?"

"Women."

"Why?"

She doesn't beat around the bush.

"Because they don't have privilege engrained in them as thoroughly as men do."

"What do you mean?"

I take another sip from the cup of tea I've been toying with. "A long time ago, my first husband—a liberal, 1960s, hippie/musician type—and I tried an experiment that involved gender roles."

"And?"

She's apparently paying attention, so I keep talking.

"One day, after several long discussions, we went to the local Dairy Queen to eat and did something really simple that taught us a lesson I've obviously never forgotten."

"Yes?" Her forehead wrinkles.

"After we discussed our radical idea, he let me place our order. I mean that he stood back while I walked up to the counter, asked for our usual burger and fries, and paid."

"Definitely simple. And?"

"I went over and picked up our meal for us, and it turned out to be a really awkward situation."

"In what way?" The lines in her forehead deepen.

"Our role reversal felt totally unnatural, to both of us. He said he felt undermined, useless, and I admitted I felt like an overbearing bitch."

"Why? What do you mean?" Grace pushes back a strand of her brown-gray hair from her left eye.

"I suppose because of the way I was raised. My mom prepared all the meals, and my dad paid for all the ingredients. I never saw him do anything in the kitchen but sit at the table and play solitaire while she cooked three meals a day. I can imagine that if she had defied him in any way, he would have considered her a bitch. That's why the idea of totally reversing those roles made me feel like my husband and I had turned the world as I knew it upside down.

"I know that sounds silly, but this was very early in the '70s. *Kramer vs. Kramer* didn't come out until almost 1980. In small-town Texas, people were just beginning to question traditional male/female roles." I sip my lukewarm tea. "But our little experiment showed us how hard it'd be to be married yet equal."

"What happened?"

"We didn't give up. I remember going to what was called 'sensitivity training.' It was a weekend workshop held in Galveston, about a two-hour drive from us. There, we were supposed to learn how to overcome the roles our society had taught us and get in touch with our 'authentic selves.'"

Grace raises a neatly plucked eyebrow. "And how did that work out?"

I rub my cheeks, remembering only a smattering of the events. "A large man walked up to us during one of the breaks and almost sneered. 'You two don't belong here. Especially *her.*' He pointed at me. 'She looks like a silly little housewife,' he told my husband, then turned to me. 'You ought to run home to Mommy and Daddy, sweetheart.'"

Graced frowned. "How rude. Do you think he was part of the so-called sensitivity training you were supposed to be involved in? I've heard the leaders liked to try to shock participants into an alternate reality by insulting them or otherwise getting under their skin."

"I suppose I'll never know. My husband was furious, and I wanted to leave early. We did stick it out, though, but I refused to go to the follow-up retreat the next weekend. Besides, it was so noisy there, with so many people never shutting up, that I was totally exhausted by the end of the weekend."

"So did your husband agree with your decision?" Grace's half smile makes me think she knows the answer to her question.

"No. He went back by himself, and the only thing I remember when he got home is his description of how one of the guys in the group hit on him."

"Hmm. And how did he react?"

"Not well. He told the guy he wasn't interested, but it did give me an opportunity to confess my feelings for one of my older female students."

"Ah. The plot thickens." Grace smooths her wrinkled napkin and nods for me to continue.

"I had fallen hard for this woman, a Cajun with two children and a husband she resented and seemed to dislike."

Grace nods. "I can relate to that. What happened between you two?"

"At that point, a lot of flirting and hand-holding. She kept saying my husband was really weird and that I needed to find someone who wanted to live a normal life instead of the deviant lifestyle he was pushing me into."

"Deviant? How so?"

"Well, smoking pot, for one. And not settling down and having kids like normal people did. She kept saying it was no wonder my parents didn't like him, which they didn't. And to sum it up, she encouraged me to break up with him. Said she'd take care of me if I did."

"Take care of you? And what did that entail?"

"That was part of the problem. She was never all that specific, and I suppose I wanted to believe she'd leave her husband too and that somehow we'd live happily ever after."

Grace's smile is crooked. "And you believed her? She certainly doesn't sound very trustworthy."

My smile stretches my face almost painfully. I like Grace's directness. "You're right. But my husband and I had adopted a baby boy, because I'd insisted on being 'normal' and having a child, and then I was promptly diagnosed with endometriosis and had to have an ovary removed. Believe me, surgery in those days was a long and painful process. He was stuck with a baby and a wife to look after, which obviously he wasn't prepared for and resented."

"Oh," Grace says. "And he probably blamed you. His exciting companion had turned into someone he didn't know how to deal with, and he was trapped in a situation he couldn't and didn't want to cope with."

I shrug. "And the new woman in my life visited me constantly in the hospital and helped me take care of the baby as I tried to recuperate."

"Of course. He most likely couldn't have been very supportive at that point, even if he'd wanted to be."

"I'm sure he did his best, but nurturing wasn't his strong suit. So I wasn't surprised that he promptly found a younger woman."

Grace frowns. "I can understand his situation and almost feel sorry for him, but I certainly see your side of the story. What a mess."

"Yes." I sigh. "Certainly not one of my finer moments, but not too unusual when I look back at that time period. The dynamics playing out between us even had a name: the generation gap. He and I were rejecting the life style of our parents with little idea of what we were doing and why, although I thought I was clinging to it harder than he was."

Grace nods. "You're right. It was long before my time, but I recall hearing one of my aunts, about your age, discuss a similar experience."

"I just wanted to be normal, and I suppose I thought being with a traditional woman who seemed to understand me and whom I thought I was in love with would be closer to normal than living with a politically radical man who wanted me to forget all my past, including my total belief system, my lifelong friends, and my traditional family."

"You didn't have much of a choice, did you?"

"That's how it seemed then, but looking back, I suppose I was more radical in some ways than he was."

"What do you mean?"

"Even then, I was choosing to live as a lesbian, whereas he simply chose another straight partner."

"What did you do?"

"Well, I started sleeping with the woman I was involved with, and he got really serious about his girlfriend. She was quite a bit younger than he was and willing to move back to Austin." I wrinkle my nose.

"It's like he was trying to reset the clock." I sigh. "At least we were able to find the baby a good home with his brother and his wife, who couldn't have children."

Grace nods. "And then what happened?"

"The woman I thought I was in love with stayed with her husband and children, though she did show up to have sex with me once in a great while."

"And broke your heart all over again each time."

I sigh and stare out the window at the rough surf hitting the white sands of a distant beach. "Yes. A totally unpleasant experience. I felt like by getting a divorce I'd alienated myself from my traditional family after all and didn't have anything to show for it but a lot of sadness and disillusionment."

Grace touches my hand briefly. "I'm sorry you had to go through that, and I appreciate your honesty. But I hope you realized your mistakes, found someone to love, and have been happy ever since, with the man of your dreams."

I glance at the clock on the wall. "Oh, Grace. In some ways I wish I had, but remember? I've been married three times." I scoot my chair back. "Hey. It's almost time to go ashore. We'll talk later. Okay?"

Just then, a voice comes over the speaker system. "First call for the green group to head to your Zodiac for loading."

She and I jump up and hurry back to our cabins, conveniently located next door to each other.

"Oh, if you or Martha Jo or Amy needs to use my shower sometime, just let me know." Grace swipes the unlock feature on her cabin door. "It might get a bit tight with three of you sharing a cabin."

I peek inside her room as she opens the door. "Thanks. We may take you up on that offer. See you on the island."

And with that understanding, Grace and I part ways. I can't remember when I've bared myself so fully and at such length to someone. I usually do all the listening. The experience frightens yet exhilarates me.

I walk into our cabin and stroll over to our small deck, where Amy's sitting and staring at the island in the distance. "What a good conversation I just had with Grace," I say. "She said we could use her shower if we need to sometime." I'm bubbling over and would like to confide in Amy all about my conversation with Grace. Yet I don't want to come across as a schoolgirl with her first crush. "What do you think about her?" I can't stop myself from asking.

Amy keeps staring into the distance, seeming miles away.

"Well?" I can't stop myself from asking.

She raises an eyebrow. "Oh. Yeah. She's cute. And it was nice of her to offer to share her facilities."

About that time Martha Jo shows up. "Time to go, girls. We have another island to visit."

We gather our gear and head out. I wish I could have talked to Amy about Grace, maybe gotten a little advice. I have no idea how to deal with my feelings about someone like her but am too embarrassed to admit how clueless I am.

Enthusiastic Greeting on Kisar

I've never aspired to be a politician or a movie star, but arriving on the tiny island of Kisar this mid-February morning lets me glimpse the type of welcome such famous figures must encounter when they meet new people in new places.

Of course, unlike us, authentic celebrities would descend from the clouds in a helicopter, not take turns climbing from a Zodiac and getting their feet dirty and wet splashing through the surf onto deep, white sand. Incidentally, the word Kisar means white sand.

But the same island people—wearing jeans, T-shirts, straw hats, baseball caps, and flip-flops—would most likely snap photos of real celebrities with their phones, just as they do us. They would also clap and cheer for their truly famous arrivals just as loudly as they do for us, although I'm sure they know exactly who we are: rich, pampered foreigners their government has encouraged to visit for commercial reasons. Yet their welcome does seem very real and heartfelt.

Wearing our sunglasses and safari hats, and carrying our water bottles and daypacks, we wave and pose for pictures with some of the more insistent individuals. "They're really excited to see us," we whisper to each other, astonished. Suddenly our flight mishaps, late mealtime in Australia, disorganized and hastily changed tours, and all the other surprises we've encountered so far don't matter so much.

The improvised transportation these enthusiastic people proudly lead us to intrigues us. Martha Jo, Amy, and I duck as we climb into the back of an old pickup, a long, wooden bench seat built into each side to accommodate eight of us.

"Can you believe this reception?" one of a trio of Canadian women we're crammed into the truck bed with asks.

"This must be one of the islands mentioned during our first briefing. You know, where the villagers haven't seen any outsiders since before COVID," Amy says.

"What did you say?" Martha Jo shouts over the combined roar of the pickup's motor and the assortment of honking scooters, revving motorcycles, and other vehicles following us.

"I feel like I'm in a high school parade," I yell to Amy, who's sitting right next to me. She nods, though I'm not sure she heard what I said either.

"What a mishmash of a caravan we are," one of the other Canadians yells as we head into the hills in the center of the small island.

"Do you have any idea where we're going or what we'll be doing when we get there?" Amy shouts at the leader of the Canadian clique.

"None whatsoever," she screams back with a smile. "But it looks like half the island's population's behind us."

Amy chats with the strangers as we whiz up and down a narrow road dwarfed by banana and bamboo trees. She acts like she's known everyone in our little group for years, which baffles me. How can she be so at ease and come up with so many things to talk and laugh about with them?

"Looks like we're finally here," Amy says as we eventually stop at a small village. "And we're going to get some exercise."

Halfway up the steep incline of a dirt road, several local performers wearing red-and-black traditional garb and sunglasses nod at us.

"Look at the men's headdresses," I say. "They're like stalks of wheat or corn growing out of their heads. How unusual."

Amy nods. "These people seem a little more reserved than the ones at the beach."

"More isolated? Or maybe nervous about performing," I say.

"Country folk as compared to city people?" The difference interests me, since I'm a small-town girl. Maybe people who grow up in more isolated areas are naturally more reticent than their city counterparts.

After the adults dance, they ask us to join them, and I feel more relaxed. Doing something with strangers is always easier than trying to converse with them. After children wearing traditional costumes sing, we browse through the traditional clothes, fabrics, and trinkets the women are selling. After a little bargaining, which Amy participates in, Martha Jo buys a gorgeous piece of cloth. "I don't know who was more pleased with that transaction," Amy says. "Martha Jo or the women who sold the material to her."

We all laugh and wave good-bye, the locals wave and shout even as we line up to put on our life jackets and wait for our turn in a Zodiac, everyone seeming to have had a great day.

Eventually, I realize I haven't seen Grace today on the island except at a distance. But, during our trip back to the ship, our Zodiac stalls in clear green water near a rocky outcropping. "This won't but take a minute," our driver says. He tries to restart the motor, but each time, it sputters out. "Looks like I'll have to purge the fuel line," he finally says.

I glance back at the engine, and there Grace sits, apparently helping him. She reminds me of a water sprite. One minute I see her, but when I look again, she's not there. And this time, when I do spot her, I jolt all over. Something's happening between us. I'm rapidly becoming obsessed, but she doesn't appear to feel the same. Did my impulsive invitation for her to come stay with me put her on guard, or does she simply not see me as anyone special?

But she does sit with us that night at dinner. And, beaming, she announces, "I've been chosen to take part in the upcoming kayak trip!"

For an East Coast native, she speaks very slowly. Her distinct emphases draw me into whatever she says, and I recognize the signs: I'm falling for her, hard and fast. *Damn it. Get a grip. I'm not thirty and divorced for the first time. I'm eighty-one. I shouldn't still have such ridiculous reactions to unavailable women.*

Why can't I stop doing the same thing over and over? I take a deep breath and twirl a piece of my hair into a curl next to my cheek. *I hate making a fool of myself like this. Is something wrong with me that I can't see?*

Stay away from unhappily married women, a small voice inside me mutters. You're just setting yourself up for heartbreak. Why not just accept her as a casual friend whose company you could enjoy short-term?

I blow out a breath. *Will I have enough sense to pay attention to that warning this time? Surely I will.*

February 19, 2023

Approaching Alor

Up early this morning, I dress and then practice tai chi in the quiet, peaceful gym. I love being the only one here. The sky begins to lighten as I finish my routine and cool down. We've left the open sea, turned into a lengthy inlet. Now on the back deck, I see white beaches and boats—long, skinny, colorful—heading in the opposite direction.

I hurry to the front, notice strange bamboo structures with thatched roofs that dot the open water, probably boat houses, another passenger suggests.

"Look. There's a small tanker," one man says, "the first ship near our size since we left Australia." Other men join us, and we all take pictures.

Though I feel a bit awkward in this situation, I don't feel compelled to carry on a conversation with any of these guys. We can let each other be and do our own thing. If this were a group of women, I'd probably feel more compelled to say something "sociable," so I enjoy this rare camaraderie.

Soon, two egg-shaped domes, one aqua and the other sky-blue with white stars, dominate the view. Beautiful mosques, I think.

"Is Islam the major religion on this island?" I ask, but no one responds. The men keep clicking, and being ignored doesn't really bother me. I feel incognito, safe, and enjoy having no pressure to converse.

Finally, long, concrete piers stretch out toward us. We ease alongside one, and crewmen toss down huge ropes the diameter of a softball. As they secure the ship to the wharf we gradually line up next to, I stand next to a retired US Navy man, who explains the process. How pleasant to listen to someone who obviously knows what he's talking about.

I've sailed on much larger ships and never noticed how the crew fastened the lines to the dock. But on a smaller vessel such as ours, everything seems more intimate. The workers on both the wharf and our ship laugh and talk as they toss and attach the huge lines that keep us tethered to land. Watching them work and listening to the veteran sailor beside me make me feel cared for, safe, like I feel when I'm with Martha Jo and Amy.

Breakfast calls, and Grace sits with us again. After we eat and start to leave the table, she casually touches my arm, as any acquaintance would. Maybe I can have a normal friendship with her instead of an irrational crush. In fact, the slight pressure of her hand seems to link me to her as securely as our ship stays moored to this new island named Alor. In this moment I feel safe with her.

The Market and the Museum

Martha Jo joins us on our shore excursion this morning. "How wonderful to have a metal walkway and a stable concrete dock," she says, as we stroll past costumed Indonesian musicians playing dissonant, clanging music. Local guides wave us to our buses with small, brightly colored flags, a banner saying WELCOME TO KALABATI stretched along a low fence.

"Look," Amy says, pointing. "Our buses may be air-conditioned!"

Martha Jo smiles, elegant as always in her broad-brimmed straw sun hat, red lipstick, gold-hoop earrings, and light-green safari jacket with its multiple pockets. "Now that's more like it." We leisurely head toward a waiting bus. This is the type of cruise we expected.

After we settle into soft, velvety seats, we drive through what appears to be a large city, overflowing with the usual odd assortment of old and new motorcycles and trucks.

"Are we already here?" Amy asks as we stop at an obvious market area.

"Looks like it." I follow her and Martha Jo off the bus, our assigned guide waiting to shepherd us through a large local market. We gawk at strange fruit and vegetables and odd types of sea creatures. It's like being in a maze or behind the backdrops in a movie set. The concrete floor is cracked and cavernous in some places, which slows us.

"Watch out," Martha Jo says. "You don't want to step in one of those holes and break a leg."

We straggle apart, and I wander alone in a dreamlike setting of distinct smells—incense, coffee, various spices—inhaling it all. I feel free, unconstrained, like I did on the ship as we approached the island and docked.

I follow the crowd at a distance, and Martha Jo, Amy, Grace, and I somehow end up at a local museum at the same time and enter together. Old photos line the wall to our left, and Grace and I stop to peruse them.

One picture shows three teenage girls, wearing belly bands and bikini bottoms. Their black hair haloes their heads, and they all wear multiple bracelets and necklaces. They are very beautiful, and I feel a kinship with them. Regardless of where individual women reside, we all live in a man's world and do our best to survive the inequities we face.

"I wonder who took that picture," Grace says. "It's definitely old."

The young women in it stare directly at the photographer. "Probably a man," I say.

She nods. "I hope he didn't bother them."

The girls are staring at whoever's taking the picture with rather blank expressions, similar to the way a woman selling odd green vegetables in the market just looked at me. As a wealthy foreigner, I don't want to come across as if I'm visiting a zoo. However, I can imagine that the people who live here and elsewhere in "tourist spots" can easily view me as such. "Yeah," I say. "I hope so too."

Another photo features a slightly older woman with dark, curly hair as well, though it's shorter. Wearing large earrings and an elaborate beaded necklace, she stares at us, very attractive with her oval face and well-shaped lips. "I wonder what she was thinking," Grace says.

I study her more closely. Grace makes me delve beneath the surface, an influence that sometimes catches me off guard. "Let me see. The way she's bending her head and looking up at whoever's taking the picture makes her seem submissive."

"Uh-huh," Grace says. "But check out how she's almost glaring at the photographer. I assume a man took this early 1900s shot, since most travelers here then were probably male." She studies the picture again. "I may be imagining things, or doing some wishful thinking, but do you detect some steel in her big black eyes under those straight eyebrows?"

I study the caption more closely, which labels her only as *A Young Woman*. "Hmm. I see what you mean. And the photographer was probably German, since the caption's in that language."

Grace nods. "Well, if it was a man out to get what men usually want"—Grace appears as fierce as the woman in the photo does—"I bet he didn't get it from her."

I give the portrait one last look. "I hope not." On that subject, Grace and I are definitely on the same wavelength, and I feel comfortable discussing it with her.

We nod like conspirators and head to the other section of the small museum. I say, "It's hard to imagine being female and living here in a city nowadays, though one of our guides did say that more women than men in Indonesia attend college because they can get better-paying jobs in urban areas than men can. Who knows? It might be better here than we think."

She nods. "Could be. But it's even more difficult to imagine how village women get along, both now and in the past."

"Just think," I say. "The young women in those photos might be ancestors of the tribe we plan to visit today."

I can't shake the photos of the young women from my mind.

But Grace has evidently already shifted gears. "Oh, look at all this gorgeous fabric," she says.

The local ikat she's staring at interests me as much as the photos of the women do.

"You know," I say, "Amy and I planned to look at the textile pieces for sale on the first island where we stopped but were distracted. Did you see any there?"

Grace nods, though she keeps studying these museum-quality examples. "The pieces on that island were beautiful, but I want something bright red and didn't find the right shade there."

"I read a bit about ikat before we came on this trip and learned what to look for."

"And?" she asks.

"A tight weave. Clear, precise motifs. And sharp edges between the colors."

She nods. "Got it. Thanks."

We move from one outstanding sample of ikat to another. The women who created these intricate pieces of fabric are really talented and must feel fulfilled when they make something so intricately beautiful. They remind me of my mom, who was a talented seamstress and loved her creations.

"Several of the islands we plan to tour," I say, "should have outstanding ikat for sale. Maybe you can find what you're looking for on one of them."

Grace gives me a lopsided, buddy-type smile, which warms me more than the heat that's beginning to build outside on this tropical morning. "Thanks for the information. I'll take your advice and wait."

Suddenly our guide rushes in. "Time to return to our bus, ladies. We have much more to see today."

We follow him and meet Martha Jo and Amy and several other stragglers outside. Though I'm not a diligent shopper, maybe I can help Grace find some interesting fabric. The process of bonding with her warms me all over again. Hopefully I can manage to not become infatuated with her but to simply enjoy her company.

Dancing at Takpale

"Wow. That didn't take long," Amy says as our bus pulls over and stops. "These local roads are the best ones we've been on so far."

Located about thirty miles from town, our final destination for the day is an easy ride away. But the narrow concrete road up to the village, too cracked and uneven for our large, air-conditioned vehicle, forces us to walk.

"What are we supposed to see here?" Martha Jo asks. "I had a short nap. Did I miss anything?"

"Our guide said Takpale consists of about fifteen families," I say. "They originally lived in the hills, isolated."

Amy chimes in. "But because they were one of the largest and wealthiest tribes on the island, the politicians in the capital city enticed them to move nearer."

"Why would they do that? Why not let them live where they were?" Martha Jo looks from Amy to me.

"So it would be easier to collect taxes from them," I say. "At least that's what our guide told us."

"It must have taken a skilled politician to make that happen," Martha Jo says. "Wonder what they had to promise to the people?"

Amy shakes her head. "We'll probably never know."

"Or more likely we don't want to," Martha Jo says. "Some things never change, no matter what country you're in."

Just then we spot a group of adults at the top of the hill, milling around wearing red and black sarongs and waving to us. We head for the shade of some nearby tall trees, and the ceremony we've come here to watch begins.

For the final dance, everyone in the village, female and male, puts their arms around each other to form a circle and dance together. And they insist that we join them, which many of us do.

When I step up to the circle, a young man places me next to a short woman. With hair as curly and almost as white as mine, she has deep-set black eyes and a broad, welcoming smile. All the local, barefoot women, who wear big, clanking bracelets on their wrists and ankles, move their feet in a basic pattern. I watch and easily imitate them, feeling as though I'm briefly one of their tribe.

Of course, these people and I have little in common, but somehow, here, our differences don't seem that important. We're all part of this world of beauty and sound, and I'm thankful to be included. Suddenly, the Buddhist belief that everything in the universe is one makes sense.

What would Grace think if I shared these ideas with her? Would she frown, smile, or simply raise an eyebrow and walk away? In some ways she and I are as much strangers as these people of Takpale and I are, but in others we seem like kindred spirits.

February 20, 2023

ENDE AND THE CRATER LAKES

Up early yet again, I notice a new companion in the gym. An Asian woman about my age walks on a treadmill while I do my tai chi warmup and routine. As she leaves, she waves, apparently my new gym buddy. On the rare occasions that we bump into each other during the rest of the trip, we nod, yet we converse only once—about the one day I don't work out because of a headache. I enjoy this little nonverbal relationship with a stranger almost as much as I do my in-depth conversations with Grace. The unspoken often says more to me than the spoken.

Last night our ship headed west, toward Bali, and this morning we plan to stop at Ende, a region of the island of Flores. As we approach—the shoreline appears very similar to the one yesterday—I see tree-covered mountains, plus black beaches, unheard of in Texas. And before we dock, official-looking people—some wearing paper masks—appear and stand on the same type of long, concrete piers we tethered to yesterday.

Our docking procedure seems to last forever, and during it, Martha Jo and Amy and I converse with an Indonesian official standing next to our balcony.

"Where are you from?" he asks. Unlike the workers in white shirts and hardhats, he wears an orange-and-black shirt, his sunglasses pushed up on top of his head, and holds what appear to be a passport and a checklist.

"We're from Texas. Have you ever been there?" Amy asks. As I've said, she can talk to just about anyone, a quality I continue to admire and have little skill in. It's like a limp or an itch I can't ignore yet can't cure. When I try to talk to people, especially ones I've just met, I panic. Even if I think of something to say, when I open my mouth, my thoughts vanish, as if they've never been there. It's almost always easier just to stand back and stay quiet. That way I don't make a fool of myself by stammering incoherently, though I often feel invisible and left out because of my silence. I wonder if that's normal or if something's been wrong with me all these years. Maybe if I understood why I feel like that, I could somehow deal with it.

"No." The man beams. "But I did fly to the United States many years ago, on business."

"Where did you go?"

He shifts from one foot to the other. "New York City and Washington, DC." He glances at a group of his countrymen who seem to be trying to catch his attention but continues to converse with us. "I wish I had gone to Texas and seen how the everyday people live, not just the ones who rush around in the big cities."

"Well, if you ever make it back, be sure to come see us."

He nods, and we all know that will never happen, though it's fun to think about. In fact, one of my wealthy neighbors recently toured Australia, where she met a couple in a bar and invited them to visit her and her family in Texas. The Australians and four of their friends accepted the invitation, and from what I've heard, everyone had a wonderful time. People from other countries often seem infinitely curious about where we live, which, after all, is as foreign to them as their native lands are to us.

The docking procedure finally ends, and Amy and I walk down the ramp to the dock and make our way to the waiting buses.

Then we drive out of the city where we docked toward green mountains in the distance.

The road winds, with constant switchbacks, through lush jungle vistas I've seen in various movies.

"This is what I expected Indonesia to look like." I point. "Check out those huge, terraced rice fields over there. They go on and on."

"And everyone seems to have a small garden in their front yard and stake their cows along the road," Amy says. "Good way to keep the grass cut and the cows fat."

"These mountain streams fascinate me." I crane my neck to watch water tumble down the side of a rocky cliff. "We're in a green fairyland."

Amy and I *ooh* and *aah* all the way up through the mountains until we reach Kelimutu National Park, wishing Martha Jo were with us.

"Brr," I say as we climb out of the bus at the park. "I bet the temperature's dropped twenty degrees. And can you believe it's cloudy and misting rain?" Amy and I take our light jackets from our daypacks, glad they're hooded.

"All right," a park guide announces. "We need to form two groups. If you don't have a problem walking long distances over rough terrain, including a lot of stairs, gather over there to my left." He then directs the other group toward an easier trail, explaining that they'll be able to see only two of the three lakes.

Of course, Amy and I opt for the longer, rougher hike, and Grace shows up too, from another bus. At first, we climb about a million stone steps through a dense forest, as the guide, who speaks excellent English, points out various plants and trees. Then the terrain becomes rocky.

We walk quite a distance up the ancient volcano, the cool weather a welcome change. "Wow. Come look," Amy says suddenly. "This first lake is the most amazing turquoise ever." She starts taking photos.

Grace and I've been lagging behind but, when we catch up, are as awed as she is. "The lake's so big," I say. "And all those gigantic rocks really set it off."

"With nothing growing nearby to distract from its appearance, it's like a huge, shining jewel," Grace says. "It reminds me of something you'd see in a Disney movie."

Our guide waits patiently while we take a ton of pictures of the lake and of each other posing in front of it. Then he points to a smaller one, its twin, to our left, a low stone cliff dividing them. It's a less vibrant turquoise, with yellow patches covering various areas of its surface.

He says, "We believe these lakes contain the souls of those people who have gone before us. One is reserved for the young souls and the other for the wicked."

"Which is which?" I ask.

He points to the smaller, yellow-and-blue one. "That one is for the young at heart," he says.

I take another look at it, then turn back to the larger, turquoise lake. "I don't care," I say. "This one's prettier. I'd rather be in it for eternity."

Amy and Grace laugh, the guide looks confused, and I wonder where that remark came from. I can't believe how good it feels to say what I actually think instead of trying to guess what most people would say and parroting them, like I usually do.

From there, he points up the mountain. "See that path? If you want to see the third lake, you'll need to climb all those steps, but be careful. They can be slippery. And watch out for the monkeys at the top. They're aggressive sometimes. I'll meet you here when you're ready to go back to the buses."

Amy, Grace, and I begin the trek up the clearly marked trail. "Thank goodness for this handrail," Amy says as we become winded.

I nod, and Grace stops to take another picture. We finally spot the third crater lake to our left. It's a somber emerald green, almost too dark to be pretty. "The turquoise one is still my favorite." Grace nods, her shining eyes the color of the lake I prefer. "I agree with you about that first lake," she says, "especially since turquoise is my favorite color."

Her remark makes me feel like she's on my side, that she's willing to trust her gut rather than let a superstition scare her.

Slowly we climb to the highest spot in the area, Inspiration Point, Amy forging ahead, and Grace and I walking side by side. "Look. Some kind of monument's up here at the very top," Amy calls. "One of you come take my picture." As if we haven't climbed enough, one by one we clamber up the huge steps of the cement edifice, though Amy doesn't crawl to the very top.

As the oldest of our trio, I insist on making that effort, shouting, "Grace did it, and I can't let her get ahead of me."

She snaps my picture, seeming amused at my competitiveness and humoring the old lady who doesn't want to miss anything on this trip of a lifetime.

On the way down, three large monkeys give Amy a hard time, mainly because she tries to get too close to them, we remind her.

Grace and I are strolling along, admiring the vegetation we pass, when suddenly she says, "I've been thinking about your divorce for the past few days. What happened after your breakup?"

A chill runs through me. Is she contemplating leaving her husband?

I try to gather my thoughts. "I floundered around, picked up men and dropped them. I certainly wouldn't recommend that type of behavior." I try to laugh but am still too embarrassed at my indiscretion during that difficult period in my life to manage even a chuckle. Instead, I blow out a deep breath. "But even though that situation devastated me, I slowly—and I mean inch by inch during the next fifteen years or so—began to accept that maybe I did like women more than men, even if the one I left my marriage for didn't follow through."

We stop to look at some mounds of ferns, admire their green and purple blooms. Then Grace asks quietly, "What were your major clues?" I inhale slowly, then try to explain. "As a teenager, I never dated guys. A gay classmate took me to our school proms and other social events, but I preferred to play tennis and study, run around with the six other girls in our clique, and moon over a girl two years older than me."

"Couldn't you have simply been immature, slow to develop?" She stops, picks up an interesting-looking rock, then tosses it to one side of the trail.

"Yes." I nod. "But it never occurred to me that I might be different in that way from most girls my age. We were all silly and self-absorbed. I just thought I was ugly and didn't know how to flirt and to attract a boy. It was so much easier and more natural to be around my girlfriends."

"And when you got older, things didn't change?" She stares at me, as if she truly doesn't understand.

"No. In college I fell in love with learning and studied every minute when I wasn't working part-time."

"And you still didn't date boys, or even want to?"

I stare back. Her questioning gaze leads me on. "No. I lived in an all-female dorm and never had much contact with guys. I did lose my virginity to one when I was a junior, but we never even had a normal date. Just a few hookups for sex. I was curious more than anything."

"So when did you get married, and how did you get engaged?" She stops and reties one of the laces on her hiking shoes, which has come loose.

"After I lost my virginity," I say, "I started to worry, because having sex was finally a real possibility to me. And, good little girl that I was, I didn't want to get into trouble." I frown. "I knew this nice guy who belonged to the same campus church group I did, so I suppose he must have asked me out." I chuckle. "I remember him looking at my legs when I wore a really short skirt to one of our meetings, which might have influenced him to ask me. But I don't remember where we went or what we did, except maybe go to a jazz club in Dallas. I just recall getting engaged not too long after that first date."

"You didn't love him?"

"I had no idea what that would feel like." I shake my head. "Most of my best friends were engaged or attached to a man. I just followed the crowd." I sigh at my own weakness. "Besides, I knew I wouldn't be able to support myself."

"Why not? You were getting a degree." We continue to stroll down the steep path, stopping again to ponder some deep-fuchsia, four-petaled flowers with large green-and-white ribbed leaves.

"I was getting a BA but didn't have a teaching certificate." I shake my head. "I couldn't work in the public schools in Texas without taking specialized education courses." I frown. "My first semester in college, I enrolled in one and was bored silly."

"After you graduated, you couldn't find a good job doing something else?"

"No. To teach at the college level, I needed an MA." I sigh again. "But without it, I was out of luck."

"You had no marketable skills at all after four years at a university?" She shakes her head this time. "I find that hard to believe."

I run a hand through my hair, which tends to fall forward. "No special skills to speak of, especially since English majors were a dime a dozen."

"Really? That's so strange."

"Believe me, in the mid-sixties, at least where I lived, we thought women couldn't be anything but teachers, nurses, secretaries, or stewardesses, who were glorified waitresses." I sip some water from the lidded water bottle I carry in my day pack. "I could work as a poorly skilled secretary, but that was about it."

"That really surprises me."

I laugh. "Luckily, my mom made sure I learned to type in high school, so, early in my marriage, I worked temporarily at businesses in Dallas as a Kelly Girl, for peanuts."

We stop to rest for a few minutes, gazing at the trail, which continues down the field of volcanoes toward some woods in the distance.

"The job was interesting at first, but when I had to type addresses on envelopes all day, I knew I needed to do something more."

"And?" She frowns slightly.

"The next school year, I took two graduate courses and taught two freshman classes each semester." I sigh. Just thinking about our first year together makes me tired. "That, plus two summers of coursework and my thesis, gave me my master's."

"Whew." She blows out a breath. "You obviously didn't have much spare time."

"You're right. My new husband and I rarely saw each other, and when he admitted to crushing on one of his coworkers, I began to realize he was even more mixed up than I was."

"Really? Did that upset you?"

"Of course, but I rarely expressed my opinion or discussed issues like that. Instead, I got furious and literally ran away when he wanted to talk about such subjects, or, later in the marriage, I'd simply listen to him. I certainly had no idea what to say and doubt if I'd have been able to express myself if I had. Not a good way to start a marriage or get to know each other."

"Sounds like you got married for all the wrong reasons. I can certainly relate." Grace says.

"Yep," I say.

Our guide's waiting for us at the end of this steep trail, so I wrap up my story. "Seven years later, when it began to dawn on me that I might prefer women, I was divorced and living in a small East Texas town with a teaching job I loved." I smile. "But I had no idea where to find anyone, male or female, who could help me discover who I was or could be in a relationship, and I obviously had few communication skills." I draw in a deep breath of cool, mountain air.

Grace shifts her daypack from one shoulder to the other. "I'm beginning to get the picture." Then she turns around, looks back up the trail, and waves to Amy, who's heading toward us. "I live near P-town, but honestly, if I were in the same situation today, fifty years later than you're talking about, I'm not sure what I'd do."

I simply shrug, relieved to have been able to explain at least this much about my first marriage.

"Well, we need to wind this up, and I appreciate you being so frank about your past," Grace says. Just then, Amy reaches us, and we approach our guide, who leads the conversation as we head back toward the bus.

Seeming in tune, Grace and I still walk side by side, two new acquaintances in a barren, rocky landscape brightened by beautiful lakes and flowers. The cord growing between us during these past few days seems stronger, more durable. Expressing myself so frankly goes to my head like smoking pot used to, and I appreciate Grace for giving me the opportunity.

Back at the parking lot, Grace boards her bus, and Amy and I climb into ours.

Our descent through the mountain jungles and rice fields awes me as much as the ascent did, only in reverse. I'm in a dream world, an image Hollywood has created of a far-away paradise, and the day has had a magical quality, my time with Grace especially enchanting.

The dream continues when we stop at an out-the-way restaurant, located beside a stream of clear, running water. However, our table for four is too small to include Grace after two other new friends join us. I enjoy the company of the women at lunch, but I miss Grace, even though I've just spent several hours with her. I can't get enough of her company.

Returning to our bus, we pass small, two-story, thatched-roof buildings. "This is a popular resort," our guide says, and Amy and I agree it would be a nice place to stay.

Wouldn't it be enjoyable to come back here with Grace for several days, when we had time to explore the island more fully? I'm obviously still lost in dreamland.

As Amy and I ride side by side back to the dock, I try to shake myself out of my fantasy world. I'm already infatuated with Grace, though down deep I don't want to be. I say to Amy, "Grace and I had another long conversation today, and I came out to her completely. Do you think I should have? I really enjoy being able to talk to her on an in-depth level instead of chitchatting about trivial subjects."

Amy turns to me. I've have been friends with her and Martha Jo for quite a few years now, but most of the time I was married to the woman I divorced a few years ago, and the four of us mostly RVed and played Rummikub together. Being single now, I feel a bit awkward talking to Amy on a personal level. Besides, since I'm rooming with her and Martha Jo and spending so much time with them, I want to try to give them as much space to themselves as I can.

"Like I told you before," Amy says, "I think Grace is cute, and she is a good conversationalist, but I don't know her well enough to say much more than that. I do know there's more to a relationship than only one thing, such as talking in depth about subjects you two have in common. Be careful."

Just then the bus stops, and everyone jumps up to unload and head back to the ship. "Thanks for the warning, Amy. I'll try to follow your advice," though deep down I'm afraid I'm not being entirely honest. Too often, I want to do what I want to do.

Dancing with Grace

Back on the ship, rested from our long hike and dressed for dinner, Amy says, "I feel like dancing. What about you, Martha Jo?"

"You're the dancer in the family, sweetheart, but I'll give it a whirl."

"You're so nice. I love you, babe." Amy kisses Martha Jo.

They both came out as lesbians later in life, after they'd reared their children and divorced their husbands. Martha Jo has written a popular nonfiction account of what it's like to embrace her true self at sixty, and Amy has quite a story to tell as well. I've never known two finer, more caring women and am lucky to have them as friends.

"How about you, Helen?" Amy asks. "Feel like shaking a leg or two after dinner? The music should be good tonight."

"Sure. Count me in," I say. And immediately I know who I'll ask too.

After our nightly briefing in the lounge, I whisper to Grace, conveniently sitting beside me, "We're going dancing tonight. Want to join us back here about nine?"

She appears startled but quickly says, "Why not? I'm meeting with a few people in our kayak group, but I'll try to make it."

I'm hoping that's a yes, but if it's not, it won't be the first time I've danced alone. Most gay people don't hesitate to dance alone or in a group or with our significant other. Moving to the music is a free, fun, exuberant time we indulge in whenever we can.

Martha Jo, Amy, and I show up at eight thirty, Amy practically pulling us away from the forward deck, where we've been stargazing

• 91 •

and enjoying the cool night breeze. "Time to go, girls. The music should start any minute," she says.

We have music in the lounge practically every evening, except when one of the crew leads a large group activity such as participating in the old game Clue. A crew member plays a mean keyboard and has a huge repertoire, emphasizing 1950s hits for this crowd.

Only a few people, sitting near the back of the lounge, are there when we arrive. But Amy says, "We need to be up front, so we don't have to walk so far to the dance floor."

We congregate around a small cocktail table near the keyboard and enjoy a familiar rendition of "Autumn Leaves," one of my dad's favorites, from the 1940s.

"It's one of my favorites, too," Martha Jo says, her gray eyes shining.

But Amy doesn't sit still long. When a more upbeat song begins, she's up and on her feet, dancing in place. "Come on, Martha Jo. I need a dance partner," she calls.

But Martha Jo shakes her head. "In a bit, Amy. You go ahead and warm up the floor."

And Amy proceeds to do just that. Energy pours from her as she hops around, seeming like an icon of joy at being alive. As she dances, couples begin to wander into the area, perhaps attracted by her vitality. Single women as well as married ones drift toward the small dance floor and begin showing off their moves. I can't resist and bounce around like a teenager, though I'll pay for all this activity in the morning. One woman even does a hilarious rendition of a pole dance for her husband as we egg her on.

While the music plays and I'm dancing, I look over at a nearby table, and there she sits. Grace. I gulp, suddenly self-conscious and shy, but keep moving to the fast-paced beat. In a bit, though, it slows, and I hear Lady Gaga's "I'll Never Love Again."

Taking a deep breath, I feel like a teenage boy at my first prom. I walk over and look at Grace sitting there alone, appearing peaceful and content. "Would you like to dance?" I ask her and stand there frozen for an eternal five seconds.

Her smile lights me up like an old-fashioned gas streetlamp. I hold out my hand, she takes it, and we're suddenly in one another's arms, skimming across the slick floor as if we've done this for fifty years.

She's so much shorter than I am, I can almost see the top of her head. She seems to weigh practically nothing, and the sensation of her hand in mine? "Your hand's so wittle," I hear myself say in a reverent tone, pronouncing the word like a child would.

"Yes. I've always had small hands," she says in a no-nonsense, adult voice.

Despite her response, I feel unusually protective, and for the first time, I understand why the boys in junior high and high school during the 1950s preferred short, small girls to tall, sporty girls like I was. The protectiveness I'm experiencing is like a drug. It makes me think I'm much stronger physically than I've ever been, like I want to shelter this woman I'm holding, give her whatever she wants and needs, be strong for her.

It's the only time we dance together, though we occasionally bounce around separately in this diverse group of older women who obviously feel free to try whatever movements come to mind. That one dance with Grace keeps me warm and glowing the rest of the night.

I feel so wonderful I try to ignore the random thoughts and questions that threaten to dim my glow. Is this what it's like to flirt with someone? While growing up, I watched some of the girls my age supposedly try to entice boys, but the entire ritual seemed confusing and pointless. Are Grace and I flirting with each other?

Or am I simply lonely and trying to make an innocent though intimate connection, even though I don't know how to very well? Does Grace have any of the same type of thoughts about me, or am I trying to fool myself into believing she even thinks about me occasionally except as a friendly face in a new and unfamiliar place?

I don't dare open my lips again, afraid of what words may rush out. I simply enjoy being close to this dainty, delicate-seeming woman who is untethering me from my usual moorings more completely every time I'm around her.

But why am I having such an extreme response to someone I barely know? Granted, I feel close to her because I've shared my feelings about my first marriage with her, and she's admitted that she constantly thinks about divorcing her husband. Almost all our conversations have been gut-level and intense, but she hasn't indicated that she's interested in the opposite sex, or in me, except as a source of information about divorce.

I've told her I'm probably bisexual and that I was married to a woman for many years. However, I don't know if she even realizes I'm attracted to her.

But am I? She and I discuss a lot of intimate subjects, and I may fantasize about having a relationship with her. However, the luxury of having someone listen to me so intently may attract me most strongly to her. I obviously crave that type of connection. In fact, most likely I want to get to know and understand myself even more than her.

February 21, 2023

SAWU'S VILLAGES AND DANCERS

Early the next day, we Zodiac to Sawu, a small, remote island surrounded by smooth water the color of a blue tang fish.

"We're visiting a very small compound this morning," our guide announces after a brief bus ride. "Four, maybe five families live there."

Inside a sturdy stone enclosure, these people's thatched-roof, square wooden homes consist of four walls, a ground floor, and a loft, where the entire family sleeps. However, teenage girls have a special section for privacy.

"You may go inside this one," our guide says, so I stoop to avoid hitting my head on the door into the dimly lit home. It's cool inside, the lower room almost empty. A few pots and pans and chipped dishes sit grouped together at one end of it. "I suppose that's the kitchen," I say to Amy, who's right behind me.

A ladder made of old limbs leads up to the loft. Up there, sleeping mats are rolled neatly along one side of the large room, the home obviously inhabited. Grace enters as I leave and raises her eyebrows questioningly. "It's simple," I say, "but has everything you really need."

In a practically identical home on the other side of this walled, circular village, six people—a woman and five men—perch outside on the unfinished boards of a shaded porch. Two men wear shorts and T-shirts, the rest dressed in woven cotton sarongs and sandals or house shoes. Watching us saunter by, they swing their feet, appearing curious, accepting, or annoyed.

Amy takes pictures of the compound's central building, which resembles an upside-down boat. But Grace magically appears beside me and murmurs as she and I wander toward the far end of the enclosure, "This is awkward, don't you think?"

I nod, and we stop to listen to one of our guides comment on the cemetery in the middle of the village. He points out elaborate and probably very expensive grave markers, some made of gray stone and others of green or yellow marble. At least half of the large slabs have a matching, inscribed headstone.

"Remember yesterday, on Flores, the island with the crater lakes, when our guide said many families bury their dead in their front yard?" Grace asks. "Why would they try to make their graves as conspicuous as possible?"

I shake my head. "If we did that at home, we'd probably be arrested. But I have seen family cemeteries on large farms in some of Texas's rural areas."

Just as we stop and I bend to look at an inscription more closely, our guide says, "All the people in this compound are animists."

I stare at our guide, and Grace comments, "The living and the dead seem to be located very near each other in this culture. Why is that?"

He glances around as if trying to judge how much longer we'll be here. I suppose it's as if someone had asked a local American guide in Nebraska to clarify Christian beliefs about eternity in five minutes.

"Many of my people believe we never die, that all our ancestors still dwell nearby." He points to the prominent grave markers. "That is why we often bury our loved ones near where we live."

He glances toward the mountain in the distance. "Everything has a soul—a tree, a cloud, a mountain. Everything in the universe is alive and never dies. That is part of animism."

I open my mouth to ask a question, but he glances at his watch. "These are the old beliefs, and many people on this island and others think they are the right ones. They may even go to the Baptist church in town, but in their heart, they are convinced their ancestors from hundreds of years ago still live with us, in our villages and in our mountains."

"But why—"

He turns. "We must go now. I wish we had more time."

Grace and I nod and thank him. Behind him, we leave the compound through a very narrow opening in the tall stone wall. This spiritual side of Indonesia intrigues me.

Farther in the countryside, we listen to music played on metal gongs, wooden drums of coconut wood and leather, and odd stringed instruments made of huge, pleated palm leaves. Their music sounds otherworldly.

Young women in black-and-gold sarongs, gold crowns on their heads, perform a Balinese-type dance. But then a short little gray-haired man, wearing a white undershirt, a turban, and two black-and-white figured shawls, sings and dances, his huge personality captivating us.

After the show ends, everyone flocks to him. "Will you take my picture with him?" Grace asks and hands me her camera, then stands beside him. He resembles my second husband, so I click a couple of shots for myself because he's such a look-alike. How strange that someone from my distant past can seem to appear in such a far-away place. I'm unsure if my ex-husband number two is still living, but for a few minutes he's alive in my mind. I think of the local belief that no one ever dies. I suppose we carry everyone we've ever known with us, and that way they stay alive.

After briefly wandering around the site, we return to our buses and then to the ship for lunch.

That afternoon, the Zodiacs taxi some enthusiastic passengers ashore again, to the island's beach, but I rest and then walk to the ship's two hot tubs. However, they're not operating. Here I am, all dressed up in my old bathing suit, surrounded by beautiful blue water, with no place to get wet.

Then suddenly I remember that I need to check out the ancient snorkel equipment I brought on this trip. The Zodiacs are still ferrying passengers to and from the local beach, so I rush down to my cabin, grab my mask and snorkel, and head to the mudroom.

Where we land and wade ashore, the sand is rather hard and gummy. But I pull my snorkeling gear onto my head and wade out waist deep. Floating face down in the calm, clear, tepid water, I check for leaks. None. *Sometimes it pays to invest in top-of-the-line equipment.*

Sprawled on the surface of the shallow water, I study the seafloor and spot a small purple starfish, several of them. *Are they dead or alive?* I don't want to touch them to find out, so I simply float. It's so quiet here.

Rested, I lower my feet to the sand, careful not to crush a sea creature, then take off my mask and snorkel. It's good to be alive and in such a beautiful spot. I am blessed, and I have a new friend—Grace. Perhaps she and I can snorkel together at the Pink Beach on Rinca Island, where we plan to be the day after tomorrow.

Finally, not wanting to miss the last Zodiac of the day, I wade back onto the shore. I'm putting my mask and snorkel into my daypack when someone says, "Hello. Did you enjoy the water?"

I grab my white ship's towel and rub my hair somewhat dry, then drape the towel around my bare shoulders. A young, dark-haired woman, along with at least eight children and teenagers, stands about six feet from me. She and the others are beautifully tanned, wearing colorful T-shirts and rubber flip-flops—ideal for the beach.

I'm barefoot, my white legs and arms speckled with scars, bruises, and age spots, my old, faded bathing suit six sizes too big for me. I've lost a lot of weight lately and haven't bothered to buy a new one.

After we all gawk at each other for several long seconds, the young woman a head shorter than I am asks, "Are you from the ship out there?"

I nod. "Yes. And I suppose you live near here?" I push my fingers through my damp curls several times, the familiar motion soothing me a bit.

The woman, her light-blue jeans fashionably torn at the knees, clasps a large cell phone in her left hand. She would blend in with a crowd in any US city. The younger ones with her appear as shy as I feel, but the woman could probably carry on a conversation with the Statue of Liberty.

"You are from America?" she asks immediately, and when I nod, she peppers me with questions about where exactly I live, what it's like there, is it as wonderful as everyone says it is, and so on.

I answer as honestly as I can without sharing the current negative aspects of the US.

"Oh, I have to go there one day," she says. "I have been practicing my English for many years now, and someday I will visit your land. Maybe I can live there instead of here." She points toward the small town behind her, the beautiful beach, the group of young people with her.

I merely smile and nod, twirling my wild curls again, wishing for a brush. She has no idea what she might encounter in the US, and I don't want to disillusion her.

We chat a bit, and I feel as shy as most of the young people in this group appear to be. I'm showing more skin than any of them, my hair a mass of wet, silver ringlets, wearing no shoes, with only an antique dive mask and snorkel, a flimsy coverup, and my daypack. If the ship left me here, I'd be in as much of a predicament as this woman would be if she landed at DFW tomorrow wearing only her jeans and T-shirt. At least she has a cell phone. And as self-confident as she appears to be, she would probably do well in a new, strange land.

I'd like to ask her more about herself, but my brain refuses to cooperate. I squirm, make excuses. My social skills are far below par. Always have been, even though I've tried to improve them. My brain and mouth petrify in situations like this, and the harder I try, the less I'm able to be at ease around strangers, no matter how eager or well-meaning they seem to be.

I push my wayward hair from my face, the familiar motion helping to ground me. If I stayed on this island two weeks, I might become somewhat comfortable speaking with these young people, but now I can think only about getting back to the ship, to Martha Jo and Amy, who are my rocks, and to Grace, with whom, by some miracle, I can converse with some degree of ease.

"Hey, how about a picture?" I ask, desperate to end this impromptu, awkward conversation and let this young woman keep her illusions. I'm glad I stuck my cell phone in my daypack and walk over to retrieve it.

I feel sorry for her. She seems so sincere, so idealistic, so ignorant of how my country has as many flaws as hers does, only in different areas.

She frowns briefly but says, "I know you must go." She herds the youngsters into a tight group, and we enlist a deckhand from the ship to snap a group shot. Sighing in relief, I grab my daypack and coverup and walk back to where the final Zodiac is waiting near the shore.

Why am I so shy, so terrible at meeting people, so unable to communicate with them comfortably? I interrogate myself as I splash through the gentle surf and climb into the waiting raft. This day on Sawu has evidently pushed me to my limits. Surely I can't get any more socially awkward than I am at this point.

February 22, 2023

HELEN AND GRACE AT THE POOL

After Amy and I unenthusiastically view some wild horses on the island of Sumba, our bus drives us to what looks to be a convention center. There we eat a ho-hum buffet lunch in a huge, stark, noisy room crammed with portable tables and folding chairs.

Then we mill around the gift shop/reception area. Amy goes to search for a restroom and souvenirs, and Grace drifts over to me.

She and I admire some sculptures of galloping wild horses made from driftwood, and then she says, "Would you like to go check out that infinity pool near where we just finished eating?" She points to a large swimming area. "I kept noticing it through the window while we ate."

"I saw it too and wanted to dive in," I say. "Sure. I'll go with you."

We stroll toward it, pausing to take pictures of the horse sculptures from a different angle. When we reach the pool, she kicks off her sandals and walks along one side of it. "Check out this gorgeous turquoise and dark-blue tilework."

"Yeah. It matches your shorts and blouse. You wear blue a lot."

She sticks her toes into the clear water. "Yes. Like I've said before, turquoise is my favorite."

"It looks good on you," I say. "Matches your eyes."

"Why, thank you. And your orange blouse really sets off your white hair. Is it naturally curly? Or do you spend hours fixing it?"

"Are you kidding? It's lucky if I even brush it." I run my fingers through it and enjoy the way it feels—like my mom's used to when she was in the nursing home and I'd brush hers.

"And you're lucky to have it. Has it always been like that?"

"Not this wild. I got these extreme curls last summer, courtesy of chemo and radiation."

She's sitting on the edge of the pool now, dangling her feet in the cool water, so I pull off my shoes and join her.

"I'm sorry." She squeezes my hand. "Cancer, I assume. What kind?"

"A rare type. Anal cancer. I preferred surgery, but that wasn't possible. So I went with the doctors' recommendation."

"Ouch." She waves at some type of insect buzzing near her face. "And how was that?"

I don't even want to think about it, but I do, running my fingers through the pool's clear, blue water and basking in her sympathetic gaze. "I had twenty-seven days of radiation, and the crew that treated me was wonderful."

"But?"

"After twenty-three days of radiation and four chemo infusions, I fell apart."

"Fell apart, as in…?"

"I'd skipped two days of radiation because I'd been getting steadily weaker, and by that Saturday afternoon, I could barely walk. In fact, my sister loaned me her husband's walker."

Grace dips her hand into the water, then lets it rest on the warm edge of the pool, inches from mine.

"I was lying in bed that Saturday evening, where I'd been all day, and suddenly my heart started racing." I squeeze my own hand into a tight fist.

"You must have been really scared."

"Terrified. I couldn't cope with strange things happening to my body because until last year I took good health for granted."

"I can relate to that," she says. "It can be both a blessing and a curse."

I describe my chemo and radiation treatments and how they landed me in the hospital for almost a week. Usually, I have difficulty recalling details when I converse with someone. I can express myself much more easily and clearly if I write what I want to say. But somehow, with Grace, I can speak rather coherently, especially about this topic.

She shakes her head. "What was wrong with you?"

"Evidently I couldn't handle the chemo, primarily because of my age and who knows why else. My oncologist discontinued that treatment permanently."

"Yes. I've heard a lot of people say that."

"Also, the radiation had burned me so badly that it was affecting my heart."

She frowns. "Whoa. That must have been really painful."

I splash some water on my bare legs. "You better believe it. It makes me hurt just to think about it. I'd read online that urinating in that situation feels like you're peeing razor blades, and it's true."

I laugh but recall how I cried when that happened to me in the hospital.

I can't believe I'm pouring all of this out to a near-stranger, but she's a sympathetic listener, and I'm finally in the right mood to talk about this horrible experience.

"So you're okay now?" she asks after I've talked about my experience for a while.

"It's been eight months at this point, and all my scans show I'm completely clear. Except for a few scars in invisible places."

"Well, I'm glad it worked out well for you. I know how frightening the diagnosis can be and understand the relief of being 'cured.'" She makes quotation marks with her fingers.

I take a deep breath. "Yes. I can't believe this time last year, I'd just found out about it. It's been a long twelve months."

She looks off into the distance. "You seem to be doing well. I've had it too, breast cancer, but it was a small area, and they got all of it. Not much of a story there." She gazes back at me. "I'm glad it turned out well for both of us."

I take a deep breath. "Me too. I've been so busy these past couple of months getting ready for this trip, I haven't thought about it much. My docs said it would be good for me to relax and take it easy in an interesting new place."

Grace splashes a handful of water in my direction. "Yeah. We've done so much relaxing."

We both laugh. "I can't wait to tell them I've been on an expedition instead of a cruise, and that it's been one of the most strenuous trips ever."

We laugh harder. "You have to see the humor in things if you want to survive," I say.

"Amen, sister," she replies. Then she turns serious again "By the way, I've been wanting to know what you finally did after your 'wild' period following your first divorce."

I take off my sunglasses, close my eyes, and pinch the top of my nose. "That seems so long ago, but eventually I married an older, more traditional man."

She groans. "And?"

"Our formal marriage didn't last long. Though after it ended, we kept seeing each other occasionally—mainly to go dancing or skiing or scuba-diving." I smile at the rush of memories. "We had a good time traveling together and sleeping together. But our relationship wasn't based on anything lasting."

"You and your second husband were companions after you two divorced? Did you date other people?" She moves two fingers slowly through the pool's clear water.

"Absolutely. And I went to several summer workshops out of state." Now I'm beaming. "That's where I began to meet long-term gays and lesbians and when my life began to really change."

"What happened to husband number two?" she asks, I suppose thinking about her own husband.

"He married a much-younger woman."

"Ah, so he could train her." She frowns.

"I'm not sure. They worked in the same lab at a small refinery in the area." I pause. "Both of my ex-husbands married women from work. Huh."

"Guess that was a common place to hook up back then," she says and shrugs. "No Internet or cell phones. What happened after that? Did you stay friends with either ex?"

I shake my head. "No. I'm not sure the older one's even alive. Though, according to Facebook, the younger one still lives in Austin, where he moved after we split. Apparently, he's been married several more times."

She glances up toward the gift shop, where our bus is supposed to pick us up soon. She seems to be paying close attention to my story, and I don't mind sharing it. All that happened ages ago—forty to sixty years.

"And then?" She moves her bare feet through the water, makes a few ripples.

"Oh, I had several affairs with women and with men, the kind of situations you ask yourself later, 'Why did I ever get myself into that mess?'"

Grace smiles and nods, her eyes gleaming, but I'm not sure how to interpret her expression. Has she experienced similar hookups? I rather doubt it, but you never know. I've shared more of my private life with her than vice versa.

She asks, "Your third marriage, to a woman. How was it?"

I cringe. Our breakup's fairly recent, so it's hard to be objective, at least about the later years. I start at the beginning. "Not bad. But I was such an emotional wreck when we met, it's a wonder she didn't run when the new wore off and she began to really get to know me."

Grace puts her hands on the cement behind her and leans back, like we have all day to sit here and talk. "Where did you meet her, since you lived in a small Texas town?"

"At work, the center of my universe. At first, I was technically her boss, but she was a bit older and a ton more experienced and assertive than I was." I move one foot slowly through the water. We should start heading back to the bus soon.

Yet I continue, and Grace doesn't rush me. "She thought she could 'fix' me, and I let her try. Yet there's a fine line between 'fixing' and 'changing' someone." Grace nods, and I say, "She gradually crossed that line, and I began to fight back."

Grace nods even harder, rolls her shoulders.

"She took good care of me for a long time," I say, "and we broadened each other's horizons a lot."

"That's good. So, what happened?" Grace rotates one shoulder, as if she's ready to get up.

"She became even more domineering, and I started thinking that sometimes she acted more like a typical man than either of my husbands had." I clench my right hand into a fist.

"You obviously don't want a relationship with a person who tries to dominate you." Grace rubs her left cheek. "What about the sex?"

My shoulders stiffen. *She definitely doesn't pull any punches.*

"I'm not ready to talk about that, but I will say this. Whether you have good sex depends on the person, not the gender."

She straightens her shoulders. "I mean, are you a lesbian or a straight woman?"

"Labels aren't easy."

One of our buses has driven up, so we really do need to leave. Yet I keep talking, though I grab one of my shoes to put it on. "If I had to choose, I'd opt for bisexual and androgynous."

Her turquoise eyes brighten. "Those sound like good choices. I could probably qualify for the asexual one too."

I'm puzzled. Does she not know the difference between the words asexual and bisexual? Was that a Freudian slip? Did she intend to say she could be bisexual too? Or does she mean she might be able to relate to both sexes in the same way but prefers to be asexual whether she's with a man or a woman?

Straight women aren't easy for me to read, and I'm about to question her, but our bus driver honks, and we pull on our shoes and hurry to our respective buses. As we ride to our next destination, I wonder why Grace is quizzing me so much about my personal life and why I'm willing to share it so fully with her. Is she merely gathering information about the passengers on board that interest her? Is she truly interested in leaving her husband? And if she does, would she ever consider being with a woman? I shake my head. Why am I even asking myself these questions? I'm confused yet drawn to her like a bee to clover.

CHEWING BETEL NUTS

"I thought we're supposed to spend the afternoon at this island's most picturesque beach," I say to Amy as we stop at another village.

"I suppose those government officials on board ship at our first stop 'suggested' this change of schedule too," Amy says.

"The guide said this is a 'royal' village, where the king of the area used to live. In fact, we're scheduled to meet the honorary king and queen of this region today," Amy whispers.

And we do. As a group, we're introduced to the royal couple—quite young and lovely. But one of the next events grabs my attention more fully.

Girls circulate through the crowd offering us samples of a betel nut—their legal alternative to marijuana and also a token of hospitality.

"I'm going to take one," I whisper to Amy, and she also holds out her hand to the girl offering them. Then I realize we're not getting just one hard, white sliver of a single nut, but also a leaf and some salt or maybe ground shells or lime.

I hold the objects in my palm and ask Amy, "What do we do now?" She shakes her head, and I glance around. Very few of our fellow tourists, especially the retired nurses, have accepted the villagers' gift. Should I go ahead and try the betel nut? After all, we're the guests of these people, and I don't want to be rude. I decide to do what I want. One tiny bite won't addict me to this narcotic forever.

"Yuck." I spit it out. "It's bitter, Amy."

Another girl comes up and mimes how to wrap the white piece in the leaf and sprinkle the powdery stuff on it. I try again, and this time it tastes a bit less repulsive. Then she mimes spitting it out, which I gladly do. This is like having my first beer and cigarette, I think, and I take another bite, then spit. She nods as if I'm on the right track, so I finish, my way of respecting their customs and satisfying my curiosity.

"Did you see the original version of *South Pacific*?" I ask Amy, who nods. "Bloody Mary got her name from chewing these nuts, because they turned her mouth and lips red." I run my tongue around my lips and poke them out. "Are mine red?"

"Nope. She probably ate a lot more than you did," Amy says.

"That was just a tiny piece."

I run my tongue over my lips, which are tingling a bit. Why did I just do something potentially dangerous?

I'm evidently so used to doing whatever the people around me do, I didn't even stop to consider the possible consequences. It suddenly hits me that I've done that as long as I can remember. Why can't I think for myself instead of following someone else's suggestion or their lead?

"Uh, it was bigger than you think," I say.

"You chewed up the whole thing?" Amy asks, and I nod. "It's terrible. One teeny taste was enough for me. I'm saving the rest of mine to show Martha Jo." She wraps hers in a tissue and sticks it into her pocket.

Amy obviously thinks for herself more often than I do.

"Hey. They're dancing and want us to join them," she suddenly exclaims, jumping up and running into the common area to do her thing.

But I just sit there. Am I feeling a buzz, or is it my imagination?

Have I done something really stupid? I've read in novels about how Asian women used to chew betel nuts to make their teeth turn black, which was a sign of beauty. But that's no reason for me to accept drugs from a stranger. Obviously I need a keeper. But as quickly as my inner critic appeared, it vanishes, and I'm heavy and boneless. It's like smoking pot. I relax back in my hard chair and seem to float on a cushion of clouds. My legs and arms feel rubbery, and the noise of the performers and my fellow travelers sitting nearby dies down, as if I've just dialed back a portable radio. I take a deep breath and let my head drop, close my eyes, and allow the sounds around me to recede. I'm on vacation, I tell myself.

Finally, I open my eyes and gaze languidly over at Amy, who's out there fast-dancing with the performers and some other tourists.

But I have no desire to join them. I just sit there with a nasty taste in my mouth, mellowed out.

I'm floating in the warm, blue water that is our host for this idyllic vacation. And then I look over and see someone beside me. It's Grace, and each of us rests on a grass-green air mattress. Wearing sunglasses, we let an arm dangle in the warm water, utter a few words occasionally but mostly lie there with closed eyes, the sun warming us, the gentle waves lulling us, encouraging us to rest, to relax. The lively music in the background seems far away, as does the laughter of our fellow tourists. She and I are alone yet connected by the sea's gentle motion and the sun's warmth.

I'm not sure how long I remain in this idyllic state, but suddenly I revive, disoriented. My main concern? Where's Grace in all this crowd?

Suddenly I spot her, on the other side of the compound, where another clump of tourists has gathered. So, as the music winds down, I stroll over to watch several women demonstrate how they spin the cotton they've grown and dyed with natural colors into thread, as well as all the other steps they follow to make ikat. Earlier our guide had mentioned that the ikat from this island is among the most desirable in Indonesia, so Grace must be doing some heavy-duty shopping.

As I watch the textile workers, I spot her again, clutching a plastic bag. Obviously, I was right, and then she almost immediately disappears again. She's a hard woman to keep track of.

By this time, Amy has walked up. Tired, she and I wander toward the buses and are about to board when suddenly Grace rushes up. "A man in our group has fallen back there. Have you seen our guide? The man needs help!"

I recall how she became very involved in the kayak group she was part of earlier in the trip. In fact, she seemed to be mediating some disturbing group issue. This is a different side of her, one I haven't gotten to know at all, and only adds to her appeal.

Our trip is winding down, though, and so am I, but I'm not ready to part ways with Grace. However, after three more days, we'll be in Bali, and then we'll fly home.

February 23, 2023

SNORKELING AT THE PINK BEACH

After spending the morning hiking through a tropical forest to see several large, frightening Komodo dragons in the wild, we eat lunch on the ship, then jump into a Zodiac again and head to Rinca's Pink Beach, which does have a pinkish tinge, caused by powdered red coral.

There, the snorkeling equipment Advantage hands out is substandard, so I'm glad I have my own mask and snorkel.

Grace has brought a small rubber raft, a smart idea, which she's been floating on. So after her snorkel equipment malfunctions, like most everyone's does, she decides to stick with the raft.

I spread my towel next to hers on the sand under a palm tree and sit down. "Do you snorkel much?" I ask her.

Martha Jo and Amy have wandered down the beach looking for red coral and unusual shells.

Grace nods. "I even went scuba diving at the Great Barrier Reef a few years ago, which is supposed to be the best spot in the world for that sport."

"Oh. I'm jealous," I say. "I've dived in Belize and Honduras, but from now on, I plan to stick to snorkeling. This is a rare treat."

Grace glances at my equipment.

"Why don't you use my mask and snorkel for a while?" I ask.

She shakes her head. Whatever her reason, I don't argue. I'm drawn to the clear, sparkling water out there like a fish is to a shrimp-baited hook.

"No. You go ahead," she says. "We can snorkel on one of the Gili Islands the day after tomorrow, on our last day of the cruise. I'll probably be able to rent some decent equipment there."

I don't argue, and, wearing an orange, long-sleeved shirt my sister loaned me, I wade into the clear blue water. One of a very few out here now, I feel like I'm entering paradise.

The previous evening we'd had a lecture about noise pollution in the ocean. Until then, I had no idea of its adverse effect.

Thinking about that lecture, I stretch out in the cool water, which isn't very salty, and simply breathe, leaving the distant laughter and conversation behind. Gradually, nothing but the sound of my own breath engages me. Inhale, exhale. In, out. The water's as clear as anything that comes out of a faucet, the waves gentle, and nothing seems to exist but my breath. It's like being part of an enormous meditation session.

Brightly colored coral sways in the water's gentle motion. Small, vibrant fish—orange, blue, yellow, green, pink—flit around the coral, seeming to chase one another like schoolchildren at recess.

I lie stretched out, face down, let this calm water take me where it wants. Absorbing the silence, I breathe it in, greeted into a world I've never imagined—complete acceptance, total, blessed peace. I feel normal, accepted, and understood. The outside world recedes. My inner world, linked to consciousness only by my steady breath, expands. I float, concerned with nothing except inhaling and exhaling slowly and steadily.

I drift over some dead coral—brown, black, gray—damaged, like I often feel inside. A divorce, a car wreck, and cancer will do that to you. As will being so socially awkward and finding it so difficult to communicate.

But most of the ocean floor overflows with flashy, colorful creatures who seem to welcome me. I feel such a part of this realm that I'm tempted to stay here forever. If death provides anything like this state of tranquility, it's certainly nothing to fear. I don't want to leave, so I don't.

Finally, though, I lift my head, look around. The sun has dropped, and only a few people linger on the beach. I've drifted near the outer limits of the rocky outcropping that protects the sheltered bay. Reluctantly, I murmur good-bye to this idyllic world and backstroke toward shore.

Martha Jo and Amy rush over as I emerge from the water, an aged Venus on the half shell.

"We're about to leave. The next-to-last Zodiac's almost here," Amy says. "We were worried about you."

I look around. Grace has obviously already left, and a stray, chill breeze hits me. Martha Jo and Amy care. Grace…

"I'm certainly glad you wore that orange blouse," Martha Jo says. "It helped us keep track of you."

"I'm sorry. I lost all sense of time. Being out there…" I glance at the approaching Zodiac, and a word I seldom use pops out of my mouth. "It was like being *untethered*," I say, wondering what I mean.

Martha Jo gives me a rare hug. "Well, we're glad you're back on land, safe and sound. We'll see you on the ship."

On the way back, I tell the smiling young woman who drives us, "Best day ever." But the wind that hits us as we bounce across the waves is a bit chilly. I have to resume living in a world where I'm never quite sure I belong.

Listing and Wine Bottles

"I need to stop by our cabin a minute," Amy calls as she and Martha Jo and I head to the dining room that evening. "Meet you at our table."

"Okay," Martha Jo says. "See you soon."

She and I are chatting as we stroll through the bar area on deck four, when the ship suddenly lists drastically to our left. Breaking glass shatters the calm I savored at the Pink Beach.

"Sit down! Everyone sit down!" someone yells.

I plop into the nearest chair, immediately begin raking my hair out of my eyes, over and over, as if my continued motion can prevent what seems to be happening. Am I going to permanently join the coral and fish I mingled with all afternoon?

We hang suspended for what seems like a lifetime, my fingers in my hair the only thing keeping me from jumping up and running around aimlessly. *I can't believe this! What's going on?*

We remain tilted at a forty-five-degree angle or more for only five or ten seconds, but this could be the last few moments of my life. Yet I distract and calm myself in a novel way—catching wine bottles. At least it gives me something to do with my hands.

They've toppled from the racks behind the bar to my right, and only one bottle breaks, but all the glasses are smashed. *I saved the wine.* Strange epitaph for the grave marker of someone who hasn't imbibed since I learned I had cancer. Whatever. At least stroking my hair and performing the heroic deed with the wine bottles helped calm my usual panic in such an extreme situation.

Amid all this high drama, suddenly the ship rights itself and continues moving forward as if nothing has happened. In reality, though, something *has* happened, regardless of my success in coping with the near-tragedy, and it has captured everyone's attention. People don't forget near-death occasions.

We soon learn that we hit a strong current when we emerged from a protected bay of the island and that dinner will be an hour late.

When we finally begin to eat, I think of the *Titanic*. What if we'd tipped over? We'd have had to tread water for a long time.

I push my paper plate away, my appetite gone.

February 24–25, 2023

STAYING ABOARD

Thanks to a fierce headache, I don't visit the final two islands where we stop. And we learn that some of the tourists who cruised from Bali to Darwin were quarantined with COVID, yet the company allowed them to stay on the ship for the return trip to Bali instead of quarantining them in Darwin. I also eat lunch with a group of strangers and surprise myself by being able to converse somewhat coherently about current novels and our experiences during the cruise. That's quite a victory for me.

    I also get a lot of rest, but I don't see Grace at all, and I miss her company, though she seems to have a ton of friends by now, and I've overheard her gossiping with several of them at our last few evening meals. That's the one thing I don't like about her, but she evidently senses my lack of interest in gossip and refrains when she eats with Martha Jo, Amy, and me, which is seldom now.

February 26, 2023

Arriving in Bali

We reach Bali early, pack, and leave the ship. "Just think," Martha Jo says. "Only two more days, and then we'll be flying home."

I nod. *And I'll have a certain woman on my mind nonstop.*

Our large, air-conditioned buses transport us directly to a temple that is, according to our guide, "one of the six most sacred places of worship for Hindus on Bali." And that's saying a lot, since Bali is loaded with temples and statues of various unfamiliar gods.

I watch a group of young girls learn to perform their traditional dances, and then I wander over to the lovely temple.

As I saunter through the grounds, enjoying the cool breeze from the sea below and the recent rain shower, I suddenly bump into a woman whom Grace seems to have spent a lot of time with during the past few days aboard the ship. And I suspect they spent a lot of their time gossiping about the other passengers.

"Beautiful view, eh," I say. "Are you looking forward to seeing more of Bali?"

She stares at me coolly. Or maybe that's how she looks at everyone. "No. I've been on the island before. I'm leaving with the ship this afternoon and heading on to Singapore for a few days."

"Oh. Well, then why don't you let me take your picture?"

We stiffly say our good-byes, and I can't stop thinking that I may have Grace all to myself on the final full day of our trip. I'm as satisfied as a monkey who's just exchanged some stolen sunglasses for a couple of bananas, a popular sight here at this temple.

❖

On my way back to the bus, I follow an alternate route, walking with the local crowd. One young Balinese woman stands by herself beside the road, as if waiting for someone. I stop and, in tourist sign language, ask permission to take her picture. In her long-sleeved white blouse, ankle-length green, blue, and gold sarong, gold sash, and sandals, a pink flower in her pulled-back hair, she's lovely. To her, though, she's probably just wearing her best Sunday-go-to-meeting clothes, plus a flower in her hair, which everyone most likely does.

After another block or so, I come across a family—the mother and daughter dressed similarly to the young woman I've just encountered, the father and two sons wearing white, short-sleeve shirts over white sarongs, plus small white turbans. They all smile and laugh, seeming happy to pose. It's like taking a picture of a family back home after church.

"Hey. Where have you been?" Amy asks as I climb back onto our bus.

"Just a little detour and a couple of photo ops," I say.

"Well, I'm ready for lunch," Martha Jo says. "How about you?"

We're driven to a small buffet restaurant, and as soon as we're seated at a large, round table, the hostess rushes over and places a pink blossom behind one ear of each of us, just like the one the young woman I photographed wore. "We have to have a picture of this," Amy says. The professional photographer from New York, whom we talked to our first morning in Australia, is sitting at our table and takes our picture. I dislike being the center of attention even so briefly, but the shot will remind me of good times with good friends.

Conversation with the photographer and his wife, as well as another couple, is much easier for me than before. In fact, I noticed that when I stayed aboard the ship those final two days, I was able to carry on a halfway fluent conversation with a stranger on several occasions. Now, excited, we all discuss how eager we are to see the luxury resort where we'll spend the next two nights. And then I share some of my adventures during the sixties, when I hitchhiked around Europe and the Middle East for a year with my new husband and we kept bumping into people on their way to becoming hippies. The photographer seems interested, plus I can usually discuss foreign travel with just about anyone without too much hesitation or stress. Maybe my social skills aren't quite as dismal as I've always considered them.

After lunch, I go upstairs to find the toilets and then wander around an upper dining room. A beautiful, framed ikat piece hangs there, much more intricate than any I've seen in the open markets. *Grace would love this.* I search the restaurant for her, but she must have already left, so I snap several shots of the piece. Maybe she can find something similar to buy near our hotel. Obviously, I can't get her out of my mind and am eager to please her.

Back in our bus, we drive south from Denpasar, Bali's capital, through crowded, noisy streets lined with shops and small hotels, surprised when we arrive at the Four Seasons Resort Bali at Jimbaran Bay. Wow! The huge complex, set into wooded hills like a fine jewel, faces a large bay with a cloudy view of a fairy-tale mountain far away in the northeast, as well as the nearby international airport.

My private villa perches at the very top of one of the hills, and after we check in, I'm amazed when my Balinese host drives me up to the colorful gate that leads into its grounds, complete with my very own small infinity pool.

He lets me into my huge bedroom and bathroom complex, explaining how to use the tub, the outdoor shower, the indoor shower, and on and on. And as soon as he leaves, I explode in a picture-taking frenzy. Otherwise, no one back home will ever believe I've stayed somewhere this fancy. Imagine me—who started my vagabond days sleeping in youth hostels, on beaches, in a remote monastery on Crete, and even on a ping-pong table in Denmark—spending two nights here.

I have a huge bed covered with about sixteen enormous pillows, surrounded by white, gauzy mosquito netting. And the ornate bedroom ceiling? Made of three distinct tiers of dark-wood slats, placed several inches apart and aimed up at a glossy, rectangular board at its peak, it's so high and symmetrical it reminds me of the interior of a vacant pyramid. On second thought, it could be the doorway to heaven, or the Hindu equivalent.

DINNER IN THE FOUR SEASONS RESTAURANT

"Look at the way that dancer moves her fingers," Amy says. "I can't imagine trying to make mine do that."

I stare at the lead Balinese performer in her elaborate gold and purple silk batik skirt and vest-like top. She waves and flaps two huge, golden fabric wings, as tall as she is, swooping around the floor with them outstretched, as flamboyant as a peacock. Her intricate gold headdress glitters, curling back over her head like the letter C. Her thick, heavy makeup and impossibly backward-curving fingers make her seem supernatural, and her distinct, abrupt eye movements emphasize her otherworldliness. I admire her poise, her command of the audience.

"We should be honored to be here," I whisper to Martha Jo. "In the old days, these legong dancers performed only for royalty and their most highly regarded guests."

"Well, I am honored," she says. "After this morning, seeing those little girls trying to learn to dance like this, I can appreciate how much training and practice it must take."

Just before the energetic dance ends, I glance across the performance area, and there stands Grace on the other side, seeming as absorbed in the performance as I am. She meets my gaze and nods slightly. The remaining dance is a blur, as my focus has shifted. Grace nods again and smiles as the final performance ends, and suddenly she's at my side, despite the crowd of people trying to make their way to the nearby dining area.

"Mind if I sit with you three tonight?" she asks immediately.

My AFib heart bumps even more out of rhythm than usual. "Of course not. We always enjoy your company."

Martha Jo and Amy nod.

"I'm rather tired of the people I've been associating with lately." She glances over her shoulder at a couple of them in the distance. "They're a lot of fun and all that, but I need a change."

We claim an empty table, then scatter to fill our plates with a huge international selection—seafood, vegetables, soups, salads, and so on.

Back at our table, Amy says, "What a feast. I wish we could stay here longer."

The rest of us barely respond because we're so engrossed in the various tastes and textures we're experiencing. And our perfect view of the bay makes our leisurely meal even more special.

"How about dessert?" Martha Jo asks.

We all moan.

"Why not?" Amy smiles. "The day after tomorrow, we'll be eating airplane food. Even in business class, we'll definitely wish we had a plate full of some of this." She gestures to our empty dishes a waiter's whisking away.

She and Martha Jo jump up and head toward the dessert room at the other end of the open-air restaurant from where we've been sitting.

Grace and I rise more slowly and stroll toward a large koi pond, located between us and our goal. "Aren't those orange-and-black fish over there gorgeous?" she asks. "Sometimes I wish I were one. I'd love to live in the water, and I imagine these beauties are well fed. That might be a pleasant life."

"You like the water that much?" I think about my snorkeling experience at the Pink Beach. Too bad she couldn't have shared it with me.

"Oh, yes. And my daughter and granddaughter do too. We all love to spend time at the beach."

To reach the dessert area, we walk past the large koi pond and over a little arched bridge to an entirely different section of the pavilion. Neither of us moves very fast at this point, and we pause to watch the huge fish drift past lily pads and other vegetation, as if they're as sated as we are.

When we finally arrive at the dessert room, we wait in line. It looks like most people are really loading their plates. They must be thinking about the airline food that's in their near future too.

"You haven't said much about your daughter," I say as we stand there. "What's she like?"

Grace frowns and blurts out in a rush, "She almost had a nervous breakdown when she went away to college. I had to go get her out—"

Suddenly it's our turn to choose our desserts, and each of us picks up a plate and starts making some very hard choices.

"I've never seen so many wonderful-looking sweets and types of fruit," I say, though I'd rather find a private spot and hear about Grace's daughter. Combined with Grace's comment when we first met about hating history, I'm wondering if she has an anti-intellectual bias. If so, it's a wonder she and I seem to have grown so close. I love intellectual subjects, though I've known a lot of pseudo-intellectuals. They give the love of learning a bad name.

"No wonder we had to wait," she says, standing next to me. "I want one of everything."

We separate then and make our choices, drooling over them as, side by side, we finally head back to our table. By the time we get there, our aborted conversation about her daughter and her college experience seems forgotten. I regret not bringing up the subject, mainly because it might shed some light on Grace's occasional seemingly anti-intellectual remarks, as I was just worrying about. But it's easy to let all the activity swirling around us sidetrack me.

After dinner, as the four of us stand at the bottom of the Four Seasons complex discussing our plans for tomorrow, Grace says, "I'm tired of riding all over the countryside in a bus. Besides, I signed up for the four-day extension here on Bali, so I'll get another chance to see more of the island. I think I'll stay here at this fabulous resort tomorrow and enjoy the beach for a change."

"That's a great idea," I immediately say, and Martha Jo and Amy grin, seeming to know what's on my mind. From time to time, I've mentioned my growing attraction to Grace while conversing with each of them, especially Amy, and they've both teased me a bit about being "sweet" on her. However, at other times they've both been rather noncommittal when I say something about her. Also, they've been busy with their own concerns, so I've hesitated to burden them with my petty ones.

I gaze at the waves on the bay, shining in the distance. Relaxing on the last day before a long flight home truly might be a good move, especially since I'm still not back up to par after my killer headache the other day. "Maybe you and I can go bodysurfing, Grace," I say. "Those waves look like they have a little kick to them."

She brightens. "You mean it? That would be such fun. Well, I'll see you tomorrow then." And just like that, she turns and starts walking toward her villa, which is evidently quite a distance from ours.

"She's like a firefly, isn't she?" Martha Jo remarks. "Now you see her, and now you don't."

I nod, and we stroll up through the maze of narrow roads and rock stairways, studded by strange stone statues and perfumed by tropical flowers. It's so quiet and peaceful here, almost eerie, especially after the constant noise of people on our small ship.

Back in my luxurious quarters, alone, I watch the sun set. Then I undress and slide into my pool, which is the perfect temperature. The unfamiliar stars above and the lights of the arriving and departing jets across the bay slowly transform my world into a fairyland of fact and fiction. But I can't think of anything except my upcoming date at the beach with Grace on the final full day of this strange trip to the other side of the world.

How did she destroy all my defenses so easily tonight? I've spent the past few days trying to convince myself that she doesn't set my world on fire every time I'm around her. I'd like to be able to hold my own around her, but right now, the cool water of my infinity pool can't possibly decrease the heat of my rising interest in her. In fact, I've totally lost my cool, as we used to say.

I gaze across the bay, the distant mountain there making me think of the crater lakes we saw the other day on Flores. We had to climb such a long, steep, rocky trail to view them, but it was worth it. Right now, I can almost feel the power of the long-ago volcanoes that formed those craters, how they must have spewed molten lava high into the air. Now some of that lava seems to pulse through my veins. That ancient eruption would have eclipsed the sun and the stars, just as my burning feelings for Grace are probably blinding me now. I feel helpless, unable to do anything but let the fire rage inside me. I've lost control of myself, let her dominate my thoughts and feelings, and I don't like my helplessness. It's like I've handed control of myself to her, allowed her to do what she wants with me, as I stand by and watch. I'm her faithful, obedient puppy dog.

I inch out of the water and sit on the edge of the pool. What if Grace were sitting here beside me? Has a simple memory of the time I've spent with her caused this odd burning sensation in my arms and legs? Am I suddenly hot with fever simply because I've let myself be seduced into thinking of her being here, especially if we touched each other right now? I can almost hear the sizzle, smell the scorch, see my flesh blister, blacken, peel off in strips. Red-hot lava seems to coat me, inside and out.

I kick the water and cool off immediately. I'm thinking in clichés. This attraction isn't physical, is it? It's similar but also very different—deeper, more complex. This urge to be with Grace seems almost metaphysical—beyond the senses. Knowing her on a deep, intimate level will help me know myself better. That's probably what I truly crave.

I shake my head. No! That doesn't seem right. That's not what's going on here. I'm sure of it, though the truth keeps wiggling out of my grasp as if it were a fish I'm trying to hold.

I gaze up at the stars. Do my failed marriages prove that I can never have a lasting relationship?

But why not be positive and pat myself on the back for trying to have one, and then for getting back up, learning from my mistakes, and trying again?

In order to succeed, though, I probably need to identify my main problem. I slide back into the pool, hoping the water will keep me cool and help me think. Two birds chatter at each other in a nearby tree. *Communication! Lack of it has been my biggest problem.*

Because I grew up with parents who obviously didn't seem to know how to talk to each other on a personal level, how was I supposed to learn that crucial skill? And I think it's something more than that, something wrong with the way I'm wired. I can have the most brilliant concept all worked out in my head, but the minute I open my mouth, the idea flies away like those two birds I've been hearing just did. It's always been like that for me, and I've never been able to do anything about it. Whatever's going on there, it sure gets in the way of me trying to converse easily with someone. It's so much easier to just carry on a conversation with someone who wants to do most of the talking. I'm a really good listener and have polished that skill all my life.

I take a break and swim a few very short laps to clear my head before I start thinking again. That's probably one reason I'm so drawn to Grace. She asks me meaningful questions and listens when I respond. If I'm ever going to improve my conversational skills, she's the kind of person I need to associate with. And she likes to talk about significant subjects, which really appeals to me. I can't stand chitchat or, God forbid, gossip.

Plus, I can rely on Grace to carry on a conversation in a group, so I don't worry about doing it myself, since I'm so weak in that area. But if I really have something to say, she lets me take a turn and gives me her silent support, as if she understands how hard it is for me to say what's on my mind. It's like she's my coach, in a way, and I can feel her supporting me.

I draw a deep breath, relieved to have taken one small step toward solving this lifelong mystery. Now I just need to try to remember what I've been thinking about and to put it into practice.

Because I finally have a little insight into why I'm so drawn to Grace, I wish I could spend even more time with her. I feel like a toddler just learning to walk, but my special adult is leaving me on my own. Deep down I know she'll fly home to her husband and probably stay with him indefinitely, but she has to live her own life, and I have to let her go. Hopefully, I've given her something she needs in return for the time and attention she's given me.

I take a deep breath and stare at the setting sun. At least I've cleared one small section of this patch of weeds I've been trying to pull from my mental lawn. Maybe our afternoon at the beach tomorrow will give me some more clues about how to improve my communication skills with someone I care for. I'm looking forward to it.

February 27, 2023

Perfect Afternoon in Bali

On our last full day in Bali, Grace and I eat an early lunch with Martha Jo and Amy. Then the two of them decide to return to their villa to rest.

"Are you sleepy?" Grace asks me. We're standing just outside the restaurant, the sun warm, the sky a clear Bali blue.

"No." I glance over her shoulder at the waves, the color of her eyes, washing onto the white sand in the distance.

"Neither am I," she says. "I can't wait to jump into that water. Want to go to the beach right now?"

"Sure. But I need to stop by my place and get my things. Would you like to come with me?"

She hesitates just long enough for me to imagine that a seduction scene may be playing in her mind. A lot of straight people think gays have nothing but sex on their mind. But then she shrugs. "Sure. Lead the way. I want to compare your pool to mine."

We stroll down the shady walkway side by side, silent for a few beats. "Oh. Look at this concrete bust," I say. "This woman's huge headpiece and necklace remind me of some of the ones the legong dancers wore last night."

"Except these ornaments are concrete and theirs were gold." Grace smooths her fingers over the woman's cheek. "I'd rather have the dancers' jewelry than this statue's carved finery."

"Yet the actual dancers, who knows how many years ago, probably dressed to please the king and his court, or whatever they were called. I bet those girls didn't own anything expensive, and the gold last night was most likely fake." I study the statue's expression. "This woman looks so peaceful. Check out her little smile and kind expression."

"You're right. She seems happy with herself instead of trying to impress a powerful man." Grace frowns, then shakes her head. "Want me to take a picture of you with her? She looks like your type."

"Sure." *What does Grace consider my type?* I drape my arm over the concrete statue's shoulder, wishing I could touch Grace this comfortably. Yet simply sharing this moment with her makes me happy.

We climb to the top level of the resort, where I unlock the large gate in the wooden wall that surrounds my villa. She passes me and walks down the flagstone path directly to my pool. "Oh. You have a plunge pool too, though you do have a much better view of the bay and the rest of the resort than I do."

She looks around my outdoor dining area and beautifully landscaped grounds as I struggle to open the ornate door to my living quarters. "I have a hard time working my lock too," she says. "I'm tempted to not fasten it from now on." She follows me inside. "Having a lock on the door in my fence should be enough."

She glances around. "Your place looks just like mine. I love the outdoor shower in the tropical garden. Don't you?"

Busy gathering sunscreen and finding my bathing suit, I nod. "Oh, yes. This suite feels almost decadent, which isn't necessarily a bad thing. Yet two showers and a huge tub seem like overkill, especially for only one person."

"I agree, but I plan to enjoy every minute of it." She heads toward the slatted sliding door and out to my pool. "I'll wait for you outside."

Is she nervous about being alone with me, or does she simply prefer to be outdoors enjoying the view? *Shut up. Enjoy the day and the luxury you're immersed in with an interesting woman.*

Trying to be casual, I change into my swimsuit and stuff everything I need for an afternoon on the beach into an old-fashioned string bag I've saved from the sixties to remind me of those long-ago hippie days. Then I pull on a hot-pink, batik cover-up I bought during an earlier trip to this part of the world and walk outside.

"Ready?" I ask.

She jumps, her back to me. Evidently she's been staring at the beach and the airport that sprawl in the distance.

She whirls around. "Sure. I was just daydreaming."

About what? I'd love to know but am too shy to ask.

The noon sun has begun to heat the stone paths we wind down

as we descend to Grace's villa, though the banana and palm trees provide welcome shade. My heart beats faster than usual, from either the sun, our destination, the exercise, or her nearness. "It's hotter than I expected," I say inanely.

"Well, we are near the equator," she says, her calm coolness making my heart pound even harder. Why do I feel like a gawky teenager with a crush on my music teacher? I don't enjoy the sensation, yet Grace attracts me like the water and our afternoon date do. I tend to get carried away when I'm around her for very long.

We silently walk down a quiet, shaded path. "And here we are at my villa," she says. "Want to come in?"

Her expression is neutral, so I simply state my preference. "Sure."

I want to see how she lives. Does she leave her clothes scattered over chair backs like I do, or has she kept them in her bags, or folded them neatly on her closet shelves? Are empty bottles and used dishes from snacks lying around or in the trashcan? She's like a thousand-piece jigsaw puzzle I'm trying to fit together in a very short time. Tomorrow she'll be taking a bus north to Ubud, and I'll still be here, packing to leave for the airport. I may never see or even hear from her again.

Her pleasantly cool living quarters almost make me shiver. Sitting on the bench at the foot of her king-size bed, I try to look like I'm patiently waiting for her to gather whatever she needs for our outing.

I hear her spraying something, and a familiar scent drifts into the room. "Hey, is that Beach Walk you're putting on?" I call.

"How'd you guess?" She returns from the bathroom area wearing long black pants and a long-sleeved blue shirt. "It used to be called that. Now it's marketed as Replica Beach Walk."

"I'd know that smell of sun-kissed, salty skin anywhere." I sniff the air like a drug dog.

She laughs. "So, you have a good nose, eh?"

"When I was young, I worked behind the cosmetics counter in a department store for a few summers. I know more about that subject than you'd suspect."

She grins. "What kind of perfume did I wear last night? And yes, this *is* a test."

I scratch my head, push my ridiculously curly hair back from my forehead several times. "Yves Saint Laurent's Black Opium."

"Hmm. I *am* impressed."

"That was easy." I grin. "Everyone knows it smells like coffee and vanilla."

"If you say so, but not many people pay attention to details like that." She picks up her water bottle. "Ready to go?"

"Huh?" My head suddenly swimming, I recall a woman I knew many years ago who wore Beach Walk too. Of course she was "happily" married, but I still had a major crush on her.

Grace's enticing scent has insinuated its way into me, seeming to urge me to find the bottle it lives in. Lucky it, to touch intimate places on her. Though not exactly in lust, I'm hyper-aware of her. I want to absorb her with all my senses, imprint her essence on myself—if I could understand what her essence is. Beach Walk and Black Opium merely provide clues.

This isn't a crush, I keep reminding myself. I thought I'd figured that out last night. Basically, Grace is teaching me how to communicate on a personal level. But have I learned anything? What would she think if I admitted my attraction to her, my urge to simply be honest with her? Could I do that? Or would she think I'm delusional?

She's leaving tomorrow. It's too late to try to start a relationship. She's going home to her husband, and if I open up too much this late in the game, I'm just asking to be hurt more than I've already been. If I show her who I actually am, she'll probably be appalled.

I better play it safe, just try to have a good time and end things on a positive note.

❖

The grounds of the resort stretch much farther than I suspected. We stroll down the hill and bear to our right, passing large, shaded buildings and then a long, narrow lap pool, built right next to the bay. Maybe we can try it on our way back, after we've played in the water.

The sand begins now, so I pull off my sandals and stuff them into my string bag. The white sand squishes between my toes, its warmth welcoming me to the beach.

We keep walking, shaded by tall palms, past lounge chairs where some of our fellow cruisers stretch out, hovering male attendants delivering them colorful drinks.

As we continue down the beach, we climb over small boulders. The cantinas that dot it become shabbier, then almost ramshackle.

"I don't think we're in Four Seasons territory any longer," Grace says.

"What was your first clue?" I grin.

She gives me a side-eye, then laughs. "Oh, I've seen my share of beaches for common people. Haven't you?"

"Ha. More than my share. My dad's idea of our yearly family vacation consisted of getting up well before dawn and driving four or five hours to Galveston. When we got there, we'd stop at a small grocery store, and we kids would stay in the car while he and our mom shopped. They'd come out carrying a big box of food and drinks, and we'd head to a deserted part of the beach, park, and spend the rest of the day there." I stop, pick up a truant plastic bottle, toss it into a nearby barrel.

"We thought we were in heaven," I say. "I remember one day when the Gulf of Mexico had absolutely no waves. It was so eerie, magical. Walking as far out as possible into the calm water, we stared at glossy shells and live sand dollars and other odd sea creatures several feet down, burrowing into the mud and sand. I can't recall a happier childhood family vacation."

"So where did you spend the night?"

I love how Grace listens intently and asks questions.

"Why, on the beach, of course," I say. "Or maybe in the car. Wherever we could find room to stretch out a bit. Luckily it never rained."

"In a way that does sound like fun." She seems lost in a memory of her own. "We never spent the night outside like that. Maybe my mom was afraid to, without a man along."

"Why didn't your dad go with you? Did he have to work?"

She kicks a candy wrapper embedded in the sand, and we walk in silence. "We didn't really have a dad. I was so young when he and Mom divorced, I don't remember much about him." Her mouth and forehead twist into a near-scowl.

I touch her shoulder for a second, and she flinches.

"I'm sorry," I say, for both her lack of a parent and my presumption in touching her. Her turquoise eyes glitter, then glisten. I'm unsure what to say, so I fall back on a vague generalization. "My dad was a bastard a lot of the time, but sometimes we really enjoyed being around him."

"I'm sorry for pulling away like that, but I suppose you never get over some things." Grace draws in a deep breath and straightens her shoulders. "However, this is the last day of our fabulous trip. Let's walk back to the Four Seasons section of the beach and wallow in luxury while we have a chance. No sleeping on the beach for either of us tonight."

We turn around and stroll in silence until she says, "Look over there. Someone's leaving those two lounge chairs under that big sugar-palm tree. It's a perfect spot. Private, yet shady."

She hurries over and grabs a chair, then pulls it closer to the other one. A Four Seasons attendant rushes up, holding two fresh towels. "Please, madam. I am here to help. Here is a new one for you and another for your friend."

Grace raises a dainty arm, I suppose to motion him away, but stops. "Why, thank you," she says. We stand back and let him strip off the old towels, then stretch a fresh, fluffy white one taut over each chair. She tips him. "Thank you."

Sitting on the edge of her recliner, she reaches into her bag, pulls out a tube of 50 SPF sunscreen, and exhales at length. "You only live once." The smell of fresh coconut joins the salty aroma from the waves—a perfect cocktail.

After slathering her face, neck, hands, and feet with the creamy lotion, she turns to me. Her long sleeves and pants cover her thoroughly. "Want me to put some of your sunscreen on the places you can't reach?"

I go where her question might take me for only a second, because it's obviously a straightforward one. I know the difference between flirtation and friendship and don't want to taint our innocent intimacy. I merely nod and lie on my stomach so she can anoint my back, glad I brought my old black swimsuit that plunges to my waist. Her touch is gentle, smooth, firm.

Suddenly, I recall her small hands that I enjoyed holding while we danced that one time aboard the ship. What was going on with that episode? I've never felt that protective of a woman. Is it because she's so petite, so unhappily married, or do I simply like her a lot, feel a kinship with her? I want her to be happy and safe.

"There." She lightly slaps my bony shoulder, startling me from my musing. "You're covered. Ready to hit the surf?"

I turn and plant my bare feet on the powdered-sugar sand. Only the finest for a Four Seasons beach. "Definitely. Let's do it."

We stride to the shore, the waves calling us to play. As we near it, small rocks and broken shells begin to bite into my bare soles, so I hurry in. "Come on," I call to her after I've swum out some distance.

"That's not fair," she calls. "You're a lot taller than I am. I'm going to catch a ride right here. See you on shore."

I nod and stand in waist-high, sandy, blue-green water, try to judge the power of each swell by the strength with which it tries to suck me out into the depths. When I experience a tug, like noticing a fish on a baited line, I face the shore, ready to leap up and stretch out on the water's surface, pretend to be a log or a leaf or a stick. The more relaxed I become, the more easily the power of the surf can propel me ashore. The exhilaration of letting go reminds me of the lift of an airplane when it finally decides to leave the runway and trust itself to the sky.

However, the wave I've committed myself to turns out to be too weak to provide much of a ride. "That was a bummer," I say as I squat in the tepid, waist-high water near the beach and let it wash around me.

"Plenty more where that came from," she says. "Let's try again."

So we do.

After repeatedly getting my hopes up for a powerful ride, only to be practically abandoned halfway to the shore, I give up and simply float on my back.

She swims over to me. "Not doing it for you, eh?"

"Afraid not."

"My mom would have told me to let it go. The harder you try to force something to work for you, the more it'll refuse."

"Your mother sounds like a wise woman."

"She was. When I was growing up, all my friends used to come over to see me after school." She smooths her hand through the elusive liquid. "But I always suspected they really showed up to be around her."

"And how did that make you feel?" I stroke an imaginary beard, and she chuckles. I'm trying to lighten the mood so she won't think I'm always serious.

"Well, Doctor. A lot of the time it made me feel like shit." She seems to take my question to heart though. "That was when I was thinking like the teenager I obviously was."

"And?"

"At other times I was proud of her for being such an outstanding person that my friends would enjoy her company."

She seems to revere her mother yet perhaps felt rather upstaged at that tender point in her life.

"Ah. I suspect an adult was beginning to hatch from that juvenile egg."

She grins, and I hope I've helped improve her attitude toward that insecure teenager she seems to have been. "I suppose you're right, Doctor."

"And what became of you and of your mother?" This is the most at ease I've felt around Grace, so I'm glad we still have a long portion of the afternoon left.

"Well, I was bored silly in my same-old, same-old hometown in Delaware, so I married the first man who came along that I was the least bit attracted to."

I admire her honesty. "The same one you're thinking about leaving?" Part of me is simply curious, but the other part still hopes she decides to do what she's been contemplating for evidently quite a long time. However, I still don't fully understand why I want her to leave her husband. It's her choice, her life. Maybe I simply want her to be brave and do what she really wants, as I hope I can from now on.

She frowns. "The one and only. As I've mentioned, being an armed-forces wife wasn't as glamorous as I'd imagined. You should have seen some of the boring places where we lived. They made me wish I'd never left home."

"So why do you stay with him?"

"Oh, the usual. He made a decent salary, which now provides a comfortable retirement. He lets me do practically whatever I want. I always had a date back then, when it mattered, except when he had to be on duty, and then it didn't matter, because everyone knew I belonged to him. Even when I went to functions by myself, people always treated me as if he were there with me."

"So. Money, freedom, and an uncomplicated social life. I suppose that's better than the kind of marriage most women settled for until not that long ago." I think of my own mom.

"Except my mom refused to settle," Grace says. "I think she preferred to raise us on her own, though she and I never discussed the subject. Part of me wishes I'd been more like her and split with my husband long ago, but I'm not sure I'll ever be as strong as she was."

"You seem strong to me. Coming on this cruise by yourself. Solving your own problem about the messed-up flight in Australia. Being our star ocean-kayaker and meeting tons of new people on the trip. Each time I divorced, I had to go through a major adjustment, but it's doable. Looking back, I don't regret any of my breakups, though none of them have been easy."

"Yes," Grace says. "I wish Mom were still around so I could talk to her about it now, but she's been gone fifteen years." She sighs. "Did you ever talk to your mother about your divorces?"

I look around at the blue water, the white sand, the green palm trees. We're in paradise, surrounded by a surf inviting us to play in it, yet here we stand in the middle of all this beauty discussing divorce and our mothers. Strangely, though, this is one of the most enjoyable few hours of the entire trip for me, one I'll never forget because it's so full not only of beauty but of meaning. I only wish I could be braver and more honest, let Grace know how I really feel and trust her to discuss the situation straightforwardly.

"Yes. I talked to my mom about my first one," I say, "when I was in my late twenties. She and I were sitting in my car at the local root beer stand, each holding a frosted mug. After I finally worked up the courage to admit what was tearing me apart inside, she said, 'I understand. If I hadn't been already pregnant with you, I probably would have left your daddy. But I was, and soon we were at war with Germany and Japan, and then things got too complicated for me to do what I knew I should.'"

Grace flattens her hand and smooths it across the temporarily placid water. "And how did that make *you* feel?" Her tone is just light enough to let me know that she sympathizes yet understands that I've processed this experience and left it behind as much as I can.

"Surprised and hurt at first, because who wants to know you're not wanted? And finally, after many years, I felt sympathy for both my parents, because apparently neither of them was ready for the life they'd gotten themselves into."

"Sounds like they must have made the best of a bad situation," Grace says. "At least you don't seem too badly scarred."

"At least not visibly." I lower myself until the brackish water reaches my chin. Here's a perfect opening. I can finally show her who I really am. But I don't risk it. "I'm still working it all out. But what about you?"

"I can't decide about the divorce thing. My married life was, and still is, comfortable—except that my husband and I don't know each other very well or like each other very much."

I run my hand over the smooth surface of the liquid that surrounds us. "Do you think you'll stay with him?"

"I truly don't know. Like I might have told you when we first met, if I don't intend to, I better do something before it's too late."

"Too late?"

"Oh, you know. Too late to find someone I really love. Someone who helps me feel like I thought he would all those years ago."

"Which is?" I stroke my imaginary beard again, to give an illusion of frivolity. I'm not sure if she enjoys this type of sharing as much as I do. Her friendship with the other people she's met on this cruise seems to focus on laughing and joking. And, to be fair, for most people, I assume, that's what a vacation trip should entail. She probably thinks I'm too serious to be any fun.

She half smiles. "I'd like to be content to be around him, or her. Want to travel together to places we'd both enjoy. Look forward to growing old together. Happy and fulfilled." She splashes me. "Oh, I don't know. Let's change the subject. This is getting too deep."

"The subject or the water?" We've evidently been moving as we talk, or the tide is affecting the water level. But I really doubt she likes to stay quite as deep on a personal level as I do. I should lighten up, try to be who I think she wants me to be.

"I don't know about you, but I'm beginning to prune all over," she says. "Have you had enough of waiting for a giant breaker to come along and sweep us to shore?" Shading her eyes with one hand, she peers out into the bay. "I don't spot any likely prospects."

I sigh, hating to leave this warm water that caresses and refreshes us and keeps the busy world at a distance. "I suppose you're right." Suddenly I spot a larger-than-usual swell. "Just one more try?"

"Sure. I'm up for anything today." She grins and faces the shore, glancing over her right shoulder as she tenses to leap into the wave heading toward us. Poised beside her, I let it suck me backward, and then I gather my energy and dive forward with it, giving myself up to its power. One with the rushing swell, I let it propel me to the beach, where it turns me over and delivers me onto the sand like I'm in its hand and it's rolling the dice.

"Wow. That's the one I've been waiting for all day," I spit out, along with a mouthful of brackish water.

She's sputtering too, and it's like we've just washed up onto Waikiki Beach—sandy, pleasantly tired, and ready to head for a cocktail and a sun bath.

We pick ourselves up, and I jerk down the bottom of my swimsuit while she rearranges her blue shirt, which has ridden up toward her breasts.

"Great finish, eh?" I ask, and she nods, pushing her soaked hair back from her face.

"Absolutely. Totally worth the wait." She glances toward the loungers where we've left our blue beach towels and other belongings. "Ready to rest a bit in the shade?"

I nod, gearing myself up to try to walk barefoot again on the shore without stepping on too many sharp rocks and shells.

Minutes later, safely back at our lounge chairs, we plop down and stretch out. She grabs her thermos and takes a long sip of water. "Ah. That's better. This is the life, isn't it?"

We chat for a while, and then she arranges her beige straw hat to shade her face from the sun reflecting off the water. Her eyes close, and I study her pink cheeks, her slightly sunburned aquiline nose, and her subtly pointed chin. Gentle wrinkles emphasize her closed eyes and mouth. The bent trunk of a palm tree and the light-blue sky mottled with puffy clouds to her left, plus the edge of the vibrant-blue towel to her right, frame her face perfectly.

As I capture this image of her on my phone's camera, I think, this is the way I'll always picture her and our afternoon in Bali. A sweet sadness engulfs me as I settle back into my own reclined chair and let this afternoon in paradise flow over me like a milk bath.

Too soon, we head back to the resort, though on the way we stop to rinse off the salt and then plunge into the resort's long, narrow, clear-aqua lap pool. There we swim a bit, then cling to the concrete side facing the bay and stare out at the calm water.

"What's your deepest fear, Helen?" Grace asks, out of the blue.

My brain freezes, and I say, "I really can't think of one right now. Maybe later."

That happens to me a lot when someone puts me on the spot. I have no idea why. Usually it takes several hours for a viable response to percolate up.

"How about you?" I ask, partly to divert attention from my inability to answer such an easy question and mainly because I want to hear her answer.

"Heights," she says immediately. "I wake up in the middle of the night and catch myself on the edge of a cliff or in an airplane with the door open, staring down at the ground, which seems to be a mile away. It's a horrible sensation, and I usually can't go back to sleep for a very long time."

"Do you think it has anything to do with your husband being in the Air Force?" I ask.

She shakes her head. "I've considered that possibility, but somehow it doesn't seem to explain how scared I am. I wish I could understand what's going on there."

I think of a novel I read in the early seventies, *Fear of Flying*. I came across it just after my first divorce and recall the phrase "zipless fuck," because I was briefly experimenting with that reality. But later I realized that it was more about women who were stuck in unhappy marriages. Grace might find it interesting.

I'm trying to process this sudden stream of information so I can share it with her, but she suddenly says, "Race you to the end of the pool," and dives underwater.

She wins, we grab our towels, and the magical afternoon fades as we stroll, side by side, to our separate villas, our separate lives. I've lost my chance to reveal who I truly am. And I don't think I'll have another one.

BATHING AT THE FOUR SEASONS

In my villa again, alone and pleasantly exhausted from the sun, the water, and the conversation, I stand in my lush backyard garden.

Bamboo, palm trees, and flowering ginger surround me, make me feel like I've wandered onto a set from the old 1950s movie *South Pacific*. My skin tingles. The salt and the sand, the sun and the waves have manipulated it, manicured it, marinated it. In short, I'm sticky and itching and burning, though I seem to glow under my thin covering of skin. I may have to use all three of my bathing facilities to scrub myself clean and release that glow.

Outside, I strip off my limp bathing suit, then twist a simple metal handle. As water cascades over me from an artificial bamboo spout high on the wall, I rinse off the remaining salt and sand of the afternoon. However, I can't—don't want to—wash away the memories of being with Grace that float in my mind. I luxuriate in them.

The lush jungle vegetation helps transport me to a more languid, richer plane, just as the coral reefs and tropical fish I snorkeled with on the Pink Beach did last week. My heart rate seems to slow, and my shoulders gradually lower as I stand and let this stream of tepid water pour over me. Thinking of one of *South Pacific*'s most memorable songs, I'm not in the mood to wash anyone, male or female, out of my hair. I just want to enjoy the glow from my afternoon with Grace, dimmed only by the regret of my lost opportunity to show her my true feelings.

Dripping, I turn off my shower, stroll inside to my large bathroom, and survey my oversize, white, ceramic soaking tub. Its shining silver knobs release a gush of hot and cold water. I stand there, meditating on how it gradually climbs up the tub's sides. Slowly, I sprinkle in bath salts, watch the shiny crystals dissolve and faintly color my private bath the hue of the Pink Beach.

I lift one leg into the tub and turn, cautious, then sit and slide down its gently sloped end. *Aah. The water's just right.* The fragrant bath salts have spread throughout the swirling liquid and seem to challenge any remaining specks of sea salt.

Again, memories of Grace—not just of this afternoon but of hiking with her at the crater lakes—flood me: the barren volcanic landscape, the rich, deep colors of the three bodies of water, the centuries-ago presence of the searing lava, the gentle fire of our casual conversation that colored my day golden. I luxuriate in these reminiscences as fully as I engulf myself in the water sluicing around me.

Then I light a stick of cendana incense, its gentle scent of gardenias and bananas mingling with the soft, woody aroma of sandalwood and vanilla in my bar of organic Bali Passion soap. Leisurely scrubbing myself with a thick, pure-white washcloth, I grow increasingly calm, peaceful. Finally, I declare myself clean and slide into the depths of the tub, head tilted back, lie there with only my nose not covered by the water until it cools, and I warm.

Dripping again, I desert the tub for my nearby large, blue-tiled indoor shower. There, I stand under its huge rain-head and rinse until I'm waterlogged. Then, finally, I step out and cuddle into a fluffy, white, oversized towel.

Compared to the small shower in our tiny chamber on the cruise ship, this one's the height of the Eiffel Tower, and right now I seem to be standing at the top of that icon of beauty, gazing out at Paris sparkling all around me.

I don't want this dreamy day to end. I want to prolong my afternoon with Grace, let it glide into our upcoming final evening, which I hope to share with her as well, lost in the magic spell Bali has cast over me.

This afternoon, when we reached Grace's villa, I told her I'd save her a seat at dinner tonight, and she nodded.

Will I see her there? What if I don't?

Last Dinner of Our Cruise

"No fancy dancers tonight, eh?" says a man already at the table where we choose to sit.

Martha Jo slides into the chair to my left.

I pull out mine and put my sun hat and sunglasses in the one to my right.

"Well, dancers or not, I'm not impressed with this banquet hall," the woman to the right of the seat I'm saving says.

I glance at her. It's Heather, the Californian we first met in Brisbane on our way to Darwin. "We're going to be stuffed in here like a bunch of dirty clothes in a suitcase," she says.

How strange to begin and end this trip with her and her husband.

"I agree that it's cramped," he says. "The restaurant last night was so much larger, more of an open-air pavilion than this closed-in place. The noise level in here's already too high."

I nod and half-turn in my straight-back chair, hoping to glimpse Grace walk through the only door to this rather plain facility. We could be in Cleveland instead of Bali.

"So, are you two flying back home tomorrow, or do you have other plans?" Martha Jo almost yells to Heather and her husband.

I glance at the entryway.

"We're staying for the Ubud extension, since we'll probably never visit Bali again," he says.

No sign of Grace.

"Ubud would be nice," Martha Jo says. "I've been hearing that it's beautiful there in the interior, but I'm ready to get back to Texas." She practically screams her comments to be heard over the increasing noise level of a hundred people talking and laughing.

I crane my head again toward the entrance. *Nothing.* I push my hair back several times, the minutes becoming hours. *No sign of Grace. Where is she? Did she fall asleep?*

Our first course, a fresh fruit salad, arrives, and I can barely distinguish a piece of pineapple from a mango—all bland and uninteresting. To be sociable, I eat only a few bites of a banana, my stomach roiling in time to my own steady motion as I push my hair back out of my face.

I twist around again. There she is! Near the front door. I drop my fork, start to wave. But…a rather obnoxious woman that we had dinner with a few nights ago on the ship stands beside her. Ugh. They look around and say something to each other, nod, wave to someone.

Immediately they head to the other side of the huge room and join another group. I let my shoulders drop, remove my belongings from the chair to my right.

"So, have you enjoyed your trip?" Heather almost yells to me.

We converse across the vacant chair as best we can, and it finally hits me. This pleasant woman has been more central to my trip than I realized. She was the first person from the group of fellow cruisers I met and one of the two other avid snorkelers at the Pink Beach, which Grace left early. That day, during our Zodiac return ride to the ship, Heather and I carried on an intense conversation, focusing on our common experiences with cancer. I really like her and feel very comfortable with her instead of on edge much of the time like I do with Grace.

I make some innocuous remark about hippies, and suddenly she asks, "What was it like to be in San Francisco during the famous Summer of Love?" I must have mentioned that adventure during our Zodiac conversation after snorkeling. I was so high from all that time in the water, I don't recall much of what I told her.

"Not many people ask me that question," I say, then proceed to describe that memorable time. "We didn't live in the infamous Haight-Ashbury District, and we didn't smoke marijuana then," I say. "That came later."

As I share some of my experiences in San Francisco that summer, Heather, obviously quite a few years younger than I am, truly seems interested, as does her husband. At least they appear to listen, unless they're simply pretending to, like Grace may have been all this time.

Talking with them distracts me, but I can't ignore Grace's behavior. I thought we had something special, but for her to prefer another woman's company to mine on our final night together?

As I continue to talk with Heather and her husband, I vaguely wish I hadn't focused so intently on Grace during the trip, but hindsight truly is twenty-twenty. Nothing can blunt the effect of Grace's blatant rejection. Even tonight's dessert isn't nearly as varied and delicious as last night's was.

Back in my villa, I slide into a lounge chair on my deck, kick off my sandals, and stare across the bay, jets steadily landing and taking off as dusk turns to dark. Low-hanging clouds blot out the moon and the stars as I slump there in the hushed night, totally alone. I don't like myself very much.

February 28, 2023

STARTLING DEVELOPMENT

My room phone rings.

"Hello," I say, not yet fully awake. I didn't sleep well last night.

"Amy just tested positive for COVID," Martha Jo says. "We want you to fly home and use our car to drive yourself back to our house. You can pick up your own vehicle there."

I sit up straight in my huge bed, jerked into a reality I don't want to face. "Are you sure?"

"Yes. Amy wasn't up to par yesterday, but we thought she was just tired." Martha Jo takes a deep breath, as if she's been climbing several flights of steep stairs. "But when she woke up this morning, she had a fever and started throwing up."

"What makes you think it's COVID?"

I get up and head to the bathroom. Maybe a damp washcloth on my sticky face will help me think a little more clearly.

"I used one of those home tests we brought, and she showed positive."

"Are you sure you can trust them?" I wipe my face, instantly more awake.

"That's what I thought, so I called the front desk, and they sent a doctor right away. According to his test results, that's what's wrong, though he took another sample and sent it to the lab to be sure. She feels terrible, so he left her several types of medicine to start taking. Plus, Bali still has strict quarantine rules, so as of now, she has to stay in isolation for ten days."

"Ten days! That's a long time." I glance around my new living quarters. "But being stuck here wouldn't be quite so bad."

Martha Jo laughs weakly. "That's what I told her. At least she picked a great place to get sick. The doctor said if the results from the lab today come back positive too, he'll test her again in five days."

"Hmm." I take my last clean blouse from my suitcase and try to press the wrinkles out of it with one hand. "Let me go eat breakfast. Then I'll talk to you again. I need to think about this situation. I hate to leave y'all here by yourselves. After all, it was my big idea to come on this trip, and it seems like we've had nothing but one problem after another." I pull on a blouse and my least-wrinkled pair of khaki trousers.

"Well, it's up to you, but you should leave. We'll be fine. What's there to do? When Amy gets well, she and I can take a taxi to the airport here. Then in Dallas we can figure out a way to get home. My daughter can pick us up, or we can use the long-distance shuttle."

"But it's at least a two-hour drive one way, in all that Dallas traffic. Probably longer. You need to have your own car."

"Like I said, don't worry about it. But go ahead and eat. You've got until early afternoon to decide."

My head spinning like a washing machine, I dress and then rush down various flights of stone steps, through lush grounds studded with strange-looking statues and flowering shrubs. I'm in the middle of paradise, but I focus only on the news about Amy. What should I do?

It would be simple to fly back to Texas alone. But to take their car? No. I can't do that. Surely I can arrange my own transportation. Plus, I think about a horrible experience last fall, while returning from Brussels to Houston after spending time with a dear friend in Belgium. Not only did I miss my connection in Seattle, but then, because a hurricane was hitting the US East Coast, I had to take an expensive last-minute redeye from Seattle to Dallas, switch airports there, catch another flight to Houston, and then wait an additional six hours for my luggage before I could drive three hours home. All because the booking agency didn't allow enough time for the transfer in Seattle, for which they refused to claim responsibility. Flying alone again so soon after that nightmare does not appeal to me.

While I'm hurrying to breakfast, that too-recent experience crashes in on me. Wouldn't it be a lot less stressful to just stay here in Bali and fly back with Martha Jo and Amy? I'm tempted. More important, what kind of a friend leaves her buddies in the lurch? I doubt they'd desert me if I had COVID.

My head's still spinning as I wait in line for an omelet and glance around the open-air restaurant. Suddenly I spot Grace, sitting at a table for two with her back to me, gazing out at Jimbaran Bay—the busy airport on one side and the still, silent mountain basking in the sun on the other one. *Stay or go? Which should I choose?*

I accept my breakfast plate from a smiling young Balinese server and walk over to Grace at her table for two.

Final Meal with Grace

"Hi, there," I say. "You're up early. Want some company?"

Grace turns around in her chair as I place my overflowing plate on her table. "Of course. But I don't mind sitting by myself, you know."

I'm not sure of her subtext. Would she rather be alone? Does she think I'm simply trying to be "nice"? Or should I accept her words at face value?

"Where are your friends?" she asks as I sit.

"I just learned that Amy has COVID, so she and Martha Jo have to stay here until she tests negative. She's evidently really sick and is already taking some powerful meds."

"What a shame," Grace says. "I hope she's better soon. What do you plan to do?"

I shake my head. "I haven't decided whether to be a Good Samaritan and stay with them or be selfish and fly home. That's what they want me to do, but deserting them doesn't seem right."

"That's a noble thought." She bites into a decadent-looking croissant. "Yet how can you help them? They're grown women. For what it's worth, I'd head home. That'd give them one less thing to worry about."

I spread my napkin on my lap. "I don't know."

"That's up to you." She shrugs and takes another bite of her croissant. "Well, you have a few hours to make up your mind. I hope everything works out well for all of you."

"Missed you at dinner last night. I saved you a seat. What happened?" I'm pushing my luck, but I want to know where I stand with Grace.

"Oh, that. Oh. Uh…uh…I took a shower and rested. Then I stopped by the resort's tourist shop."

I cut into my omelet, which is perfectly cooked, but suddenly I'm not very hungry. "Some last-minute souvenirs, I suppose."

"Yes. That's it. Yes. I found a few more things for my granddaughter." Grace sips some deep-golden juice. "I didn't think, uh, you'd be interested in shopping with me after dinner."

This is the first time I've seen Grace rattled.

"You're probably right, but I wouldn't have minded," I say. "My sister's a grandmother, and I know how much she adores her grandchildren."

"Yeah. Well. Yeah. I ran into a woman from the ship there, and I really do feel sorry for her, so I, uh, asked her to have dinner with me. You're always with Amy and Martha Jo anyway, and under all that bluster, this poor woman's rather pitiful. You've seen how she is. I can't decide if she's lying about half the things she says that she does or if she truly is an exhibitionist. I knew you'd understand…"

I fork a piece of my omelet and force myself to eat a bite, letting her excuse drop. Grace and I really don't have anything between us except some shared experiences and interesting conversations. Plus, we haven't found any places we'd like to tour together in the future, so this is evidently the end of the road for us. Except what do I do with all these feelings that getting to know her has stirred up in me?

We chat about how much we've enjoyed the trip, how good it's been to spend time together, and other usual clichéd subjects. Soon, we finish eating, and it's time to leave. We walk out of the restaurant together, and she initiates a friendly good-bye hug. "Take care of yourself," she says.

"You too. Enjoy the rest of your trip," I say without much enthusiasm, my energy level nose-diving.

She nods, and just like that, we're untethered from one another.

As I'm climbing the third flight of stairs back to my villa, it hits me—the same type of headache I had on the ship the other day, but at a magnitude of ten instead of five. I almost run down the narrow street to my gate and barely have time to unlock both doors and rush inside, then race to the toilet and fall on my knees before I throw up what I ate of my breakfast. Afterward, I somehow make it to my bed. COVID has obviously made my decision for me.

The Doctor Visits

"Have you packed?" Martha Jo asks when I finally get the house phone to stop its terrible screeching. "The Advantage rep's wondering what you've decided. The people flying home are leaving for the airport in an hour, so you need to call a courtesy cart to come pick you up before long. Then the rep's going to Ubud with everyone else. She's a basket case right now, so we're pretty much on our own."

I drop the phone, rub my fingers along my eyebrows. The slight pressure makes me lower my hands. "Helen! Helen! What's going on?" I dimly hear.

I inch my fingers over to the instrument of torture and manage to lift it to my head again. "I'm sorry, Martha Jo. But I'm not leaving either. I'm afraid I have what Amy has."

"Oh, no. I should have known. You poor thing. And all by yourself."

I hear her relaying the news to Amy and almost let go of the phone again. I just want to sleep and not wake up for a very long time.

"Helen. Listen to me," she says. "Don't worry about a thing. I'll arrange things with the Advantage rep and whoever else I need to. And I'll have them send a doctor to see you soon. You just rest."

My shoulders relax, and I'm so relieved I almost drop the phone again. "Oh, Martha Jo. You're an angel. What would I do without you and Amy? Talk to you later. Bye."

I click off and make it to the toilet just in time to empty whatever's left in my stomach. I don't care if I ever eat again.

Martha Jo, the doctor, and the Advantage rep show up just as I'm drifting in and out of a dream of Grace and me hanging on to the side of the resort's large lap pool discussing our deepest fears. I've just told her mine—that I'm most afraid of talking to people, especially in a group setting—and she's laughed and said that's ridiculous. In the dream, she admits that I do seem a bit shy, which is what people usually say, at least the few I've trusted enough to confide in.

The doctor gives me a self-test, and sure enough, it shows positive. I stare at him, say, "I've taken all the shots and boosters, worn masks, self-isolated—done everything possible. Hasn't this illness run its course worldwide? Isn't it safe to travel abroad now?"

Yet he simply mumbles something and swabs my nose again. "We have to send this one to the lab, so we won't know the final results until late this afternoon. However, the self-tests are usually accurate. I highly recommend that you not fly home today as scheduled."

The doctor leaves, but the rep stays. She's a heavy-set young woman from Eastern Europe, whom we've barely seen because we opted out of the official tour yesterday. She gives Martha Jo and me the details of my upcoming confinement, assuming my second test will be positive also.

"They've had a lot of cross-contamination with this strain of the virus here on Bali," she says, "so we don't want you and Amy passing it back and forth. Luckily, Martha Jo was sick last month and recovered, so she should be fine to stay with Amy. But you shouldn't see either of them until you're well, Helen."

I blow out a breath. "How long will it be before we can leave?"

"Five days minimum."

The rep sounds like she's had some recent experience with the situation here on the island, and I imagine she's thinking about the tour members who caught COVID during the trip just before ours and were quarantined in our ship on its way back from Australia.

She crosses her arms, continuing her mandate. "On the fifth day, both of you can take another test, and if you're negative, we'll put you on an airplane immediately."

"What if we're not?" Martha Jo asks.

"I hope that doesn't happen, because I have to fly back to Budapest that day," she says. "But if it does, you can take the test again every two days and leave when you're negative."

"How long will that be?" I ask, envisioning myself a permanent resident of Bali.

"After ten days, you won't be contagious any longer, so you can leave then, if the airport officials here will let you." She stares at me. "Are you okay for now? Do you need any medicine? The doctor gave Amy several strong drugs to help her."

I shake my head. "I don't know. What do you think?"

"He'll probably see that you get the same meds he prescribed for Amy." She looks at her watch. "I need to finalize arrangements for the group that's touring the Ubud area. I have to be with them all the time, but if any of you need me, you can call or text. Good luck." And with that, she's gone.

Martha Jo and I stare at each other. "Well, I thought we could at least get together and play Rummikub while we're stuck here," she says. "This would have been a perfect opportunity."

I nod. "It was a good thought. Thankfully we have phones, so let's stay in touch."

"Of course. Keep me up to date, and I'll do whatever I can to help."

"Thanks," I say. "Maybe someday we'll laugh about all this."

Martha Jo's smile isn't very broad or bright. "I hope so. And I hope our trip insurance reimburses us as well as the Advantage salesman promised."

So, now, the three of us are officially exiles in paradise, and I'm stuck in solitary confinement, though I may receive a reprieve.

Yet I highly doubt it.

Suspenseful Afternoon

After a long nap, I feel better, so I study my villa again, read all the available information about it. Apparently, it resembles a typical Balinese home, the decor consisting of framed authentic textiles and paintings that some of the prolific artists on the island have produced, along with its handmade, high-quality furniture. I also learn that the Four Seasons at Jimbaran Bay regularly ranks as one of the world's finest resorts.

After surveying my surroundings, I study my limited resources. Of course I have a big-screen television set, but I don't normally watch much TV. I have no computer and no books. Only a paper notebook and pens and my cell phone. At least I can text. And I do like to write poetry.

In fact, I wrote a few short poems during the cruise but haven't revised them. Yet now I have nothing but time in this laid-back setting. I peruse my recent, unedited poems and begin a new one. My muse seems to have moved in with me and become my best friend.

In my first poem here in Bali, I focus on—of course—Grace,

describe how she causes a volcanic explosion inside me and I'm a "sacrificial lamb" on the altar of her charm.

Rather melodramatic and extreme. On her way to Ubud right now, immersed in a new adventure, Grace has probably already consigned me to her mental album of "interesting memories."

But COVID must be causing me to lose my mind and persist irrationally, because after I take a breath, I pen another short verse.

Caught!

I feel like a fish on a hook.
Your golden barb keeps me from freeing myself,
no matter how hard I wriggle.

Obviously I feel trapped.

Not yet definitively diagnosed with COVID and confined to quarters only a few hours, I'm already going bonkers. And when a messenger later knocks on my outer gate and leaves a small paper bag and an envelope addressed to me, I feel like a young man back in the day receiving his draft notice.

The test results, quantified in numbers, show my score as nearly 20, about thirty points below a negative. That's it. No doubt. Science has spoken. I need to recuperate.

I immediately text Grace, let her know my status.

She responds quickly.

Thanks for the warning. I still feel great. Will keep my fingers crossed.

Then she relays the latest conflict to disrupt the tour group—some of them have private pools, though others don't. It's a gossipy bit of news that doesn't interest me.

She writes again. *Hope you're better soon.*

I respond. *Should be the most leisurely vacation ever.*

Though I'm tense about this change of plans, that night, I do sleep soundly in my huge, comfortable bed.

However, before I drop off, I think, in prison, only the most troublesome, hardened inmates are placed in solitary confinement, aren't they?

March 1, 2023

Pool, Photo, and Poems

I wake up early, feeling the tiniest bit better, and bow to habit.

Obviously alone, I slip into my gym shorts and a tank top and venture out onto the veranda. Low-growing palm trees and red-and-yellow bird-of-paradise flowers surround me as the clear water in my pool disappears over the edge. It whispers to me as I very slowly perform my gentle warm-up exercises. Then the rising sun greets me as I glacially move through my familiar tai chi routine, stopping several times to rest.

A sea of thatched roofs decorates the view between my villa and Jimbaran Bay. The surf crashes against the distant white sand. I finish my cool-down and bend to inhale the fragrance of a lone gardenia.

If only I could turn back time and repeat my afternoon in the waves with Grace. As that memory washes over me, the distant swells seem to thunder through me.

The sun warms as the gray sky turns blue. I slide out of my clothes and into already warmish, light-green water. The sun heats my back as the water does its disappearing act, carrying with it a peach-colored bougainvillea blossom.

Water constantly flows into the pool from the mouth of a pot-bellied, animal-headed, concrete statue, painted black, resting his hands on each side of his pregnant-looking belly. Probably a minor Hindu god or a guardian figure, but I've never seen anything similar. Fanged, with a bear-looking head, one eye open and one closed, and bare-chested, he appears ferocious. Yet his four-toed feet pressed sole to sole, four stubby fingers, and embroidered garment make him seem almost childlike. However, I respect him: he supplies my pool with never-ending water.

Resting my throbbing head on my pool's coping, I float weightlessly. Only the endless rush over its edge and an occasional bird's chirp break the silence. I could be the only person in this huge complex. A major cataclysm could have destroyed the rest of the world overnight, and only I might have survived. The moment timeless, I'm caught in a dream, and my thoughts center solely on Grace, who has gone away, leaving me and my cement guard to keep one another company.

I wallow in my solitude, think only of her and the slight fever that heats, then chills me.

Why not relax? Embrace the joy my memories of our recent afternoon on the beach brings? Accept everything and judge nothing?

I try to do just that.

As I float like a palm frond on the water, a poem begins to gurgle up from deep inside me. I rush inside to my bedside table, and when my pen touches a bare page in my notebook, words stream out like the water rushing over my pool's seemingly infinite edge. I let them flow, a willing conduit and, sometime later, read my account of my perfect afternoon with Grace at the beach. I want to give it to her, something she can't buy in an overpriced souvenir shop.

After rewriting and polishing my new poem, I sink back into several cloud-soft pillows, click through the photos I took of her yesterday as she reclined in her lounge chair, and crop a head shot of her a million times.

Then I phone the front desk for breakfast.

It comes promptly, and, now outside again, I eat a bit—save the rest for later in case my appetite reappears.

Sitting at my patio table, I study my gray-concrete, moss-covered "spirit house," similar to ones I've seen in Thailand. It stands on a pedestal about four feet tall, surrounded by lush vegetation, obviously an important focal point.

The Hindus of Bali place fruit or flowers in their family's spirit house daily to honor and appease their deities, so I decide to respect their custom. My breakfast includes a small silver container, wet sand covering its bottom, with nine small, cone-like heads of a deep-purple flower resting in it. They remind me of crimson clover, widespread in Texas, so I place these familiar-looking flowers on the little porch around the small birdhouse-look-alike.

While doing that, I spot a small yellow-and-beige striped snail and take a shot of it. *It's a kindred spirit.* How appropriate for it to be one of my companions during my "exile."

The little creature has been inching along the front wall of the shrine, seeming to feel its way through the world by instinct instead of using a map or a set of rules. I can certainly relate to it.

During my late twenties, my first marriage winding down, I wrote a brief autobiographical poem in which I crawl "snail-like toward the light." Others sometimes step on me and crack my "seemingly tough shell," yet I keep moving, "leaving only a faint track." My poem ends, "Snail of myself,/why do you crawl?" Obviously, I have an unusually close attachment to the small creatures.

Suddenly exhausted, I take my COVID medicine, stretch out in my lounge chair, and let the distant waves and warming breeze lull me to sleep. After waking up, I text Grace my new poem, the close-up photo of her, and my new shot of the snail, remarking that I've felt a connection to these small creatures almost my entire adult life.

Then I go inside and indulge in a very long nap.

Final Flurry of Texts

Late that afternoon, I receive a text from Grace. She likes the photo of herself and my poem: *What a wonderful memory you've painted/created; thank you for sharing. I'll treasure it.*

Of course her remark pleases me, as does another one that stands out in her longish message. *You are def a survivor. Warrior quality, but you're far too tender.*

Well, who doesn't like to be called a survivor/warrior? But "far too tender"? What does that mean? I should ask her immediately, but too often I ponder life's mysteries forever instead of speaking up.

Grace says she's also seen several snails here and detests them because she used to step on them on their basement steps when she was a child. *Yuck!* she writes.

I can understand such an experience being unpleasant, but her comment hits me the wrong way, maybe because I don't feel well. I respond. *If you hate them so much, why did you take so many photos of them while we were on one of the islands?*

    I'm not a planner. Never have been. I feel my way through life and rarely know what I'm going to do until just before I do it. But when something finally feels right, I jump in immediately. My instinct's not always on target, but I've always operated that way and have stumbled into some amazing experiences, though some have not been so amazing.

    After pondering this truth about myself, I think, "Grace said she hates snails," and being a brilliant logician, I conclude, "therefore she hates me." At least that's how I feel right then, my poor health perhaps to blame. She just wrote that she'd often stepped on them, and suddenly it's like she's stepped on me.

    I'll probably always wonder what she meant by the word "tender" and regret not admitting how her "snail" comment affected me.

    Instead, I go off the rails and bombard her with lengthy texts that probably come across as the ramblings of an insecure woman whom no one would want to associate with. I don't hear from her again, and I understand why. I must sound deranged.

March 2, 2023

Conversation with Martha Jo

My phone rings mid-morning on our second day of confinement, and I answer it immediately.

"How are you holding up?" Martha Jo, my major connection to the outside world, asks.

"About the same. The medicine seems to be taking its time. What a letdown after island-hopping for two weeks. How's Amy?"

"A little better. The pills seem to be working, but she's still miserable—Yes?" She speaks to Amy.

Now Martha Jo's back on the line. "Amy says hi and that she hopes you aren't as sick as she's been. Being worn out from all those shore excursions probably hasn't helped."

"Yeah. We didn't have much time to take it easy, did we? It's kinda nice to kick back and do nothing, though I'm really feeling cooped up."

"I know," Martha Jo says in her best mother-hen voice. "It's hard, but try not to worry. You'll both probably test negative on the first try, and we'll be flying home before you know it."

"I hope you're right. What are you doing to pass the time?"

Martha Jo says something to Amy again, then tells me, "I brought my Kindle and have been watching a lot of TV too. We get tons of channels, and I've already found some movies I've been wanting to see. You should take a look."

I sigh. "Thanks, I will, though I'm not much of a TV buff. But I don't have many options at this point."

I don't want Martha Jo to know how much time I've already spent trying to understand my tangled thoughts and feelings about Grace.

During the cruise, I did occasionally confide in both her and Amy about my attraction, and they seemed interested and supportive. But I need to untangle this mess I've gotten myself into on my own. Besides, I certainly have a ton of free time to devote to the subject.

"Well, I better get back to Amy. She's like a child when she's sick, just like we all are, I suppose."

"Of course. I understand. You two take it easy. Thanks for the call."

"Any time. If you need anything—"

"I know. I'll get in touch. You're the best. Tell Amy I'm thinking about her. Bye."

And with that, I'm back to myself, my luxury villa, and my confused thoughts, mainly about Grace. In fact…

Wish List

I had just finished my morning tai chi routine when Martha Jo, who's usually an early bird, called. Now I strip and sit on my small, underwater pool bench, tired after my slight exertion.

Resting here, the hard lip of the concrete pool gently biting into my back, I immediately wish Grace were here beside me to share the silence of early morning in Bali.

I look down at the aging skin on my stomach. If Grace were here—if she felt comfortable enough for such casual intimacy, which I'm sure she wouldn't—she could look at herself too, though her skin couldn't possibly be as worn as mine. The blue-green water magnifies my stomach wrinkles, and I run my hand over them, trying to tighten them. If she were here, she could do the same to her own aging flesh, and we could laugh together at the futility of fighting time.

I wish Grace could enjoy the early morning sun's warmth on her back as I do, how it contrasts to the slightly chilly pool water.

We could speculate about the animal-headed statue, water spouting from his mouth, discuss why he clutches his pregnant-looking belly with both hands and what he might represent to people who understand Hindu spiritual beliefs.

I stare at the small garden to the left of my pool. Grace would appreciate the richly colored white-and-yellow frangipani blossoms on the gnarled tree shading my spirit house. She mentioned that she likes to garden, so we could admire the deep purple of the Mexican petunias growing low to the ground at the tree's base. And then we could scoop up a coral-colored blossom that my bougainvillea tree has dropped into the water, discuss how it looks and feels like parchment paper.

We would both spot the black, white, and orange birds with orange beaks as they flit from my thatched roof. "Listen to them coo," one of us would say. "They sound like the doves back home."

"And did you notice how much their little topknots look like the metal sculpture on the peak of the thatched-roof villas here," the other would remark.

I find this scene perfect as I sit here, alone.

But with Grace beside me, it would be even more perfect.

Suddenly a dragonfly swoops down and just as quickly speeds away.

As if the dragonfly has collided with my shoulder, I think that Grace and I both have to fly halfway around the world and tend our own gardens and flowerbeds, enjoy our own families and friends, share with them our experiences in this foreign country.

Sighing, I slide from my underwater bench, glide into the clear water, swim a few strokes.

It was a pretty fantasy.

But I still miss Grace.

Thinking About My Family

Grace still on my mind, I drift to the other side of my pool. But thinking of her reminds me of my sister Kitty, back home taking care of everyone, as usual.

When I'm there, her husband Matt and I constantly ask each other, "Where's Kitty?"

"I don't know," one of us says. But in a bit, she turns up—from the yard or a flowerbed or the garden or the chicken pen.

When we really need her, though, she's always there, ready to help or answer a question.

Both she and Grace resemble quicksilver.

Back inside my villa, now wearing my long, old, batik house dress, I call the front desk, suddenly hungry.

"Yes. How may I help you?"

"I'd like to order the American breakfast, please." Breakfast comes with the room, and maybe eating a bit will help offset my homesickness.

My food arrives not long after I've applied sunscreen and brushed my tangled curls, and I stay on the far side of my yard as the server brings in an overflowing round, wooden tray. My scrambled eggs look as fresh as the ones Kitty and Matt's hens lay every day, my sausage four times as big as the sausage Matt has made from the one deer he kills each fall. Plus, my four pieces of bacon, pile of toast, yogurt, fresh fruit, as well as mango juice and a pot of tea, look delicious. Apparently, the cooks here think Americans have huge appetites.

My server places my various plates and containers just so, then nods, his hands folded together under his chin like he's praying, and wishes me a good day. I didn't eat anything last night but now am able to down part of the eggs and a bit of toast.

Satisfied, I'm sipping my herbal tea when a lone, fluffy-looking, white bird—its wings and tail tipped with black, and a deep-blue patch around each eye—lights on the wooden tray near my shaded table. My mom the birdwatcher would love to see this sight.

Suddenly, it hops onto my table, so near I could touch it if I dared. It gleams in the sun, the blue around its eyes startling.

"Hello, ma'am," I say. "What a beautiful country you live in. I'm honored to stay here for a while. Thank you for stopping by."

However, the unusual creature seems more interested in a bit of toast I've dropped than in me.

After it begins pecking the crumbs on my table, I reach for my camera, and it darts away.

I pick up my teacup again, succumb to the mystical spirit of Bali. "I'm fine, Mom," I call after the bird. "Thanks for checking on me."

I finish my tea, then go inside and lie down, exhausted. After a long rest, while leafing through some literature on my desk, I notice a small, folded pamphlet: *The Enchanting Jimbaran Forest*. Apparently, this vicinity is a centuries-old sanctuary for native animals, as well as a spiritual retreat for Balinese people.

The blurb about the area birds interests me the most. *Burung* is Balinese for "bird"—the first word I learn in their language. And birds supposedly carry messages from ancestral spirits.

Ah. I shiver despite the tepid breeze flitting in from outside. So that's why I spoke to the little creature. My mother loved all birds, so why wouldn't she choose that way to touch base with me? Her gentle spirit fills the room, spreading contentment through me. Maybe I'll recover more quickly than I've dared hope.

Getting to Know My Roommates, Plus Some Fruit and the Moon

Standing at one of my two spotless bathroom sinks after breakfast, brushing my teeth, I spot a small, shiny, black-brown bug on its back near my feet. It's wiggling its legs frantically, evidently panicked.

After putting away my toothbrush, I carefully pick up the bug with a tissue, walk outside, and place it on the ground near my outdoor soap stand.

Upright now, it begins to crawl but then starts limping and falls over again. At least it can die out in my peaceful garden instead of on a hard, ceramic floor.

What will its spirit transform into now?

On Bali, it's easy to believe all life is sacred, transitory.

Already in my garden, I remove my house dress and rinse off the pool water from earlier. I don't stay long, but while I stand here, water gushing onto my back from the fake-bamboo spout, a brown-and-yellow-striped snail inches up the rock wall to my left.

My kindred spirit must want a word, so I shut off the water and, dripping, focus on the beautiful snail's slow pace, its silvery trail. Does it have a fixed goal, or is it simply ambling along, taking life as it comes? I stand still until the small creature inches behind a large banana leaf on the ground.

After returning, still damp, to my regular bathroom, I leisurely towel off and pull on my house dress again. It's comfortable and one of the only pieces of loungewear that's still clean after our cruise. Obviously, I didn't do much lounging on the ship.

Still thinking about the lovely snail, I pick up the pamphlet from earlier. The Balinese word for "snail" is cute—*pici pici*—and its blurb mentions the saying about "slow and steady" winning the race. But is that concept always true? The fast and the daring usually win most of the races I'm familiar with. That's the American way.

Yet the phrase does have its own truth. And here on Bali, it makes sense. The pamphlet says the snail reminds us to "embrace a slower, more relaxing pace of life" while we're here, and the snail I've just seen embodies that advice perfectly.

I put down the booklet, thinking about Grace's aversion to snails as opposed to my identification with them. What does that difference say about my clearly overblown feelings for her? Maybe I'll eventually find out.

The snail has obviously made me think about Grace. I hoped I'd get a reprieve today, but no.

❖

It's late afternoon now, and I've been trying to relax by taking another long nap. My house phone rings, and, groggy, I feel around for it. My bed is so large, I have to crawl quite a distance to grab the phone.

"Hello. This is Katherine," a strange voice says.

"Katherine?"

I'd assumed it would be Martha Jo, or maybe Amy, if she's better, but this voice sounds only vaguely familiar.

"Yes. Remember me? We spoke yesterday when I checked you in, and then this morning when you called in your breakfast order."

"Oh, yes. I'm sorry. I didn't recognize your voice." And I didn't remember her name, either, an unpleasant side effect of getting older. To be fair though, I've never been very good at the social niceties. Most of the time they seem rather trivial and insincere.

"I understand. I just wanted to see how you are doing."

"How thoughtful. I'm a little better. Just trying to get as much rest as possible."

"Was your breakfast all right?"

"More than all right. I probably won't need anything else to eat for the rest of the day. What I had was delicious."

"Well, we do not want you to go hungry. I am sending you a little something to help make your stay more pleasant," she says. She's one of the managers and probably has more important things to do than worry about me.

"Oh, thank you. But you didn't have to do that."

"It is no problem. One of our staff should be there any minute. I just wanted to let you know. If I can do anything at all for you, please call me."

I gulp. "Why, thank you, Katherine. That's very thoughtful. I certainly will. Thank you again."

"You are most welcome," she replies and ends the call.

I've just gotten up and am running a brush through my thick, messy hair when the doorbell chimes.

"Just a minute," I call.

"No need to open the door, madam," a male voice says. "I will leave the tray on the table. Have a good day."

By the time I walk outside, my front gate is clicking shut, and a large, covered plate sits on my black, round table. Its silver dome hides an assortment of colorful fresh fruit—orange, yellow, red, fuchsia, green, purple, and cream. Banana slices, pineapple chunks, and a few grapes, plus wedges of mango and papaya, are familiar, but the other four types of fruit baffle me.

Several fleshy, fuchsia hunks are dotted with small black seeds—maybe dragon fruit? A large, spiky one, the same raspberry color as the black-seeded hunks, has what looks like an eyeball (the white part only) inside it. Perhaps rambutan? A scaly looking one with a seemingly tough brown skin cut open to show three beige cloves that resemble garlic presents a bigger puzzle. Perhaps snakeskin fruit? But a large one in the middle stumps me. Outside, it resembles an orange, but it contains greenish seeds similar to those of pomegranates, encased in a thick, transparent, slimy-looking film.

Lying beside the fruit plate, a seemingly hand-painted card depicts a local boat sailing on a lovely turquoise sea near two tropical trees. And on the back is this handwritten note.

Dear Ms. Helen,
 Greeting from Four Seasons at Jimbaran Bay. We hope you will fully recover and fly back home soon.
 Best regards,
 Katherine.

How kind and thoughtful. Her personal gesture makes me feel less alone.

Spearing a piece of pineapple, I think of home. And the spiky, fuchsia one—rambutan?—which tastes really sweet, like jelly, interests me because it's different.

I take the platter inside, out of the heat. This, along with my breakfast leftovers, will be a pleasant evening meal.

To escape the heat, I flop back onto my bed, search the various TV channels. A nature program focusing on the Amazon rainforest looks interesting, so, settling back with a cool drink, I let the documentary carry me to another part of the world. As it ends, I pick up my nearby notebook, intending to write a note about the program, but a pressed flower falls out. I write a poem about it instead.

During the cruise, I mostly jotted notes about our activities—journal-type entries.

Yet on Bali, poetry has obsessed me, especially since I've been sick. A poem hits me, and I have to write it down or lose it. At home, my creations originate the same way. When I had cancer and was driving myself to chemo and radiation treatments, I had to stop by the side of the road several times to jot one down. Buddhists call it being in the moment, and apparently extreme circumstances like having cancer and being stranded far from home can encourage this urge.

Right now, it's like I'm on a horse I can't control. If it wants to gallop, I guess I'll have to stay on it or miss the ride. So what? I suppose I'll just stay in the saddle until I leave Bali or the horse grows lame. Who knows? I may have COVID forever and remain here to enjoy this overwhelming source of inspiration.

My mind keeps racing. When that pressed flower fell out of my journal just minutes ago and inspired this rant, I flashed back to our first restaurant here on Bali, where the hostess placed a pink blossom behind our ears when we entered.

Now, just a few days later, brown splotches have formed on the pressed flower I wore that day at lunch. Holding up one hand, I study my age spots. The sight depresses me. But the flower's natural color stands out more than the splotches do. And the same goes for my ageing hands. I still look somewhat young in spite of my advancing age.

After writing a poem about that comforting realization, I wander out to my covered veranda, stretch out in a lounge chair. Cooler now, Bali's heat can't rival July and August in Texas, and the light breeze from the bay is refreshing.

I gaze at said bay—and think of Grace, of course.

As we stood in the waves several days ago, talking, the female photographer we first encountered in Darwin waded out to us. Throughout the trip, she seemed standoffish, with a rather sour expression, but there in the water, Grace struck up a conversation with her as if they were old friends. The woman's lined, rigid face softened in just the brief time she and Grace conversed.

Grace obviously inherited, or learned, her mother's magic that lured her teenage friends to her home. Maybe that's one reason I'm still under her spell, though I certainly don't want to be.

That thought flies away, and then a dragonfly, its iridescent wings a blur, flits right in front of me. I've brought my journal outside, as well as the little pamphlet about the animals and flowers of this area. According to it, the dragonfly (*capung*) is one of the world's fastest-flying insects.

Grace has been darting in and around my life during this entire trip, and she still seems to be nearby in this small insect, wrenching my head and my heart as I try to keep up with her spurts of speed, followed by brief rest periods.

According to the pamphlet's few comments, the sun energizes the dragonfly, enables it to keep its intricate, transparent wings fluttering all day. And, come to think of it, I can't recall a time when Grace wasn't active. Perhaps that's one reason she attracted me. Maybe being around her energized me as well.

These idle thoughts come and go as I doze, then sit and stare at the bay, where, just a few days ago, I was with her, under her spell. Surely she's like a dream that will fade as we continue on our separate ways.

Phone Call and That Bali Moon

How long will I sit here and daydream?

My house phone rings, and I slowly make my way inside.

"How's it going," Martha Jo asks. "Are you doing okay?"

"Sure. I don't have much choice, do I? I can think of worse places to be. Can't you?"

She laughs. "It's not all bad. I'm certainly catching up on my reading. I'm so glad I brought my Kindle. Did Katherine send you a fruit basket?"

"She certainly did." I smile. "Wasn't that nice?"

"It was." Martha Jo chuckles. "Amy was impressed, even though, after throwing up again yesterday, she still doesn't have much of an appetite. I told her not to worry, that I'd take care of it for both of us."

"I know what you mean. In fact, I plan to try to eat a bit more of mine before too long. Katherine's really sweet, isn't she?"

We chat about this and that, and Martha Jo recommends a couple of movies she's already watched.

"Well, I won't keep you," she finally says. "I just wanted to let you know that we're thinking about you."

"Thanks," I say, and I mean it. With such good friends and beautiful surroundings, how can I be anything but content?

"Have a good night," she says. "Talk to you tomorrow. Wish you could be here so we could play Rummikub."

"Me too." I sigh. "You take care, and thanks for calling."

As I hang up, I'm glowing inside. Martha Jo and Amy always have that effect on me. I'm truly grateful to have them as friends.

Then I sprawl on my bed and, relaxed, fall into a deep sleep.

Later, after I've gone outside, stretched out on a lounge chair, and picked at my fruit slowly and messily, I walk back inside and wash my hands and face. There, I slip into my bathing suit, lie on the edge of the pool, enjoy the cool evening air, and then watch the slow parade of planes taxi down the runway far across the bay and lift themselves into the sky.

Their pace hypnotizes me, until finally I gaze up, and there it is—the egg-shaped moon, speckled with gray, which I've barely paid attention to during my trip.

As I slide into the water and float faceup, the moon seems to be nesting high over my head. It appears, then disappears, as if a hen keeps perching over it, trying to will it to hatch.

Suddenly a dark cloud sits on it, and a tropical downpour drives me indoors.

I stand there and peer through my glass patio doors, wish I were still outside—sitting beside Grace and gazing at the moon.

But I'm not. I'm inside, trapped, and very much alone.

March 3, 2023

BAD DAY

Today I sleep late, stay in bed, and eat small amounts of my breakfast throughout the day. Maybe my body wants me to rest so my next test result will be negative.

As I lie here, my sheets and light blanket as tangled as my feelings, I'm overwhelmed—as isolated and lonely as if I were on the moon. Plus, I'm scared. Even though I'm lounging in a world-class resort, I have no idea what turns my life will take. And I'm lonely. Grace is gone, and I've been banished from my two friends' presence.

Also, Grace has quit answering my texts. It's like RADIO SILENCE. Of course, she's busy on a tour, but she should be able to spare a little time at the end of the day.

In my dreams, Grace suddenly turns up again, stays in Bali with me, goes back and gets a divorce, and we work things out and live happily ever after.

I get up and straighten my wrinkled, tangled sheets, remind myself of my caring, supportive friends both here and at home, plus my numerous family members, who want the best for me.

But at this point I'm not very happy, especially when it comes to Grace. Plus, I'm scared. I'm sick, and I'm about as far away from home as I can get without leaving this planet.

I want to blame someone for my predicament, and Grace is my easiest target. So I aim my next poem in her direction and take a cheap shot.

Betrayal

*Your apparent obsession for gossip
makes me shut the steel gate of my heart;
lock it;
promptly forget the combination.*

There! *Take that, Grace*, I think.

Until now, I've emphasized Grace's strengths and ignored her weaknesses, but her tendency to gossip is at the top of that list. On the ship, at first she would share a tidbit with us at mealtime, but we rarely responded enthusiastically. As time went by, she tapered off and probably found an outlet with her other acquaintances there, with whom she began to socialize more frequently during our cruise.

When I was young, my mom rarely, if ever, gossiped, and I remember clearly the one time I did relay an unkind remark about one of my friends.

Mom frowned at me and said, "Don't judge anyone until after you've walked a mile in their moccasins."

She didn't have to tell me twice. Especially after that advice, I've never understood why anyone would want to talk about other people behind their back. If I hear something questionable about one of my friends or acquaintances, it makes more sense just to ask her or him about it, especially if the comment doesn't sound accurate. But most of the time I simply ignore it. I'm usually too focused on my concerns to waste time listening to and repeating things that most likely aren't even true and might hurt whomever the gossip is about. Speculating about other people like that bores me.

In fact, I'm ashamed of writing this little poem. I suppose I thought it would make me feel better, but it doesn't. "Helen," I say out loud, as if I'm channeling my mom. "You should be ashamed of yourself."

But then my mom's voice rings through me. "You know Grace has a lot more good qualities than bad," she says. "I always taught you not to gossip, and I think you've usually followed my advice. But I also taught you not to judge someone until you've walked a mile in their moccasins. Have you done that with Grace?"

My mom was the softest and kindest of women, but even though she's been dead since right before COVID hit, I can still hear the steel in her voice.

I ball up under my feather-soft, white duvet and feel like sucking my thumb. *My mom never did take my side. I could be dying here all by myself, and she's telling me not to judge Grace because Grace won't do and be what I want. I want sympathy, not advice.*

I get up, drink a bottle of water, and put my hand on my forehead. *Do I have a fever again?*

But Mom's still not through with me, which is unusual. When she was alive, she rarely gave me advice. She usually let me work out my problems on my own.

Now that I'm back in bed, she says to me, "You know you're not all that sick, don't you? You've always been as healthy as a horse. You're a survivor, so quit feeling sorry for yourself and try to be rational. Writing ugly things about other people just because they won't be or do what you want is silly and pointless. I'll say it again. I taught you better than that."

I turn on the television, tired of her interference.

"Okay. I understand you need time to work things out, Helen, so I'll leave you alone," Mom says. "Take care of yourself, and by the way, I do love you."

And with that, Mom's voice in my head disappears, and I promptly go to sleep.

When I wake up, I'm glad she visited me, because she's right. I do need time to think about this situation with Grace more carefully. And I'll try to do just that after I get home too. Or better yet, I'll stop thinking about her altogether.

March 4, 2023

Mount Agung

The next day, I wake up feeling better and begin my day early, doing tai chi by the pool. This peaceful atmosphere makes me more aware of my surroundings, the sights and sounds of the smallest things magnified. Or perhaps being almost completely alone is causing this hypersensitivity.

After some additional stretching exercises, I lounge in my bathing suit and robe and stare across the bay at the cone-shaped mountain in the distance. I haven't paid much attention to it before today, but now it stirs my curiosity.

Someone rings the bell at my front gate. "Come in," I call.

One of the older staff members, bringing clean sheets and towels, greets me in fluent English, so I point to the mountain, ask its name.

Though he keeps his distance, he seems glad to answer my question.

"Mount Agung, madam. Today is the first time this week we can see it so well."

"How far away is it?" *It seems very near.*

"About fifty kilometers. In the north part of our island."

Hmm. Thirty miles or so. Who would have thought it was that far?

"And how tall is it? Do you know?"

He nods. I've evidently picked the right person to ask. "Yes, madam. It is about 3,000 meters, or 10,000 feet tall."

"About the same as Pikes Peak, in Colorado, back in the US," I say, suddenly homesick. "I climbed it when I was a teenager, which wasn't easy. My friend and I didn't know it was a fourteen-mile hike and thought we could make it up and back down that day. But we were lucky. When we finally reached the top late that afternoon, some girls we ran into in the souvenir shop gave us a ride to Colorado Springs in their old car. If they hadn't, we would have had to spend the night on top of the mountain without any equipment or food."

He laughs along with me. "We also do strange things here when we are teenagers."

He stares at the mountain for a moment, like he's communing with it. "Mount Agung is the most sacred spot in all of Bali," he finally says. "It would be a blessing for you to spend the night on it. Our ancestors sleep in it for eternity."

"How do you know so much about the mountain?"

"I guided hikers up it for ten years." He glances toward my front gate, as if he needs to leave.

I ask only if he enjoyed being a guide.

"It was the best job I have ever had. But it took much energy. I loved being on the mountain. It has started to erupt again after many years, though, so it is good to no longer be so near it."

"Erupt! It's an active volcano?"

"Yes, madam. But it has been calm for the past few years, since 2019. It is the home of the gods, so it is a magic place, though unpredictable."

I really do need to let him get back to work, so I thank him and hope we have another chance to talk. From now on, I'll have more respect for Mount Agung.

Still stretched out in my lounge chair, I stare at the mountain with fresh eyes. Its jagged peak seems to gnaw at the clouds that surround it, saw-toothing them away to let the mountain occasionally shine in the morning sunlight. But clouds still hide its base.

I lower my gaze, notice plumes of blue-gray smoke billowing from several spots along the beach on the other side of the bay, orange flames under the smoke barely visible. Are people paying tribute to the gods and the ancestors of the Balinese people or simply burning trash?

Suddenly I ache, as if stabbed in the heart. I feel like Grace has just sat down beside me and is staring at me as if I'm a stranger.

"Why are you ignoring my texts?" I want to ask her. "You remind me of that mountain—distant, surrounded by clouds, smoke drifting up in front of you from the beach, blurring your features."

Then I direct a fanciful thought at her. "Maybe those are funeral

Untethered

pyres for old women like me who've jumped off the top of the mountain, sacrificing themselves because of a broken heart."

Wow. Now that's a little extreme. I try to dial myself back and focus on how the smoke from the fires on the beach is making it harder to see the mountain now. I remember glancing at it the day we arrived here, but I wasn't concentrating on the scenery at that point. I sigh. I felt so fresh then, almost young, infatuated with Grace, looking forward to our last day together.

But now my obsession with her reminds me of the smoke and the clouds that are trying to blot out my view of the mountain. Will I ever see it again? Will I ever see *her* again?

A jet glides in low from the east in front of a line of white, puffy clouds. A plane like that will soon carry Grace away from Bali, back to her home and her family and her real life.

Just a little over two weeks ago, she plopped into that hard seat on that hot minibus beside me, and we truly connected for the first time. Right now, it seems so much longer since that happened. Like in "Jack and the Beanstalk," my thoughts and feelings about her have magically taken root and shot up taller than the mountain I'm staring at.

The beach fires burn. The smoke thickens. The volcano disappears.

Has Grace left my life forever?

❖

Well, today may be a crying-in-my-beer day. Poems about missing Grace flood out so fast, I may set a new world record for writing the most heart-achy outpourings in a single day.

Just a minute ago I sat in the tepid water of my pool staring at the odd male guardian figure with water spouting from his mouth. But suddenly, almost hypnotized, I reach over to the narrow deck, grab my notebook and pen, and jot down a poem.

Water

I miss our conversations—
sweet, cool, fresh—
as if from a deep, rock-lined well,
glimmering as the words flow from our lips.

• 173 •

And I do miss our conversations more than anything about our relationship. Grace and I almost competed to see who could dive the deepest and come up the wettest, as my mom used to say. We shared like strangers talking on a long plane ride, saying things we, at least I, would never confide in anyone else.

I think about Grace's mysterious text the other day: *You're too tender.*

Then, almost immediately, I spew out another short poem.

Question

You say I'm too tender.
Do you prefer your filets
tough as well?

I know. My mom would say I'm being tacky, but I truly don't have a clue what Grace meant by that comment, which irritates me.

The day's beginning to heat up, and I'm not wearing any sunscreen, so I dry off and go inside to change into my long, batik house dress. It's cool and covers me almost entirely. That way, I'm less self-conscious when one of the staff brings me whatever.

I've ordered breakfast and am waiting for it to arrive when my phone rings. "Hi, Helen. It's Amy. How are you?"

"Amy! It's great to hear from you. I'm a little better, but tired and don't have any energy. Maybe that's from doing nothing though. How about you?"

"I'm better too. No more upset stomach, and my fever's just about gone. We should do fine on our COVID test the day after tomorrow. I'm looking forward to leaving here."

I hear Martha Jo talking in the background and ask, "What's she saying?"

"That we can celebrate with a few games of Rummikub, even if you and I don't pass the test."

Amy tells Martha Jo, "It's a date."

"Okay," I say. "But I just learned something that might interest you."

"What is it?" Amy asks. "An instant cure for COVID?"

"I wish. Can you see the mountain in the distance?"

"Hmm. Yeah. I looked at it earlier."

"Well, I just learned it's an active volcano."

"You have got to be kidding. When was the last time it was active?" she asks.

"2019."

"No. Be serious. Really. When was it?"

"I *am* serious. The guy who brought me some fresh sheets and towels earlier told me."

Amy sounds like she may choke. "That's about right. All we need to cap off this grand adventure is to wake up in the morning with chunks of lava spraying down on us. How far away is it?"

"Thirty miles."

"Sheez. That's closer than it looks. You're really not messing with me?"

"Nope. But I'm sure we'd have some kind of warning if they even suspected it might suddenly go active."

"And the flights out of here would be jam-packed. The next time you suggest we go somewhere, I'm going to do a lot more research before I say yes." She's laughing, but she obviously means it, and I don't blame her. I plan to do more research too.

"At least we haven't been bored."

"You can say that again, Helen. And twice more. This has definitely not been a boring trip. Wait till I tell Martha Jo. She'll probably think we're trying to pull her leg."

"I wish. Well, have a good day. Here's hoping we get well and make it home before anything else unexpected happens."

"Amen to that. Talk to you later."

Suddenly the bell at my outer door rings. "Oops. Sounds like my breakfast's here. Later. Thanks for calling."

I hurry out to unlock my door, then walk back so I'm standing a good distance from my table, where I wait for my attendant to unload a seemingly endless number of dishes and bowls and glasses and utensils and condiments. It's enough food to last me a week. "Thank you," I say, and we exchange small nods before he leaves, smiling.

Settling down to eat what I can, I glance at Mount Agung. "Good boy," I say, as if it's my pet Doberman. I want the volcano to stay calm.

The Dragonfly

After I finish what I can eat of my huge meal and store some of it in my refrigerator for later, I push one of my lounge chairs into the shade and enjoy the cool breeze that's kicked up. My stomach full, I'm about to doze off when I spot a small movement on the concrete deck near my pool. It's a dragonfly, lying partially under a drying croton leaf. She can barely push one of her limbs out from under the leaf and is most likely thirsty, even though she's sprawled out only a foot or two from the pool that holds more water than she could ever drink.

She struggles to crawl from under the withered leaf, where she's probably been hiding to protect herself from predators. But now she must smell water nearby—a small puddle from last night's rain shower. Her forelegs most likely ache as she tests them, but they don't seem damaged. She labors, leaving the protection of the croton, dragging herself to the nearby water source.

Finally, she dips her proboscis into it. I imagine it tastes fresh, like she's sipping from a petal after an early morning dew. Amazed, I watch her shrunken body expand into its normal size, like a piece of dried apple rehydrating.

She pauses, then drinks some more and clearly spots a small fly nearby, its iridescent green-black body gleaming in the sunlight. She inches forward, flicks her tongue at it, and misses. She collapses. Will she die on this quickly heating concrete? Should she head back to her makeshift shelter?

Yet then she apparently senses movement to her left and focuses on another fly, sucking nectar from the fallen yellow bloom of a nearby sugar-palm tree. The dragonfly seems to tense and hold her breath, then strikes with surprising speed.

She devours the fly, and I imagine her feeling her power return. Her wings, slender body, and even her antennae seem to plump, grow stronger. She takes off and soars over the pool, not as fast as usual, but she's on her way again.

I hope she'll soon be speeding through the air, proving her reputation as the world's fastest-flying insect.

I lean back, letting my shoulders go limp after my vicarious involvement with the dragonfly. I know what it's like to be drained, to be a shell of myself, and then to recover. Maybe that's how I can get over this fixation on Grace. Is that what she meant when she said I'm "too tender"? Is nature truly "red in tooth and claw," as a major poet described it a couple hundred years ago? Do I need to be more assertive socially in order to survive?

Afternoon Fears

The heat rises, driving me inside my villa. I embrace my best friend—sleep—but it allows only a brief nap. I turn on the television, but nothing interests me. Restless, I rummage through my luggage, then my toiletries, realizing I haven't taken my usual morning pills—mainly vitamins. I pick up a pill container, my last one, with my emergency supply. After opening a compartment, I dump the remaining contents into my hand: two vitamins, a baby aspirin, and half of a twenty-five-milligram metoprolol succinate to treat my AFib. Then it hits me. I have the other half of this pill to take tonight, but that's it. No more aspirin either, my only blood thinner.

When packing at home, I obviously didn't consider that I might get sick on this trip and assumed my few extras would cover any special needs. I haven't been ill abroad since I was in my twenties. *Oh, well.* I take such a low dose of heart medicine, it doesn't matter. In fact, a little poem pops into my mind.

Stranded with AFib

I've run out of heart pills.
Hope my ticker
doesn't out-pitter its patter.

I grin and dismiss my pill situation. Then I sort through my clothes, checking to see if I have a suitably clean outfit to fly home in (I do), and enough clean underwear to make it for the next few days. I don't, so I rinse out several pairs. I'm doing absolutely nothing to dirty my sleep shirt and batik house dress, so I'm good there. And the hotel supplies me with clean robes.

My laundry finished and my toiletries lined up like passengers in the first-class section of an airplane, I drift back to my current best friend—my huge bed. It's too soon to even try for another nap, so I just lie here and stare up at the impressive wooden ceiling that rises above me like the loft of a Gothic cathedral.

Yet I can't stop thinking about the remaining half of a pill in my travel pouch. What if I don't test negative? What if I get really sick? What if I get worse, develop heart problems, and die over here?

With nothing else to occupy my attention, I spiral downward, drifting like the yellow bloom I saw earlier this morning, the one that fell from the sugar-palm tree near my pool that my dragonfly friend snatched an unwary fly from.

Untethered. The word springs out of nowhere and begins to echo in my head in time with my heartbeat. *Untethered.* I've suddenly come loose from the stable spot in the world where I'm usually moored and am drifting farther and farther from it. I think of how our ship almost tipped over in an isolated sea with a strong current. And then I recall how I've regarded Bali for almost thirty years.

I first visited this island in 1995. Our small cruise ship, the *Ocean Pearl,* anchored off the east coast of the island, and we tendered ashore in a small boat on two consecutive mornings. We toured Ubud and a few temples, watched a dance-drama performed on the grounds of one of those temples, ate a delicious buffet meal in a mountainous area, and glimpsed women bathing unashamedly in rivers visible from the road. I found the island beautiful but the most foreign place I'd ever been.

And today, in spite of being in a much more technologically advanced part of Bali than we were back then, I still have the same wariness. I don't feel at home. I'm adrift in a very foreign place, and being here is scaring me.

My thoughts drift from the idea of being untethered and dwell on places that frighten me. And then something inside me whispers, "You've obviously been flirting with Death for several years now—divorce, car wreck, heart problems, cancer. But you've never gone this far before. Right now, Death is walking toward you barefoot, with blue eyes as bright as Grace's. Death is even speaking like Grace does, slowly and deliberately. It's trying to charm you into a new realm. You're drifting in waves way over your head and thinking far too much about your pull toward the depths. In fact, you're beginning to be able to breathe only Grace and Death."

I sit up in the middle of the huge, soft pillows that surround me on my lavish bed. *Where the heck did such suicidal thoughts come from? Because I'm running out of heart medicine, I'm suddenly afraid I may die over here? COVID is so yesterday. It's on its last gasp. I'm healthier than most people my age, and Bali isn't a backwater. If we were on one of the really remote islands we've just toured, or if our ship actually had flipped over, I would definitely have had something to worry about. But here? It's almost like being in the States. I bet the foreign tourists here outnumber the Balinese. Don't sweat it!*

Yet fear is irrational, and I wallow in it, drifting farther and farther away from rationality until I curl into a ball and hang on to keep from completely succumbing to my terror, keep myself from letting it drown me. I long to be tethered to some place, something, someone.

Grace at Night

I wake up gradually, the smooth sheet draped over my shoulder, push my arms upward, open my eyes to the beauty of the wooden ceiling high above me. What a bad dream. I roll over, swing my feet to the cool floor, strip off my house dress, and pull on my black bathing suit.

Outside, it's twilight. The air has cooled, and I stretch out in the corner of my pool. Warm water engulfs, comforts me.

But the concrete against my neck, under my hips, is as hard and unforgiving as reality. *That wasn't a dream.* "It is my life right now," I whisper.

Grace is far away instead of here beside me, and I need to accept that fact. "Suck it up, girl," I hear my old tennis coach say. "You can do this."

So I try to relax, float on my back in the cooling water and gaze up at the sky of the southern hemisphere, not that far from the equator. One by one, unfamiliar stars twinkle into view. Planets rise together, then drop below the horizon, but I'm not sure which planets they are. Evidently they have different locations in this part of the world. The moon's the same though. Again it reminds me of a white egg, like my sister Kitty's chickens lay every day, back home.

The moon beams at me as if assuring me I'll be okay. But the distant stars remind me how far from home I am. Where's the Big Dipper, the Little Dipper, the North Star? The only constellation I recognize here is Orion's Belt.

Yet that's enough to tether me to reality. It's as familiar as the sound of Grace's voice, which I still dream of hearing yet fear I never will again.

I drift over to the bench in my pool and sit on it, my legs in the water. Two unfamiliar birds flit under my thatched-roof overhang, call to each other in their special language.

Low on the horizon, two stars float in space near one another—one larger, brighter, higher than its dimmer companion. They remind me of Grace and me, though in my mind she alone illuminates the southern night sky, more than the moon, the planets, and the stars do. She outshines everyone and everything.

Then I gaze across the bay, where she and I had our afternoon in the sun not that long ago. Jet liners are dropping from the sky, rolling down the light-studded runways, red and white lights emphasizing their descent. On the opposite side of the landing fields, other planes rush down a narrow spit of land, lift off just before they plunge into the bay.

I watch their constant descent and ascent, but my memories of Grace still shine brighter than all this coming and going.

It's almost dark now, so I walk inside and raid my mini-fridge for fruit and leftovers. Then, stretched out in a lounge chair, plate in my lap, I let the still-warm air of Bali soothe me. I'm tired, as though I've been hiking up Mount Agung all day in the heat.

Emotionally, I'm evidently still trying to dig my way out from the avalanche of feelings my conversations with Grace during those two weeks together somehow triggered in me.

Along with COVID, this struggle has left me gasping for air.

March 5, 2023

Morning Blues

I wake up this morning with a bitter taste in my mouth, which no amount of toothpaste can brush away.

Not much has changed. I just talked to Martha Jo, and Amy's feeling better. We're all looking forward to tomorrow, when she and I can retest and then hopefully schedule a flight home. Everyone expects us to be negative, so this may be my last full day to lie around and feel sorry for myself.

My American breakfast arrives midmorning, after I've faithfully exercised in my to-die-for backyard. But everything tastes bland. I toy with my scrambled eggs, gag down a slice of bacon, and eat part of a piece of toast. My usually delicious herbal tea defeats me, however. It tastes as bitter as my mouth did earlier.

After salvaging some leftovers that I may be able to stomach later in the day, I retreat to my bed.

Of course, Grace is right there beside me, sharing my pillow as my thoughts agitate my feelings, and I rehash my discontent, dredging up her worst fault. Hopefully dwelling on it will help me get her out of my mind for good.

She tends to gossip. It's all I can charge her with for now.

I lie here, turn on the television, but I can't focus on the movie I try to watch. Grace still dominates my thoughts.

I plump my pillows, jump up, pull a bottle of water from my fridge, and lie down again. Memories of our last dinner on the ship, in the *Odyssey Adventurer*'s small dining room, fill my mind. Grace and I were sitting at different yet nearby tables, so close I was able to overhear her dinner conversation with a stranger that night.

"You've led a charmed life," she told that person.

Stunned by that random sentence, which seemed to fill the dining room, I immediately realized I'd heard the line before. I sat there mute, my cheeks burning, because Grace had said the same words to me after breakfast near the beginning of the cruise, when I'd confided in her about my three divorces.

I'm obviously not special to her. She uses that line on everyone.

I jump up and gaze outside at Mount Agung and the never-ending stream of airplanes in the distance. Then I walk back to my bed, smooth my wrinkled sheets, and lie down again. I have one more suspicion about Grace and recall how, near the end of our last beautiful afternoon here on the beach in Bali, she confided in me that heights terrify her more than anything.

I should have said something to her about that Erica Jong novel that flitted through my unreliable brain. It focused on women in bad marriages, and maybe it could have helped her cope with her marital situation that she mentioned during our break-through conversation on the bus. Why is my brain so scrambled sometimes? Why do I often have something in my mind that's so clear and relevant, yet miss my chance to mention it to the person I'm talking to? Ugh. I could kick myself.

I wad up a piece of my comforter, then wish I could shake all the wrinkles out of my bedding. "Forget it. You're an idiot to remain so fixated on Grace," I say out loud and slam my open palm against my soft mattress. *Has she thought about me at all since we parted ways?*

I jump out of bed and walk out to my pool. *Enough is enough.*

Stretching out in a shaded lounger poolside, I think about what it would have been like if Grace and I had had access to some equipment and gone scuba diving together at one of the beaches we visited during our cruise.

That might have been pleasant, but feeling the way I do right now, I imagine having an emergency underwater and being forced to share an air tank with her. Doing that could save my life, but being that dependent on her could also get old very quickly, especially if she doesn't want to be close. I want to be able to breathe on my own without having to rely on her!

I hurry back inside to my comfortable bed, where I flounce in and out of it for the rest of the day, craving water and kicking my thermostat down as low as it'll go. I can't stomach my leftovers and eat only a banana.

Watching the Moon

Hours later, after the day has cooled and the moon has risen, and I've finally had some restful sleep, I ease onto my veranda again and stretch out on a lounger. I could lie here forever, watch the nearly full Bali moon play hide-and-seek with the drifting clouds.

High above, the moon seems to smile at me as she glides out of the gray twilight clouds for a brief appearance.

But then she disappears without saying good-bye. And, fool that I am, I long for her, wanting her—and Grace—to shine on me again.

I feel like throwing myself off Mount Agung or leaping into its yawning crater and joining the ancestors that live there. Haven't I learned anything from my tirades this morning?

I should give up. Death is calling me to come walk with Her, like Kitty does back home, either early each morning or late every afternoon.

I take a slow drink of water, the bottle cool in my hand. I'd miss my sister and the rest of my family and friends.

I take a deep breath. *I'll get over Grace. I just need to wait out this irrational episode.*

Besides, Amy and I are scheduled to have our next COVID test tomorrow. Surely we'll both be well, and I can leave all this anguish behind.

I hope.

March 6–7, 2023

COVID BLUES

My doorbell rings, and, masked, I open my heavy wooden outer door for a slender young man, also masked. He swabs me and collects a specimen, then leaves as quickly as he came, promising my lab results will be ready by early afternoon. I nod, then sit down again and try to decide whether to order breakfast.

I have little appetite, no energy, and crave water. Plus, my face is warm, my throat sore, my nose scratchy. Obviously, I'm having a relapse and am much more ill now than when I was first diagnosed. I doubt my test will come back negative. I feel like a beggar, with nothing to offer. I evidently need something more powerful to help me recover.

I go back to bed, and in the early afternoon, as promised, my house phone shrieks, its loud, shrill ring shaking me from a restless sleep.

"I am sorry, madam. But your test still shows positive, even worse now. Would you like to have the doctor from the hospital come see you and bring you some stronger medicine?"

"Yes," I croak. "Please."

I can't think of anything I'd like better.

"The doctor should be there in one or two hours," the caller says.

"Good. I'll be expecting him. Thank you."

I collapse back against my huge white pillow, watch large, grayish clouds scamper across the eternal blue sky. They remind me of cloth sails on an old-fashioned pirate ship. Sugar-palm fronds whip around in a sudden tropical breeze, then pause as the wind seems to take another breath.

Across the bay, planes land and take off. Will I ever board one again—head for home on silver, metal wings? Or will I have to watch the same scene after two more days trudge by and I fail another test? Finally, I work up enough energy to call Martha Jo and Amy.

"I was just about to get in touch," Amy says. "I've been so depressed I don't want to do anything. I'm still testing positive. How about you?"

We exchange our test results, her scores even lower than mine.

"Whoa. You must have been really sick," I say, "if the meds have made such a small difference in you. The doctor's supposed to come see me this afternoon, so maybe he can give me something that works better."

Amy sighs. "Well, good luck with that. I'd like to just pack up and go home anyway," she says. "The US isn't as careful now about letting people enter the country, though I've heard that the airport here can refuse to let obviously sick people leave."

Evidently Amy feels a lot better than she did that first day when we decided to stay. Just the thought of a twenty-four-hour-plus flight appalls me.

"I'll let you know what the doctor recommends," I say, "but when I'm up to it, I definitely want to leave as soon as possible. You rest up, and I'll do the same. Tell Martha Jo hi."

Amy's improvement gives me some hope that we'll get home sooner rather than later. In the meantime, my universe seems to have shrunk to my bed pillows, the fluffy white clouds that I gaze at out my window, and the rumpled white sheets and comforter piled around me on my cushiony king-size bed. I'm miserable.

Pleasant Doctor's Visit

I've left my outer gate ajar, and the ringing doorbell on my inner door shocks me from a sound sleep. I jerk on my pink batik house dress and rush to open it.

Instead of the older male doctor I saw when I was diagnosed almost a week ago, a young, slender, masked woman with long, straight, black hair stands on my veranda, accompanied by another young woman, apparently her assistant.

"Hello," she says. "I understand you have tested positive for COVID twice. I am so sorry this illness has interrupted your stay on our island."

This young woman combines the beauty and grace of a dancer with the brains and skills of a doctor. Studying me with dark, steady eyes, she examines me thoroughly with firm hands and questions me about my symptoms. "Your lungs and stomach look fine, but you need to stay in the sun for an hour or so every day and get plenty of exercise."

"So it's okay to walk around the resort?" I ask.

"Definitely. If you see someone, just go the other way."

She hands me two small boxes. "I want you to take this anti-inflammatory for ten days, as well as this antibiotic for five, plus multivitamins. You should start to feel better soon, though some people's tests don't show negative for quite a while. My husband had to wait a month."

"So after our ten days are up, it will be okay for us to leave?" I trust her judgment and admire her skill and her bedside manner. In fact, I already feel better after talking to her.

She smiles. "Yes. In addition to sunshine and exercise, get plenty of rest, drink a lot of fluids, and try to enjoy the rest of your stay in Bali."

"I will, and thank you so much," I say as I give her assistant my credit card and we settle the charge. She's changed night into day for me.

Slow Recovery, with Feeling

I wish I could say that I recover overnight, though my thoughts of dying do begin to recede like spent waves. Yet strange thoughts keep washing through me, poems continuing to gush out onto paper.
In a flowery mood that morphs into sadness, I write this poem about Grace.

Untold Riches

*She led me to explore caverns
I've never visited,
gaze at pearls and diamonds
I've never imagined.
The memory of them and our last afternoon together
haunts me like dreams of a lost treasure.*

However, in an hour, I become sarcastic.

Attracted

*Her intensity drew me in,
moth-like.
Singed wings smell so unpleasant.*

My mood shifts again, to bitterness.

Warning

*Unhappily married women
will steal your heart,
then run back home to "Daddy."*

And before long, I cycle back to sadness.

Life Is a Series—

*waves hitting the shore,
pearls on a string,
ticks of a clock,
beats of a heart,
drips of a faucet,
beads on a rosary,
rotations of a fan,
signals from a lighthouse,*

> *breaths of a living being,*
> *thoughts of you.*

Exhausted from all this emotional turmoil, while lying in bed, I think of my niece Bonnie, my sister Kitty's younger daughter, who lost her husband during the early days of COVID. I text her for advice.

After a long discussion of symptoms and meds and recovery time, I ask her if mood swings are part of this disease.

> **Bonnie:** *Yes. Mood swings are a definite portion of this! The steroid and anti-inflammatory you're on also cause them.*
>
> **Me:** *Wow. Thanks for the info. I thought I was either going crazy or had become sixteen again. I'll try to be a little easier on myself.*

Then I briefly describe my situation with Grace, ending, *Oh, well. Just part of the adventure of the trip.*

> **Bonnie:** *Ooh la la! Almost like the artist's signature for your trip, along with COVID, I suppose.*
>
> **Me:** *Absolutely. Nothing like a broken heart to make me pour out a stream of poems to put things in perspective.*
>
> **Bonnie:** *Putting the pieces together in preparation for the next adventure...*

We end our conversation, especially since it's after midnight back home in Texas. I'm really relieved. She's a lifeline to the other side of the world, connects me to it and truly seems to understand.

My moods continue to parade through me. The hours pass, and gradually the meds and rest and sun and solitary walks seem to help. Am I wearing my illness down, are my meds fighting a winning battle, or will COVID defeat me?

Finally, I move beyond my focus on only Grace and begin to look at the bigger picture, still relying on poetry to clear out my emotional chaos. I write about how, for years, I've fallen for unavailable women who are ill-suited to me, and how each encounter has elated yet eviscerated me. My moods have swung like a golf club and hit me far down the course, but too often into the rough. And sometimes they resemble old-fashioned red lanterns, signaling the coming and going of a freight train. But too often I ignore these red lanterns.

Then I grow sorry for myself.

Beggar

*The unsupported self
always has to sing
for her supper.*

I wallow in self-pity.
Will I ever get well? And will I ever be back on Texas soil?

March 8, 2023

Positive Again

Finally, a bigger picture appears, and I switch from my fear of physically dying to the small death I've felt at the end of each of my major attractions to an unavailable woman. I begin to visualize death as a shapeshifter, a woman I've gradually become intimate with, known occasionally since girlhood. She's appeared as public-school teachers, older girls, married women—all beautiful, charming, unattainable objects of worship.

At this point, my psychological pain eases. I also feel better physically and call Martha Jo and Amy.

"So, how's the patient?" I ask Martha Jo when she answers.

"Amy's improved a lot. She's waiting for the results from the lab and believes she'll be negative now. In fact, she's downright feisty. I think she's formulating an emergency escape plan as we speak."

I can't bear to be disappointed again today. Surely I'm not positive this time. I change the subject. "Did Katherine send you two another fruit basket?" I gaze at the one that's just arrived, sitting on the credenza near my TV.

"As a matter of fact, she did. Have you ever met a nicer hotel manager?"

"No. I'm certainly going to give her high marks on her evaluation." I recall all the times Katherine has called to check on me and how responsive she's been when I've phoned her to ask for something.

"I agree." Martha Jo pauses, Amy saying something in the background. "Amy wants to know if you'd like to come over for a little Rummikub. You've been cooped up long enough."

I glance around my solitary room like I'm planning a jail break. "Absolutely. Let me put on something other than a robe or a gown for a change, and I'll be right there."

After we enjoy a few of the mystery fruits in Katherine's second gift basket, we're sitting on their veranda playing when their house phone rings. Amy jumps up. "Oops. That must be my test results. Anyone want to bet on the outcome?"

Martha Jo and I both raise an eyebrow.

Amy's just letting herself out on their veranda again when my cell phone starts buzzing. I accept the call and listen to the brief message. Amy's back and sits down again as I click off my phone. "Okay. You first," I say.

"Still positive." She shrugs. "Do you think the tests are rigged so we'll stay here until we go broke? I hate to think what this place charges per night and what our insurance will, or won't, pay."

I shrug too. "You may be right, but the doctor I saw could be correct too. Sometimes it takes quite a while for a negative result to show up."

"And we're supposedly not contagious starting tomorrow. I think I'll call our long-lost Advantage rep in Budapest and see what she can do to get us out of here pronto." Amy sits down, spears a slice of banana, and lays down the rest of her tiles. "I win," she says, and Martha Jo and I smile.

Maybe this time tomorrow we'll be on our way home, or at least sitting in the airport waiting to board our plane.

March 9–10, 2023

MELTDOWN IN THE AIRPORT

My house phone rings just as I begin my morning tai chi routine out by the pool, the sun gradually brightening the sky and the sea. I run inside and grab the receiver.

"Pack your bags," Amy says. "A cab's supposed to pick us up to leave for the airport at three this afternoon. We definitely want to be ready and waiting! We fly out at seven tonight."

"Oh, great." I glance around my villa. I've left my suitcase partially packed with dirty clothes from the cruise. It probably won't take more than thirty minutes to get ready to go. "I'll be there. Thanks for taking care of this. See you this afternoon!"

Getting ready takes longer than I thought because I'm so nervous and paranoid and weak from being ill. In a daze, I check every drawer and hiding place at least three times. Then I do my morning stretches, eat a final American breakfast, and stroll around the grounds while the day's still cool. Back in my villa, I recheck every item, every closet, every cubbyhole, then rest until it's finally time to call a young man in a cart to drive me to the reception area. The anticipation of leaving exhausts me.

Amy and Martha Jo are waiting outside when I arrive. "Surprise, surprise. Advantage isn't sending a taxi, so we'll have to get our own."

"It doesn't look like that'll be a problem though." Martha Jo points to the long line of cabs waiting in the driveway. "But we need to go settle our bills first."

Katherine greets us at the front desk. "I am so glad you all are doing better, and I hope you have a safe trip home." She holds out a little bracelet made of white cord and three clear beads, an intricate knot joining the ends, and hands one to each of us. "It's for luck."

"Oh, thank you," we all say, then take out our credit cards as she slides our bills toward us.

I try not to gulp too loud as I look at my total. In rupiahs, it appears to be millions, and in dollars it's not millions—just thousands. I've certainly never stayed anywhere this expensive and am thankful my card has a high credit limit.

Martha Jo appears similarly stunned as she signs and then retrieves her credit card, which obviously has an extra-high limit too.

"Well, what are we waiting for?" Amy says. "Let's grab a cab and get there early." We hug Katherine good-bye and wheel our luggage to a waiting taxi.

It doesn't take long to reach the airport through the congested streets, the busy lanes of traffic crowded dangerously close to the shops. The driver chats, pointing out sites of interest, and we gaze around, having seen very little of Bali except one temple and the resort.

After making our way through the crowd, we separate. I stand at the end of a very long line for passengers in the economy section, and Martha Jo and Amy walk up immediately to the first-class check-in desk. I notice them talking to the clerk, who returns to her computer, then to them, several times. I see a lot of headshaking and begin to feel like a leaking balloon. Finally, when Amy walks over to me and says, "They don't have any tickets for us, or for you either," all the air seems to fly out of me. I feel totally deflated.

"What do you mean, they don't have tickets?" I ask.

"Just what I said." Amy's scowling. "Remember all the problems those people on our cruise had getting from the States to Australia?"

"Yes," I say, reality slapping me in the face.

"Well, it's happening to us now." A vein in Amy's temple is throbbing, and suddenly I'm glad she's not holding a gun.

It's a good thing I still have my roller bag, because if I didn't have it to lean on, I'd fall. I drag it over to an empty corner and plop down on the cold, hard floor, my brain short-circuiting. The memory of missing my flight in Seattle just a few months earlier, my chaotic thoughts of Grace, and my experience with COVID create a perfect mental storm.

Thank God for Amy. She shifts into battle mode, and after having to borrow an airline employee's cell phone because hers won't work here, and calling multiple times, she finally reaches our contact in Budapest.

In the meantime, I slump on the bare floor in a corner of the noisy airport, people walking by me as if I'm a piece of lost luggage.

Finally, Amy rouses me from my stupor. "The Advantage rep said for us to buy our own tickets and fly home, and the company will reimburse us. Let's do it so we can get out of here."

At that point, if she'd told me they were sending a big pink elephant for the three of us to ride home on, I would have agreed. At least I'm able to stand up and pull out my credit cards. I say "cards," because that's what it took. Evidently, the sudden huge amount I've just paid the hotel has set off the security warnings for that card, so without my two backup ones, I'd be out of luck until I could find another alternative. And Martha Jo and Amy have the same problem. Amy has to forgo a first-class ticket and sit in economy with me because that's the only arrangement we can manage even with our assortment of cards.

But we're going home to Texas! Yippee. Of course, now it's too late to get tickets for our original seven o'clock departure, so we're forced to wait for the one a.m. flight. We park ourselves and our luggage in a huge, open entry area full of tourist shops and cafés and play Rummikub until eleven p.m., when we're allowed to check in.

Martha Jo speeds through the first-class line, but Amy and I have to wait quite a while. And though the clerk processes Amy's ticket quickly, she obviously has problems with mine. She spends at least ten minutes checking and rechecking her computer and my ticket, then consulting several colleagues. But, finally, the woman presses a magic button and nods for me to go ahead.

After the expected wait in a relatively quiet departure lounge, we finally board our plane and fly all night, crossing India and landing in the Middle East. And from there, we spend fifteen more hours in the air, soaring over the Caspian Sea and Russia, and then near the North Pole. The only problem—the seats in economy are so narrow my hip bones will be sore for a week after I get home.

When we land in Dallas in the late afternoon, Texas has never looked so good, despite the heavy traffic on the freeways. A three-hour drive to Martha Jo and Amy's, where I retrieve my car and drive another hour in the dark, and I'm home, which I'm tempted to never leave again.

Six and a Half Weeks Later: April 26, 2023

RELAXATION AND REVELATION

Being back in Texas for the past six and a half weeks has been a mixed bag of readjusting to my own time zone, my normal routine, and my family and friends. My major hassle has been with the trip-insurance company, to which I've had to send the pertinent information about my expenses several times and by various methods: snail mail and two types of electronic media. I still don't have my documentation completely right, but I persist.

The insurance company has informed me that, in my situation, it will pay for only five days in a hotel and allow no more than $250 a day for my room. So I'm forewarned that I've treated myself to an unexpected, very expensive vacation. My hotel stay will probably cost as much as my entire cruise did. But what can I do?

Amy, savvier than I am about how to submit her expenses, has already received complete payment for her medical costs, so that's encouraging. I'm now wondering about reimbursement for my return airfare, since I paid almost double the price of the original ticket to book it at the last minute. Martha Jo and I keep in close contact regarding that situation since she flew first class and has a lot more at stake than I do. The last I heard, though, she's thinking about giving up because she assumes Advantage must be strapped for cash.

Spring in East Texas is as lovely as usual. The leafed-out oaks and dogwoods and the blooming azaleas and roses brighten the streets and yards in our small town. The world smells fresh and new, with no whiff of the brutal heat the approaching summer will most likely oppress us with. We all revel in this moment of relief, working in our flowerbeds and gardens and playing and sitting outdoors every chance we have.

News flash! I've just received the results of my latest colonoscopy, informing me that the radiation and chemo treatments I was undergoing this time last year have totally eradicated my cancer. Though I'm still not back to full strength, I'm getting there, and this news boosts my spirits.

Sitting in my sister Kitty's den after sharing with her the good news about my remission, I suddenly recall the article I read in her copy of *Prevention* magazine just before I embarked on my Indonesian adventure. It seems like years ago, but I do remember that the young woman who wrote it had discovered she was on the autism spectrum.

What were the symptoms she mentioned? I've been so busy with the cruise and its unexpected aftermath that I barely remember them. Something about her emotional instability in high school, how noisy, crowded situations sometimes completely overwhelmed her, and how she was exhausted for days after she spent a lot of time interacting with people.

I can certainly relate to being around noisy crowds, since the cruise ended just a couple of months ago and I'm just now recovering from being around so many people practically all day during our ten days at sea, in spite of my forced isolation on Bali. I try to dismiss the article from my mind, yet it keeps nagging me. Why was I so excited about it originally? Most teenagers are emotionally unstable, aren't they? But the point the author makes about her interactions with people exhausting her resonates with me.

I pause. When I took the Myers-Briggs eons ago and tested as an INFP, I learned from the initial *I* that I'm an introvert. And that classification has always made sense: introverts lose power to other people in social settings and thus feel exhausted, whereas their opposites, extroverts, gain power in the same situation. I can recall dozens of examples of that aspect of my personality, from my early childhood until now. But does that point alone make me autistic?

Curious, and finally rested from the trip and relieved from my worries about my recent cancer treatment, I turn to two of my best friends: Google and my local public library. And what a journey they take me on—this trip free of charge except for my time.

Two Weeks Later: May 11, 2023

Wine with My Cousin

My cousin Lou and I sit in her den, her ever-present Siamese keeping an eye on us.

I've been bursting to share my discoveries during the past two weeks, after avidly researching autism spectrum disorder (ASD). During that time, I've discovered Temple Grandin and read her research about how her brain is wired differently from most people's. My sister Kitty is familiar with her, and yesterday during our daily morning walk, I mentioned the highlights of what I've learned so far about the spectrum. One of her granddaughters is on the opposite end of the spectrum from where I'm beginning to think I may be, so she's more comfortable with the subject than the average person around here.

Back with Lou now, I can't stop myself from jumping right in. I ask her, "Do you remember our discussions about the Rogers family before I left on my trip?"

"Sure. My mom and your dad may have had the worst cases of whatever was wrong with them, except maybe for their middle sister, but probably all five of that generation were affected." Lou takes a sip of red wine from her long-stemmed, globed glass.

I nod and drink some of my ice water, then set it on the small glass-top table to my right. "Well, I just read an interesting article about autism, and I think—"

She slams her glass down on her own side table so hard I'm afraid it may shatter. "What? You think they were all autistic? I inherited some of the things I hated about them, and you did too. But no way am I like *that*. And you're not either. Are you sure you don't want some wine?"

I shake my head. "No. Since my cancer, I've quit drinking, probably for good." I take another sip of water. "But Lou, seriously, autism isn't always what you think it is."

"Well, I know Kitty's granddaughter is autistic, and she's the only one in the family who is!"

I take a deep breath. The young woman whose article gave me this idea was right when she said it wasn't easy to convince people, even professionals, that she had ASD. And I haven't even told Lou that I suspect I may be on the milder side of the autism spectrum. She just assumed I was referring to the more noticeable condition like Kitty's granddaughter has.

I try to explain. "I've been doing a lot of research since I got back from my trip and have learned that autism is very different in different people. You took several psychology courses in college, didn't you?"

"Well, yes." She settles back in her chair a few inches. "But we didn't study autism much back then. What's the latest?"

"For one thing, researchers seem to agree that autism, or ASD, as they call it now, is different in males and females."

Lou sips her wine and nods. "Seems like I did read that somewhere. What's the difference?"

"In males, autism is usually more obvious." I rake my hair out of my eyes. It tends to fall forward.

She keeps nodding. "That's typical. Boys could always be a lot louder and rougher than we could when we were growing up."

"I agree," I say, continuing to stroke my hair. "Girls' symptoms are more subtle. We tend to try to fit in with what's expected of us and not be too obvious."

"Yep. I always wanted to be a boy so I could do what I wanted to without Daddy pitching a fit. 'Don't stay out too late. Don't let him put his hands on you.' I got so tired of being 'protected,' especially when I moved back here in my forties after living on my own or with one of my husbands in Houston and Dallas for all those years." She pauses. "But we were talking about autism."

"Yes. We were. I've read a lot of books about it in the last couple of weeks."

"And?" Lou reaches over and strokes her cat, who turns his head slowly toward her, then lowers it and closes his eyes.

"I've learned that Temple Grandin is the most famous American woman with ASD, and that, thanks to early intervention, she's been able to succeed in her chosen specialty of dealing with cattle, and that she's a well-known writer and speaker."

"Is she like your great-niece, who's obviously autistic?" Lou asks.

I take a drink of water. "I'm not sure, though she obviously had a lot of help from the time she was really young. Everyone seems to be different." Another sip. "Regardless of where people are on the spectrum, though, none of them know how to socialize in a natural way, and, uh, sometimes they think it's silly to try." And another sip. "They seem so awkward in a crowd, almost backward, that people usually just ignore them when they attempt to say something, which makes them feel even more inept." Lou is one of the few people I usually don't have any trouble talking to, but I'm almost stuttering now.

"Like Aunt PJ's son?"

"Yes. I hadn't even thought about him. We always just considered him a little slow, didn't we?" I listen to what I've just said. "And we didn't take him seriously."

Lou glances at the TV, which she muted when I came in.

I'm doing a terrible job of getting my point across to her. I'll try harder.

"People on the spectrum can be really intense and focused at times…" I'm searching for words, and my heart's pounding. "When they start a project, that's all they want to do, and you better not bother them." *Do I know what I'm talking about?*

"Well, I can't think of a better example of that than your dad," Lou says. "Can you?"

I take a deep breath and shake my head, relieved, and now I don't have to hunt quite so hard for what I'm trying to say. "You're right. If he found a book he liked, he'd stay up all night reading it." I remember him doing that quite often. "Or if he got interested in anything he was building or working on, sometimes he wouldn't even stop to eat. He was definitely focused."

Lou huffs. "Well, I don't see anything wrong with that. And so what if he was a hermit on Christmas Day and other times got mad at your mom for no reason she could find and wouldn't speak to her for a month? That's just the way he was." She eyes the TV set again. "Mama was like that sometimes too. But both of them seemed better when they got older."

"And their sisters were like that as well. I don't know enough about ASD to be able to diagnose them, but I really think I have most of the symptoms."

I finish my glass of water, suddenly exhausted by Lou's total denial of practically everything I've said. I sigh, yawn, and glance at the clock on the mantel.

"Hey," Lou says. "My favorite program's about to come on. Do you mind if I watch it? I want to see who's gonna get kicked off this week. You're welcome to stay."

At least I tried. But I failed. "No, thanks. I need to go. See you later."

She's already turned up the sound before she lets me out the door.

About a Month Later: June 16, 2023

MY NIECE AND HER AUTISTIC DAUGHTER

My niece, Leslie—Kitty's older daughter—has a thirteen-year-old girl, Sam, who was diagnosed as profoundly autistic at a very early age. Leslie's stopped by to help me with a computer problem, and I ask her if she's read any of Temple Grandin's books.

"No. But I've seen her on TV. She's impressive. Thanks to an early diagnosis and some great parents and teachers, she's come a long way," Leslie says. "Advanced degrees, innovative inventions, published books, fame, and fortune."

We're standing on my tiny back porch, and Leslie's eyeing her black Tahoe, where Sam is sitting and waiting for her, the engine and the air-conditioner running.

"Pretty amazing what Grandin's been able to accomplish, especially with the livestock industry," Leslie says. "She's helping make a lot of people more aware of autistic individuals and what they can contribute to society."

"Yes. The way she explains the differences between people's mental wiring and how it affects us really interests me," I say. "By the way, are you familiar with the term autism spectrum disorder?"

"ASD? Sure. But I don't know much about the other end of the spectrum. I'm too busy keeping up with Sam's area."

"Well, I really think I may fit there," I say. "I suspected it a little before I left on my trip, but now that I've had more time to research it, I'm more and more convinced that I have a lot of the characteristics of people with ASD."

I'm tall, but I have to look up at Leslie, and at Sam as well. They both hover at six feet, and their slim figures make them seem even taller.

Leslie nods, glancing at Sam, who's bouncing in the front seat and running her fingers through her hair like I do sometimes. Hmm. "It's possible," she says. "I think a lot of us may fit the description more than we realize." She takes a step backward. "Gotta run. My always-hungry son's waiting for me to bring him lunch from Chicken Express. With two teenagers, I never have much spare time. See you later."

"Good talking to you, and thanks for the computer help."

"No problem. Bye."

And Leslie races off to her busy life.

I walk out into my backyard and stare up at the fresh green leaves on the enormous limbs spreading over my head. This white-oak tree is almost as old as I am. *Leslie understands what I'm trying to say about my self-diagnosis!* I want to throw my arms around the tree, hug its rough, worn, gray trunk.

Maybe I'm on the right track. But how does being ASD have anything to do with my recent feelings for Grace? There must be a connection.

Ten Days Later: June 26–27, 2023

Tossing Out a Term

Every Monday afternoon, I meet with Amy and several other friends to freewrite. Our small group of older, retired, professional women includes gay and straight, Black and White, liberal, Buddhist-leaning former social workers, teachers, and lawyers from Texas and New York City. We chat briefly before two p.m., then meditate for ten minutes. We're all very drawn to Buddhism.

After that preamble, we take turns reading aloud a brief section from a classic book about writing by Natalie Goldberg, then freewrite for fifteen minutes on a randomly selected topic. At that point, each of us shares what we've just written, with little or no comment from the others, and then we repeat the writing/reading process. Our topics differ wildly, ranging from an abstract word such as "sacrifice" to our impressions of a visual prompt, such as a cityscape.

Before we begin today, I ask, "Are y'all familiar with the term autism spectrum disorder?"

"Yes," all but one of them say. "Why do you want to know?" the former social worker asks.

"I think I may be on it."

We don't pursue the topic, because we're not a discussion group. But the term is in the air, and these women don't miss a trick.

The next day, Klara, one of the women about my age whom I haven't known very long, calls and asks me to have lunch with her.

She and I first met at a Christmas concert this past December and clicked so dramatically, I was afraid we'd drown out the orchestra and the singers with our whispered conversation. Seriously, I don't think

I've ever related so quickly to another person. Her longtime, English-professor husband died several years ago, and she's been trying to adjust to life as a single person, evidently quite successfully. Before I left for Indonesia, she and I ate lunch together a couple of times, and I joined the writing group she was in.

Since our initial connection was so strong, we quickly bonded after I recovered from my disastrous trip, and soon we found that spending an hour and a half together once a week in our group activity wasn't enough. So we started finding any excuse we could to get together, though we live an hour and a half apart by car.

Today we meet at a Mexican restaurant halfway between where she and I live.

Klara immediately asks, "Why do you think you're on the spectrum? I'd never have suspected it, and, excuse me for saying this, but I'm not sure you know what you're talking about."

I have to laugh. I love her directness. She's a precious new friend who helps me be honest with myself and with her.

"I'm serious, Klara. I thought about it a lot during my adventure in Indonesia, mainly because of a woman named Grace that I met on the cruise. As I examined my feelings for her, especially when I was isolated in Bali, more and more pieces of the puzzle began to fall into place, even if I wasn't sure what the finished picture would look like."

Our waitress brings our drinks and menus much too quickly. Klara and I usually spend as much time as possible together over a meal. Klara sips her iced tea and gazes at me with soft, brownish eyes, a distinctive ring of light green circling her irises. "What happened with this woman named Grace? Did you sleep with her?"

I almost spit out the water I've just tasted. "Huh? I wish. But she was as straight as you are, maybe even more so. I didn't even try."

Klara's eyes brighten, the outer rings flaring. "Maybe you should have. You never know. And what did you have to lose?"

"Well, for starters, she's married."

"Happily?"

"Hmm. No. But that wasn't what our relationship was about."

"What was it about, then? I thought that's the main reason people go on a cruise alone. To find true love. Like in *Now Voyager*, that old classic Bette Davis movie."

Our waitress shows up much too quickly, fidgeting with her order pad. I try to ignore her and run a finger around the top of my water glass as I tell Klara in a pompous tone, "I actually like to visit foreign countries to experience a new and different culture, but I have to admit I did venture into 'truelove' territory."

Klara gently waves our waitress away. "Do tell."

But I wave the poor woman back. "Nothing happened, except in my imagination, especially while I had COVID for those ten long days alone."

Klara shakes her head, and we both finally order taco salads. Then she says, "You're not much fun today. But go ahead if you want to be like that. Why do you think you're on the spectrum?"

I drink some water, then make a face at her. "Okay. If you insist."

She rolls her eyes, and I can feel her focus all her attention on me. I really like this new friend.

"I've always felt really different," I say. "I've already told you all about my three bad marriage choices. But I don't think you have any idea how hard it is for me to get up in front of people at a book reading or be part of a panel discussion."

"Really? I've never seen you at a public event, but I just took for granted that it would be easy for you. After all, you were a college teacher."

I shake my head and grab a chip from the basket we're sharing. "It's not easy at all. I dread it for days, am usually tongue-tied while I'm in the spotlight, and then I'm completely exhausted for the longest time after it's over." I wash down the chip with another sip of water. "It's the same when I try to have any type of casual conversations that most people take for granted. They truly wear me out."

"Oh," she says, her tone softening. "I have noticed that you're a little shy, but I find that trait endearing. It makes you special. Too many people never shut up."

"Thanks. I love you too, even when you're a pain in the ass. But I'm serious."

"I'm serious as well. And I'll tell you what. I'll research the latest information I can find, and we can discuss you possibly being autistic however we can manage to get together next—Zoom, WhatsApp, FaceTime, phone, or in person."

"Hey. About research material. It's pretty hard to locate info about really older women on the spectrum. I just found *Women and Girls with*

Autism Spectrum Disorder in our local library and recommend it. It's by Sarah Hendrickx, in the UK."

"You want me to read it too?"

"Sure. If you have time and don't mind."

Klara laughs softly, like the sunrise cresting a mountaintop. "You know, at my age, I don't have much except time and money to spend on new books. I'll order a copy from Amazon, and we can discuss it the next time we get together."

"You're the best, Klara. What would I do without you?"

Just then our waitress puts our plates down in front of us, and Klara grabs her fork.

"You'd do okay. But it's a lot more enjoyable to share things like this, don't you think? It's just too bad we live so far apart."

"Only an hour and a half. That's a hop, skip, and a jump in Texas," I say.

She chuckles. "You're right. At least we can both still drive without any problems."

"Absolutely."

We eat our taco salads and discuss a lot of other subjects, laugh frequently, and finally leave after several hours. I've just gained a powerful ally in my new quest and look forward to discussing Hendrickx's book with Klara.

July 3, 2023

QUESTION AT WRITING GROUP

It's almost two o'clock, when our weekly writing group is scheduled to begin, but at the last minute, one of my friends sitting across the table from me says, "Helen. I just have a hard time thinking of you as on the autism spectrum. You seem so…normal."

Caught off-guard, I blurt out, "But you don't know me the way I know myself. People with ASD, usually women, and especially women from an earlier generation, like I am, learn at an early age to mask our true thoughts and feelings. And we probably do it so often, we lose touch with them." That idea has just occurred to me, so I'll ponder it later.

No one says anything, and I continue. "I've never conversed much about my personal life with anyone, especially in a group. So maybe that's one reason I like our format. I can share whatever I've written without having to try to explain or justify it. We just accept what each of us writes and keep on going."

Being so honest with a small group like this is a big step for me, and my friend's question seems oddly liberating. It appears to have come from an honest, caring part of her, which has apparently freed me to respond in the same tone.

It's now two o'clock, so we begin to meditate, and my thoughts easily slow down as I close my eyes and sit silently with these special people. Support groups such as this one are especially important to older women like us.

July 6, 2023

First Meeting with Klara

"Are you ready for our meeting?" Klara asks as we begin our Zoom chat this afternoon.

"I've been looking forward to it all week," I say, "though our family Fourth of July celebrations and a lot of yardwork have kept me busy."

"Well, today's all business," she says, though the smile in her soft, gold-brown eyes belies her words. "I hope you've organized your comments in the way I suggested when I emailed you last week."

"Absolutely. I'm glad your background in the community colleges where you've worked has taught you how to organize meetings effectively. I do need some help making sense of all this information I'm discovering about ASD. I've wracked my memory and my brain and my heart. I'm certainly glad I've had several days to prepare."

Klara nods, her cheeks reminding me of baked apples, though her eyes have a more businesslike glint now. "Then why don't we discuss your childhood memories first."

I describe how I always need a lot of sleep, then share one of my earliest memories, when I insisted on going to bed at my usual time even though my parents were having a noisy party near my bedroom.

"Such a mature little girl," Klara says.

"I've always been a little self-conscious about being such an obedient child," I say. "I was so boring and never got into trouble."

"Oh, I'm sure your mother appreciated that quality."

I nod. "But at the same time, I was like a little robot instead of a kid who wasn't afraid to express herself. When my sister came along ten years later, my mom seemed relieved that she spoke her mind and didn't seem to be afraid to be herself."

"Did your mother ever say anything?" Klara slips on her brownish horn-rimmed glasses, which emphasize the color of her eyes, especially that interesting narrow ring that circles each of them. Looking at her eyes is like gazing at planets in the solar system.

"No. But she rarely said anything personal and certainly nothing she thought might hurt my feelings."

"So this was all in your head?"

I scratch my cheek. "I've always been very perceptive. It's like sometimes I can read people's thoughts, which isn't pleasant sometimes." I take a deep breath. "I was always different from most of the other girls, though I did have a few special friends I enjoyed being with."

"How were you different?" Klara smooths a stray gray-brown curl that tends to kick up behind her right ear.

"I always tried to be perfect. I had the best grades, never got into trouble, never argued, never said ugly things about people, did what was expected of me, and so on." I shrug. "Like I said, boring."

"And your sister wasn't like that?"

"Not at all. She always seemed to say what was on her mind, would talk back to our dad—which none of the rest of us would do—and seemed to have always known exactly who she was and what she wanted."

"And your parents preferred her to you?" Klara's smile squeezes my heart.

"Yes. I'm sure they did. And they should have. She was a person, not a robot like I was."

"I'm so sorry you felt like that, but I can understand why you would. I wish I was with you now to hug you, like you needed someone to do to you all those years ago."

I tear up, because she's right. A hug would have gone a long way back then, but I would probably have been embarrassed and frozen, been rigid, which is probably what actually happened. My mom was the oldest girl in a poor farm family with eight kids. She most likely had to give a lot more hugs than she got.

Klara gazes at me with those steady, searching eyes. "Well, I'll give you all the hugs that little girl needs."

I brush away a tear. "Thank you. And I'll take them. I've learned over the years that they're some of the best medicine possible." I sniff and then wipe my nose with a Kleenex. "But let's get back to business. Okay?"

"If you're sure you're ready."

I shake my head. "Yep. Let's keep going."

"What else about your childhood makes you consider yourself on the spectrum?"

"Well, several things. Especially in my social life as I grew older. I liked to play sports with the boys and was usually one of the first ones chosen to be on our neighborhood ball teams. I was athletic and competitive and determined. But let somebody mention a party, and I felt totally out of my comfort zone."

"In what way?" Klara moves her head from side to side, as if her neck's getting a little stiff.

"The same boys I found so easy to get along with on the ball field seemed like strangers at parties and the other social gatherings that kids were supposed to enjoy."

Klara nods. "How so?"

"All the other girls kept saying silly things to them and flirting—I guess that's what that was. I never got the hang of it or figured out why everyone seemed to enjoy it. It's like they were speaking a foreign language that I didn't understand."

Klara's eyes gleam as if she'd like to smile but doesn't want to upset me.

"It's okay," I say. "It's rather humorous to me after all this time, but back then I truly didn't understand. And that upset me, because how can you control something you don't have a clue about?"

She nods. "You're right. And how did you cope?"

I tense one side of my face. "I really studied what the girls were doing, and, for a while, I tried to copy them."

"And?"

"That didn't work out so well. As they say, my heart wasn't in it, and I finally decided it wasn't worth my time. At parties, I'd hang around with my female friends and giggle a lot. That was much more enjoyable than trying to figure out how to communicate with a boy that I knew I could out-pitch and out-run."

"Good for you," Klara says. "That way you didn't have to pretend to be someone you weren't or do things you weren't interested in."

"Maybe if I'd thought about it that way, it would have been okay. But I mostly wondered what was wrong with me and didn't like myself because I couldn't be like the other girls." I sigh. "I also wondered why I was always so tired for several days after one of those parties or dances I hated going to."

Klara shakes her head and pushes her shoulders back. Then she settles in her desk chair. "Okay. You've told me some of what you didn't like about yourself. But surely you liked some parts."

I turn my head from side to side and listen to my neck crunch. I need to exercise it more than I already do. I blow out a long breath. "Well, most people thought I was really smart—gifted, some people said. That made me feel good, except…except it scared the boys away even more than my inability to flirt with them."

"And that mattered to you so very much?"

I nod. "Unfortunately, it did. And seeing my mom so obviously disappointed when she noticed me not being able to talk to a boy on the phone, and not be asked out on regular dates like my friends, and having to beg my best friend, who was gay, to take me to the prom, made me disappointed in myself. My mom loved to make fancy dresses for such events, but I certainly didn't enjoy wearing them. At least she had my little sister to make up for my shortcomings."

Klara puts her hand over her mouth and draws in a deep breath. "Well, I bet she was proud of you for being smart."

I smile. "You're right. She did enjoy having my friends come over to study with me in the kitchen while she cooked and talked to us about whatever we were learning. That was my very best social life, and I'm so glad to have had it. Much later in my life, my mom was able to travel with me and a group I was leading on a couple of trips abroad, one to the British Isles and the other to Central Europe. That turned out to be a great experience for both of us."

Klara claps. "I'm so glad you two had that experience together."

I nod. "Me too. And thanks for that. Mom and I and even my dad all loved to read, so there's that as well."

"And that's a lot," Klara says. She looks at her smartwatch. "Time to go. After reading Hendrickx's book and listening to your story today, I can agree that you seem to be on the spectrum. Why don't we deal with a few more topics next week, and after that, we can look at the situation more clearly in the future."

"That sounds good, Klara. I really value your comments and your willingness to discuss this situation with me."

"It's been a pleasure, dear one," she says and ends our Zoom session.

July 7, 2023

Cuddling with My Great-Niece

On my sister Kitty's huge deck behind her brick home, my great-niece, Sam, long, bare legs crossed in the lotus position, sits on a wooden bench made of large planks that hugs one side of this open-air, roofed area. As slim and flexible as a young willow tree, Sam glances at me, her gaze as distant as an unexplored Indonesian island.

Kitty is babysitting her but has trouble sitting still with so many plants spread over her half-acre backyard that need her attention. "Keep an eye on Sam for a minute, will you," Kitty asks me. "I want to go put the sprinklers on the tomatoes and the cucumbers. With this heat, they probably need more water than usual."

I nod and sit with Sam while Kitty flits around her yard like one of the hummingbirds that dart to and from the three feeders hanging at the far end of her porch, high enough that her two cats can't leap up and grab a hummer mid-flight.

The hot weather makes me drowsy, but I'm a bit uncomfortable being with Sam because she's, well, different from most everyone else I've ever known. However, with my newfound interest in ASD, I'm more open to this great-niece I'm now briefly responsible for.

She stares at me, then glances away toward a hummingbird that jets past us and then at a lurking cat pretending to nap near the hummer's feeder. Sitting within reach of Sam, I suddenly feel her warm, moist hand on my arm. She looks at me, then sidles nearer.

I try to relax my suddenly tense arm and inch closer to her, and before I know it, she has her slim arm around my shoulder and has snuggled into my side. It's like watching a dove take a drink from my birdbath. I almost hold my breath and don't make any sudden moves, afraid I'll scare her away. She raises her head and stares at me, says something incomprehensible, then cuddles even nearer.

I try to breathe normally and live fully in this precious moment. Sam has rarely let me touch her before, and now she's almost wrapped around me like a wisteria vine. We simply sit there together, joined like a double-yolked egg in its shell, and breathe the same air. I'm visiting a strange, new world and want to treasure every second of this unique experience.

July 13, 2023

Second Meeting with Klara

Klara and I meet on Zoom a week after our first session, and I hope things go as well today as they did last week. We chat about the highlights of our week, and I ask her, "So, what have you been doing all day besides playing with Mina?"

Her topaz-brown eyes glow even more than usual. "Well, it's been too hot to go outside, so she and I have been doing our best to stay cool. Thank goodness for air-conditioning. I don't know how we survived without it when we were kids. I've been trying to sew on some pillows, and Mina's insisted on helping me unwind the thread from the spools. I guess when she was a stray kitten, she didn't have anything this interesting to play with. She certainly keeps me on my toes."

"She's a lot of company for you, isn't she? I love calicos, and she's a beautiful one."

"And she evidently knows it, though she does let me pet her once in a while, when she's in the mood."

I laugh. "Well, I'm glad you two found each other. You seem to be a perfect match."

"She's like the sister I never had, and we're learning to get along well, just as long as I don't treat her like she's a cat. She's my equal."

"Good for her. She evidently knows how to keep you in line. Will you ask her if we can talk now?"

After a brief silence, Klara says, "We're in luck. She's just decided to take a nap, so I'm free for a while."

"Then let's don't waste any time. We have a lot left to discuss. Ready?"

I gather my handful of notes and spread them out in front of me.

One long list covers the entire back of a receipt for gasoline from Walmart, and three other small squares I've pulled from a thick stack of note paper are almost black with words and phrases—lines and arrows connecting circled words, some crossed out and others barely legible. I'd be lost without my memory aids.

Klara clears her throat and opens her notebook, which appears much neater and more orderly than mine. To each her own, I think. "I'm curious to know what you think are some of the rest of the major reasons you consider yourself on the spectrum."

I sit up in my desk chair and lean toward my computer, glancing at my notes. "The characteristics I'd like to discuss have been with me my entire life, though I've become aware of them at different times."

She gazes at me steadily. "Fine. Which one do you want to discuss first?"

"The fact that almost all my life, my feelings have always seemed frozen, like I have no contact with them. That really bothers me. It's like they're wild animals who live inside me, but I don't have any rapport with them."

Klara shakes her head. "You just handed me a large, heavy suitcase. Maybe we can unpack it so I can understand more fully what you're saying. How about starting with your feelings being frozen?"

"All right. When I was thirteen or fourteen, my junior-high-school math teacher died. He and his family lived right across the street from us, and his only child was my age and one of the boys in the neighborhood that I played various sports with." I have a mental snapshot of one scene from that funeral that I want to share with Klara. "His funeral service is the first one I recall attending, and at the graveside, I noticed a lot of people crying. I started to tear up too, but then I glanced at my parents. Dry-eyed, they both frowned slightly and barely shook their heads. I immediately swallowed hard and choked back the tears and the feelings that I was trying to keep down. They nodded, and I learned my lesson well. From then on, I tried to never express any strong emotion such as grief physically. To this day, I rarely cry, and I don't recall either of them ever crying, except once, when my mom dropped a lemon pie she'd just pulled from the oven."

Klara shakes her head, her cocoa eyes soft and moist. "I am sure your parents had their reasons, based on their upbringing and the difficult time periods they had lived through. But it's so sad to discourage a child from expressing herself."

"Other kids would have rebelled and been truer to themselves, but I was a good little girl, always wanting to please. I probably had already begun to suppress my true self, which is where I see my connection with ASD. Situations such as the one I recall simply reinforced that tendency."

"So, when did you become aware that your feelings were frozen, as you describe it?" Klara writes something in her notebook, then looks up, letting a comfortable silence wrap around us.

I take a deep breath. "I've always loved to sing, and I idolized the woman who taught our public-school choir class. Many of us were in it for five years, beginning in the eighth grade, and in high school, we participated in two major public concerts every year—one near the end of each semester. My teacher asked me to be the student conductor for several pieces during our final concert my senior year, which was a huge honor."

"Music is a wonderful way to express your emotions, so you were lucky to have such an opportunity," Klara says. "I envy you."

I nod. "Yes. I was also in the school band for the same number of years, where I played the snare drum."

"Even better," she says. "I bet you could beat out a lot of feelings on that drum."

"Yes. You're right." I recall how freeing it had felt to do just that. "But back to my choir experience. I remember vividly the first time I stood in front of the group I was supposed to direct—expressionless and rigid, unable to move. In fact, I imagined myself as one of my drumsticks—tall, skinny, and wooden."

"Music is such an expressive medium that I imagine realizing you couldn't move to it, not even to raise your arms, relayed a clear message that you were alienated from your own feelings," Klara says.

"Yes. But I didn't think about it in such an insightful way. I just remember noticing how stiff I was and being surprised." I swallow the lump in my throat that this memory causes.

"So what happened?"

Klara's velvet tone makes we want to continue.

"Our music teacher walked over and put her arm around me, then hugged me close. Everyone stared, but she looked at them like she dared anyone to say, or even think, anything bad about me. She even kissed my head, which I'd hung down, trying to hide how embarrassed I was. 'You can do this,' she whispered, and somehow I realized I could. I relaxed, wanting more than anything to live up to her faith in me, and I was able to do just that. After our concert, she told me privately that I was the best student choir director she'd ever had."

"How kind." Klara's soft eyes glisten. "Did you stay in touch with her after you graduated?"

"You better believe it. We wrote each other occasionally while I was away at college, and almost every time I visited home during all the years I lived away, I stopped by to see her."

"She must have been someone special. Did she have any children?"

I shake my head. "No, though she was married. I like to think I was like a daughter to her in some ways, that she valued parts of me that weren't the norm in our part of the country. She seemed to be close like that with some of her other students throughout the years too, usually the ones who were rather different in some way, whether they were gay or didn't fit the traditional mold. Quite a few of us owe her a lot."

I take a deep breath as I recall visiting her in the hospital just before she died. People like her have no idea what a difference they make to the young people in their lives.

I glance at Klara on my laptop screen and sense that she's thinking the same thing I am.

"Thanks for sharing those memories," she says. "Do you want to talk about anything else along those lines, how you've struggled to recognize and/or express your feelings?"

I sit there quietly for a minute, and one more incident fills my mind. "After my junior year in college, Klara, I spent a month on Nantucket Island, living and working with a small group of Methodist students my age. We were from all over the US and had a variety of jobs on the island. I was a clerk in a local department store. Overall, it was an enlightening experience, but I most clearly remember lying on the beach one weekend afternoon and watching the older married couple in charge of our group sit side by side on a sand dune and talk."

"What made that incident so memorable?" Klara asks.

My smile feels forced. "I'd never seen my parents simply carry on a conversation. I'd watched them work together many times, which they did with ease. But I'd never been aware of them having a lengthy discussion about what appeared to be an important subject, or subjects."

Klara cocks her head to one side. "Why was that so important to you?"

"When my dad got mad, he clammed up and refused to speak, especially to my mom. We would all tiptoe around him and were uneasy and careful during these periods, which could last for weeks. My cousin Lou and I talk about it sometimes, and she said her own mom, my dad's oldest sister, acted the same way, though she didn't withdraw for as long as my dad did. It could be that my dad had ASD or some other condition and that couple's conversation on the beach on Nantucket showed me an alternative. It gave me a clue that some adults could really discuss meaningful subjects and reach a common understanding. In fact, I'm beginning to wonder if that's why talking in such depth to Grace on my cruise seemed so important to me. Maybe my ideal of two people successfully solving a joint problem overshadowed other things about her and our interactions that I should have noticed."

Klara is now busy for several minutes jotting something in her notebook, so I wait and replay that long-ago scene in my mind. Though my childhood was relatively happy, it would probably have been very different if my parents had been able to communicate verbally like that couple I observed.

She looks at me over her glasses. "I may be carrying us far afield, but do you think your three marriages all ended because of communication difficulties?"

I nod and then sit very still, the possible truth of her observation sending prickly electric impulses through my arms and legs. "Hmm. I did get along a lot better with all three of my spouses when we were on the road or somewhere other than a permanent home, where we had a lot of common, everyday experiences that we needed to discuss. That point seems worthwhile."

I sip from the glass of ice water sitting on my desk. "My first husband did talk about his feelings or ideas a lot, and I simply listened. In contrast, my second one was usually rather quiet and preferred for us to participate in sports together or watch television instead of discuss anything meaningful. Hmm. My female partner and I communicated better than I did with either of the men, so maybe that's why she and I stayed together for almost thirty years, instead of seven years, maybe less, with the two men in my life. But even at the end of my marriage to her, I refused to even consider counseling. I told myself it was because she was so much more verbally fluent than I am, but it could have been because I still don't know how to communicate effectively in an intimate relationship and am afraid to try."

"Huh. I suspect you're on to something. And maybe you were on the right track just now when you said that talking in depth with Grace was so important to you that you simply ignored anything else about that interaction that you should have taken into account."

I nod. "Thanks so much for listening to me, Klara. It really helps me straighten things out in my head."

She beams. "What else are friends for? Do you want to add any other points?"

I scratch my head. "In addition to Hendrickx's book, I found a great site on YouTube, called 'Mom on the Spectrum.' You'd never suspect that the woman who speaks on it is autistic, but after you hear her comments, you're convinced. In the piece I saw, she briefly discussed sixteen overlooked autistic traits in women, and I identified with all but one of them."

"That's impressive, Klara says. "I assume you've already covered some of the ones she mentioned. Want to briefly discuss some of the others you remember?"

I nod. "We haven't mentioned stims, but I do find myself fooling with my hair a lot when I become overly stimulated in some way."

"Yes. I've noticed that trait, though it's not offensive."

"Good. It really does help calm me when I get upset, especially when I'm in public. It's a good way to give myself time to regulate my feelings and draw attention away from the panic or other overwhelming emotion that has suddenly swamped me. And it feels so good, it's one reason I've decided to wear my hair longer than I have since I was a girl."

"Stimming, eh?" Klara says. "I'll keep that in mind. I was vaguely aware of the term, but now it makes a lot more sense."

"One more thing about it," I say. "According to the YouTube information, girls tend to keep their stims as unobtrusive as possible."

"And why's that?" Klara takes a drink from the glass of what I assume is either water or tea that she's been sipping during our conversation.

"It's the old male/female thing," I say. "You know. Boys, especially back when we were young, feel much freer to act out in a grand style. Some experts even used to think that only males were autistic because they expressed themselves so much more freely and dramatically."

"Mm-hmm. That makes sense. Girls, especially those of us in the older generation, are taught not to rock the boat."

"And related to that point is the term masking." I pause and drink water from my own multicolored thermal glass.

"Masking?"

"Yes. Pretending to be someone we're not. Studying 'normal' girls so we can be more like them."

"I always thought that was just a characteristic of teenage girls wanting to be popular." Klara frowns.

I nod. "That's probably part of it. But girls on the spectrum take it to such an extreme that we totally lose sight of who we are." I shrug. "We copy and paste the behavior of girls we consider popular—their tone of voice, the way they laugh, their gestures—to such a degree that we eventually have no idea of how to be our true selves in a crowd." I draw a deep breath. "I know that feeling well. We become strangers to ourselves, and it's not easy to become reacquainted after all those years of living a lie."

"Whoa. That's enough," Klara says. "I see what you mean. And it's really sad, isn't it, what we do to ourselves, even many of us neurotypicals. Want to tell me about any of the other of the sixteen characteristics you learned about on that YouTube channel?"

I stretch my back and move my head from side to side. Then I check the handwritten notes I've jotted down while watching the "Mom on the Spectrum" YouTube several times. "Yeah. Another one is a no-brainer for me. Females on the spectrum feel more comfortable writing than talking because we feel like we can be truer to ourselves on paper than aloud."

"Absolutely. That's definitely you, as evidenced by your advanced degrees in English and your interest in various types of writing. What else, in a nutshell?"

"This next point is related to the one I've just mentioned. But I'd never recognized it in myself until I watched that YouTube."

"And?"

"Many autistic women mention that they think they have

something really great to say, but when they start to try to express it, it simply disappears. Then they have no idea where it went. I've done that a lot, and it's really frustrating. Makes me feel like a fool every time it happens. It's almost like my brain is sabotaging me."

"That must be a terrible feeling," Klara says, shaking her head.

"It is. Usually makes me angry at myself, though I'm really trying to go easier on myself lately. After learning all this stuff, even at my advanced age, I can understand and forgive myself for such things. It makes a huge difference."

Klara nods. "I'm certain it does. And I'm sure it'll take you a while to internalize all these realizations you've been having. But I have no doubt you'll work your way through them and come out even stronger and more self-aware than you already are. Anything else you want to mention?"

"Just one thing. Women on the spectrum do tend to gaslight themselves."

"Gaslight? How?"

"We're good at fooling ourselves, convincing ourselves that we can ignore what our body is warning us that we can't do. We think that just because others are able to do something, we should be able to do it too."

"I'm still not quite sure what you mean."

"Okay. I mentioned earlier that women like me can become exhausted by situations that don't bother neurotypical women. But we tend to ignore that fact and advise ourselves to suck it up. Yet then we end up getting sick or upset or out of kilter when we fail. The woman on the YouTube presentation advises us to 'Give ourselves the grace and patience to do things differently than the person next to us.' She does, however, admit that making this change is a long, slow process."

Klara holds up one hand and smiles. "I certainly agree. You've convinced me that you've done your homework. And you obviously have plenty more points and examples to share with me. But you don't need to do it all at once. Over the course of our remaining years of friendship, which I'm sure will be numerous, we'll have plenty of time to sort out all this. In fact, I look forward to exploring this new information with you."

She gazes at me with such a serene expression that my shoulders lower, and I stretch my rather tense legs out in front of me.

Klara continues, "Some of what you've been talking about applies to me. I don't see myself nearly as fully on the spectrum as you do. But I can relate to some of these insights simply because I'm female. I can imagine us continuing parts of this conversation for many years. But, for now, let's take a break and relax. I'm sure we have some other tidbits to talk about."

I hold up my hands. "You're right, my wonderful friend. I do tend to get carried away with all this talk about stimming and masking and gaslighting and so on. It's a new world for me and one I intend to explore for a long time."

Just then, I hear a soft *meow*. "Sounds like someone just woke up and is demanding a little attention," I say to Klara. "Guess I better let you get back to your better half."

She chuckles, and we sign off with a promise to talk again soon. Having Klara in my life is a pleasure and a blessing.

July 14, 2023

Mr. Wickham and Jonathan Darcy

"Have you read many books by Jane Austen?" my sister Kitty asks after we clown-foot over our neighbor's cattle guard and walk side by side on his long, manure-splashed, gray-asphalt driveway that winds down a steep hill through a cow pasture.

Short bitterweeds, with foliage like pine needles, dot the edge of the road, their yellow-petaled flowers reminding me of tiny daisies. Woolly croton weeds tower over them, their soft green, long, oblong, fuzzy leaves interspersed with blooms, resembling tiny clusters of hairy beige grapes that will soon flower. Black-and-white cows munch short Bahia grass in the distance. Sometimes the huge Black Angus bull who dominates the herd wanders a little too near the road, and Kitty and I have to detour through the tall weeds to avoid him, though luckily he's not in sight today.

"I've read Austen's novels," I tell her. "We studied them in graduate school. She wrote just six, but they're all great."

Kitty likes books as much as I do. Since both of our parents were avid readers, I'm not surprised. Even my brother, a former architect and builder, finally fell in love with reading and in the past few years has devoted himself to the Greek and Roman classics. His current hero is Thomas Jefferson, mainly because Jefferson read the classics in the original Greek and Latin.

"I found a novel at the library I think you'd enjoy," Kitty's saying, as a fresh, early morning breeze washes over us. In East Texas, this is the only time of day cool enough in July and August to exercise outdoors without risking heat stroke.

"Oh," I say. "What's it like?"

"Most of the characters are taken from Austen's novels, though the plot is similar to one in an old Agatha Christie murder mystery."

"Huh. That does sound like it's right up my alley. Is the book new?" I haven't read much mainstream fiction in quite a while, and it might be fun to catch up.

"It came out last year, and the author's already published a sequel. I finished this one yesterday and will give it to you after our walk."

❖

Several hours later, my chores done, I look at the novel Kitty's shared with me—*The Murder of Mr. Wickham*, by Claudia Gray. Mr. Wickham. Hmm. I try to remember which of Austen's books he was a character in. Maybe *Pride and Prejudice*? Google helps me recall that he was indeed the villain who caused a major conflict between the two main characters in that novel, though they end up together in spite of his machinations.

The blurb makes the book sound clever, so I open it. It's been such a long time since I've read Austen's works, I have trouble remembering which characters are taken from which book. However, one of the two main ones this author has invented grabs me immediately.

Named Jonathan Darcy, he's the son of the two major characters in *Pride and Prejudice*. As I read, I'm increasingly drawn to him. He's socially clumsy, totally inept around groups of people, especially strangers, and has to hide when he has a social meltdown because he literally rocks himself to become calm. The author introduces his condition gradually and does an incredible job of keeping my attention on him. Getting into the book, I think, "She's creating an autistic main character and pulling it off well."

I shouldn't be so surprised, because several years ago I watched *The Good Doctor* faithfully. Yet television has never been my medium of choice, and I haven't seen this series that features an autistic young male doctor during the past three or so years. Instead, I've reverted to my first love, print on paper. So, given my recent research into ASD, I'm pleasantly surprised to discover a character with ASD in a popular young author's wide-selling novel.

Again, my sister, unwittingly or not, has helped me on my journey of discovery. Obviously I've been on the autism spectrum all these years and simply never realized why I've so often felt different from and nervous around most people I associate with. The possibility of understanding even more fully oddly comforts me.

August 3, 2023

ON KITTY'S BACK PORCH

It's promising to be the hottest August on record in Texas, and this morning we're sitting on Kitty's back porch, the ceiling fans whirling at top speed, a large box fan trained directly on us as well.

"So is Sam looking forward to her first day of school tomorrow?" I ask Leslie, her mother, who's slumped in a plastic deck chair.

"No more than I am, but yes. She loves going to school and can't wait." Leslie takes off one of her expensive running shoes and feels around inside it. "Ah. Gotcha. I hate to have a rock in my shoe. That's all I can think of when I'm working out at the gym."

"Any idea why Sam likes her school so much?" I ask.

Kitty, who's just walked up from her garden, where she's been watering her pepper plants, pipes up. "For one thing, it has one of the best programs in the district for kids like Sam."

"Really? Why's that?" Suddenly I'm totally interested in my great-niece's education.

"I'm not sure," Leslie says. "But I do know she can't wait to go to school every morning and that she gets along well with all her classmates. They accept her just the way she is."

"They don't treat her any differently because of her autism?"

"Nope. She's been one of the gang since day one."

"Wow. What a change. Back in my day, of course we'd never heard the word autism, but we almost always rejected anyone different in any way."

"Lot of changes since the Middle Ages, Aunt Helen." Leslie and Kitty laugh, and suddenly Sam joins them.

"I know," I say, grinning. "I've been around forever, and I'm tickled to hear that kids like Sam are finally getting the type of support and education they need and deserve."

"Heck," Leslie says. "I bet a lot of us in our family fit somewhere on that autism spectrum. Not only is Sam on it, but her cousin, the granddaughter of your and Mom's brother, has been diagnosed with it too. Of the six children in that generation of our family, two are autistic. That's a rather high percentage. And just look at Granddaddy. He was a prime example."

"What?" I ask her. "You suspected he was autistic way back then?"

"Well, I spent half my time with them when I was growing up, so I noticed something was off. Little kids pay attention to stuff like that. Of course, I didn't realize what was wrong with him until I had Sam. But after that, it didn't take me long to figure it out."

"So why didn't you say anything?" I ask. "I've had to make sense out of all this the hard way."

Leslie shakes her head. "You barely mentioned it the one time we talked about it, so I didn't know you were that interested."

"Well, I—"

"Sam, get your feet out of that bucket," Leslie says. "Your grandmother's fixing to water her plants here on the porch with that rainwater." She motions at Sam with her head. "Taking care of this one and her older brother, I don't actually have much free time to sit around and chat."

Just about then, Kitty yells, "Put that down!" and jumps up.

I glance around. "What the heck?"

"Oh, Mama's cat just caught a hummingbird in midair. Happens more than you want to know."

Kitty shoos the cat off the porch.

"It's just a cat's nature, Mama," Leslie says.

About then, Sam kicks over the bucket of water Leslie's just warned her away from.

"Sam, I told you—"

"It's just Sam's nature, daughter." Kitty looks at Leslie and grins.

We all laugh and settle back down in our chairs, trying to catch a cool breeze.

Leslie looks at Sam, who's said something and then started flapping her arms. I wonder what she's feeling and thinking when she flaps like this. I think I can relate. She seems to just be doing the same thing I do when I run my fingers through my hair.

"You know, I'm starting to wonder if Sam has a language of her own," Leslie says, seeming to calm down, "and I'm beginning to understand it. Sometimes if I ask her to spell what she's trying to say, she can give me the first few letters, and then I can guess, and she can say the whole word."

Kitty's blue eyes shine. "That's great, Leslie. And interesting."

At this point I'm sitting here with a full heart. Some of our family members may be on different points of the autism spectrum. In fact, all of us probably are to some extent, but it's not a tragedy. Instead, it's a blessing that pulls us all together. We just need to know about it and accept it.

If I hadn't gone on that cruise and met Grace, then endured all that agony in Bali thinking about her while I had COVID, I might not have taken this inner journey to explore why I've always felt that I'm different from the norm. And as a bonus, I might not have responded to our writing group's one-word prompt this week—*nimble*—and written a totally positive sketch describing my dad's strong points. In it, I praise him for his agility and his strength, which is quite a contrast to my life-long negative attitude toward him.

I gaze at the three women sitting on the porch with me—my sister, her daughter, and her granddaughter—and can practically see the cords that bind us. We're part of a clan that includes Kitty and Matt, Bonnie and her girls, Leslie and her family, my brother and his surviving son, two granddaughters, and his wonderful wife. Plus, I have countless cousins such as Lou, and even a couple of uncles, both nearing a hundred, the patriarchs of the clan. And—I find it hard to believe—I'm the matriarch of both sides of our extensive families. Along with my friends Martha Jo, Amy, Klara, and even Grace, plus many others, we're all valuable members of the human family.

Looking back, I'm glad I cruised Indonesia and had to stay isolated in Bali. Otherwise, I might not have discovered that I'm autistic and that I'm okay with my new reality.

About the Author

Shelley Thrasher, world traveler and native East Texan, has been an editor for BSB since 2004. Having a PhD in English, she taught in composition and literature on the college level for thirty years before she retired early. She has published novels, poetry, short stories, and essays, as well as one scholarly book. Shelley lives near her family in the small town in East Texas where she grew up. Her first novel, *The Storm* (2012), was a GCLS historical-romance finalist and a Rainbow Awards runner-up for best debut novel. Three of her novels—*First Tango in Paris* (2014), *Hidden Dreams* (2021), and *Untethered* (2024)—are based on her travels in France and Southeast Asia. And her third, *Autumn Spring* (2015), which focuses on the romance between two older lesbians in small-town East Texas, was a finalist for a Lammy. Her book of poetry, *In and Out of Love* (2016), won a Goldie.

Books Available From Bold Strokes Books

Can't Buy Me Love by Georgia Beers. London and Kayla are perfect for one another, but if London reveals she's in a fake relationship with Kayla's ex, she risks not only the opportunity of her career, but Kayla's trust as well. (978-1-63679-665-9)

Chance Encounter by Renee Roman. Little did Sky Roberts know when she bought the raffle ticket for charity that she would also be taking a chance on love with the egotistical Drew Mitchell. (978-1-63679-619-2)

Comes in Waves by Ana Hartnett. For Tanya Brees, love in small-town Coral Bay comes in waves, but can she make it stay for good this time? (978-1-63679-597-3)

The Curse by Alexandra Riley. Can Diana Dillon and her daughter, Ryder, survive the cursed farm with the help of Deputy Mel Defoe? Or will the land choose them to be to the next victims? (978-1-63679-611-6)

Dancing With Dahlia by Julia Underwood. How is Piper Fernley supposed to survive six weeks with the most controlling, uptight boss on earth? Because sometimes when you stop looking, your heart finds exactly what it needs. (978-1-63679-663-5)

The Heart Wants by Krystina Rivers. Fifteen years after they first meet, Army Major Reagan Jennings realizes she has one last chance to win the heart of the woman she's always loved. If only she can make Sydney see she's worth risking everything for. (978-1-63679-595-9)

Skyscraper by Gun Brooke. Attempting to save the life of an injured boy brings Rayne and Kaelyn together. As they strive for justice against corrupt Celestial authorities, they're unable to foresee how intertwined their fates will become. (978-1-63679-657-4)

Untethered by Shelley Thrasher. Helen Rogers, in her eighties, meets much younger Grace on a lengthy cruise to Bali, and their intense relationship yields surprising insights and unexpected growth. (978-1-63679-636-9)

You Can't Go Home Again by Jeanette Bears. After their military career ends abruptly, Raegan Holcolm is forced back to their hometown to confront their past and discover where the road to recovery will lead them, or if it already led them home. (978-1-636790644-4)

A Wolf in Stone by Jane Fletcher. Though Cassilania is an experienced player in the dirty, dangerous game of imperial Kavillian politics, even she is caught out when a murderer raises the stakes. (978-1-63679-640-6)

The Devil You Know by Ali Vali. As threats come at the Casey family from both the feds and enemies set to destroy them, Cain Casey does whatever is necessary with Emma at her side to bury every single one. (978-1-63679-471-6)

The Meaning of Liberty by Sage Donnell. When TJ and Bailey get caught in the political crossfire of the ultraconservative Crusade of the Redeemer Church, escape is the only plan. On the run and fighting for their lives is not the time to be falling for each other. (978-1-63679-624-6)

One Last Summer by Kristin Keppler. Emerson Fields didn't think anything could keep her from her dream of interning at Bardot Design Studio in Paris, until an unexpected choice at a North Carolina beach has her questioning what it is she really wants. (978-1-63679-638-3)

StreamLine by Lauren Melissa Ellzey. When Lune crosses paths with the legendary girl gamer Nocht, she may have found the key that will boost her to the upper echelon of streamers and unravel all Lune thought she knew about gaming, friendship, and love. (978-1-63679-655-0)

Undercurrent by Patricia Evans. Can Tala and Wilder catch a serial killer in Salem before another body washes up on the shore? (978-1-636790669-7)

BOLDSTROKESBOOKS.COM

Looking for your next great read?

Visit BOLDSTROKESBOOKS.COM
to browse our entire catalog of paperbacks, ebooks,
and audiobooks.

**Want the first word on what's new?
Visit our website for event info,
author interviews, and blogs.**

Subscribe to our free newsletter for sneak peeks,
new releases, plus first notice of promos
and daily bargains.

SIGN UP AT
BOLDSTROKESBOOKS.COM/signup

Bold Strokes Books
Quality and Diversity in LGBTQ Literature

Bold Strokes Books is an award-winning publisher
committed to quality and diversity in LGBTQ fiction.

Milton Keynes UK
Ingram Content Group UK Ltd.
UKHW041048150824
446997UK00001B/31

9 781636 796369